The
SECRETS
of the
LITTLE GREEK
TAVERNA

The SECRETS *of the* LITTLE GREEK TAVERNA

ERIN PALMISANO

GRAND
CENTRAL

NEW YORK BOSTON

Grand Central Publishing
Hachette Book Group
1290 Avenue of the Americas, New York, NY 10104
grandcentralpublishing.com
@grandcentralpub

Originally published in New Zealand and Australia by Moa Press, an imprint of Hachette Aotearoa New Zealand Limited, in 2024

First Grand Central Publishing edition: May 2024

Grand Central Publishing is a division of Hachette Book Group, Inc. The Grand Central Publishing name and logo is a registered trademark of Hachette Book Group, Inc.

The publisher is not responsible for websites (or their content) that are not owned by the publisher.

The Hachette Speakers Bureau provides a wide range of authors for speaking events. To find out more, go to hachettespeakersbureau.com or email HachetteSpeakers@hbgusa.com.

Grand Central Publishing books may be purchased in bulk for business, educational, or promotional use. For information, please contact your local bookseller or the Hachette Book Group Special Markets Department at special.markets@hbgusa.com.

Library of Congress Control Number: 2024931744

ISBNs: 978-1-5387-5749-9 (trade paperback), 978-1-5387-5750-5 (ebook)

Printed in the United States of America

LSC-C

Printing 2, 2024

For you, Mom.
You are my inspiration and my best friend—this book is
for and because of you.

Prologue

On a planet with 195 countries and a population of eight billion people, there are a lot of places to see and a lot of stories to tell. For many of those billions, the sun rises and sets, routines take place, and the world exists for each person in a pleasantly expected way. But there are also unexpected moments, joys and sorrows, plans embarked upon, mistakes made, and life becomes a story within a story within a story. Such is life and such is our existence that we each live our own beautiful story all the time, every moment of every day.

Sometimes stories collide, like a beautiful accident nobody saw coming. They do not cure cancer or change the world. The butterfly effect of friendship does not alter the paths of most people. But occasionally that collision can alter the paths of some and can shake up a small village.

This particular story of the little Greek taverna begins in a very small village on the island of Naxos in Greece. The village is called Potamia and its three hundred inhabitants have been living their story without any shaking up for a long time, since the day a group of the women of Potamia were washing their clothes in the local river and found a spring nearby, from which they all drank when they became thirsty. Strange things began to happen in Potamia after that, things that are now so commonplace that the villagers do not even notice. Though to us, it might seem a little bit like magic.

If we begin at the east end of the little whitewashed village, nine kilometers from the town of Chora Naxos, we see many stories just waiting to be told. At a vineyard beside the river, Arie bottles his wine and puts a label on just one. It is a photograph he took of a very special woman entering a secret garden, though he does not yet know why he is doing this. Down the road, Nico and Nefeli are in the midst of one of their famed passionate arguments, creating little sparks that are inadvertently igniting fireplaces and ovens throughout the village, much to the consternation of the townsfolk. Along the main square, Mayor Andreas constantly fumbles with his pocket watch, but he is never early and never late, though the watch stopped working years ago. He mumbles hello to Georgios, the oldest man in the village. Georgios walks at the same time every day, donned in a three-piece suit and a Panama hat and cane, though he is not going or coming, just walking along, like he always has and always will.

At the west end of town, Mago sips her Kitron as she warily eyes the rising full moon, sewing sequins onto an old 1920s style flapper dress she knew she would need to wear soon but did not know where just yet. But she knew it had something to do with her neighbor, who was about to have a very bad night. On her property is a three-tiered garden and a whitewashed guesthouse and taverna that never opened because its owner, Leo Thermopolis, died at the young age of twenty-seven and his wife, Cressida, didn't know how to move forward after that.

The moment this story begins, on a Monday evening at 6:03 p.m., Cressida Thermopolis is reading a very unexpected letter.

Ms. Thermopolis,
We at the Resurgence Hotel Group would like the opportunity to meet with you at your earliest convenience to speak about your delightful property. We believe your establishment might be a great asset to our group…

Cressida finished the letter, letting out a sigh so loud that sound waves carried it around the world to the place it was destined to stop. That place happened to be about 12,000 miles away in Los Angeles, California, where a young woman was taking a morning walk.

Marjory St. James did not know where it came from, but at that very moment she felt the pull, the one she always felt when it was time to leave. Jory never knew where it would take her, but she knew somehow that it was time. Time to go. She left the beach and walked restlessly into the city center of Santa Monica until she passed by a travel agency. On the door was a photo of a beautiful yacht in the Greek Islands. It was almost as if it had been put there just for her.

And so our story begins. A story where the lost sometimes need to be found and the found sometimes need to get a little bit lost. The story of the Little Greek Taverna.

One

"I bought a ticket to Athens this morning." Marjory St. James waited for her two best friends to say something.

It was another beautiful Sunday in Los Angeles and they were sitting at their favorite cafe where they'd spent Sundays brunching for the past many years. Kate and Liz looked at one another, their glasses of prosecco mid-sip.

"You've only been back eight months, Jory. What on earth happened between dinner last night and now to inspire this?" Liz asked.

Most of Jory's friends thought there was something Jory was running away from, or some inescapable need to find something. But years before, Jory's mother had nodded pragmatically whenever Jory told her she felt called to go somewhere. "You're a

St. James," her mother would say. "And a St. James knows when it is time to leave. An instinct, a pull to a place without knowing why. Perhaps you will simply explore. Or perhaps you will find yourself in a place that needs to borrow a little bit of your gift. The gift of home that exists within you. So you never feel lost, but always just where you are meant to be."

"It has been eight months, Liz, thank you very much. And you know I don't know *why* it's time to go, but it is. As for the inspiration…" Jory grinned, pulling out the brochure the travel agent had given her with the yacht and whitewashed Greek Island on the cover.

Kate smiled at Jory. She was more understanding of Jory's lifestyle than Liz, who was utterly practical.

Jory and Kate had gone to college together, and they met Liz a year after they had moved to Los Angeles. Liz told them once she'd had trouble making friends when she first arrived in the city. It wasn't that she was shy, because she wasn't. And it wasn't that she wasn't sociable, because she was. It was simply that she was very protective of her time and energy with people. She wasn't a person who wanted to spend (or waste, as she thought of it) herself on people who weren't going to be a core part of her life. Liz was pragmatic, concise, and she wanted solid, sturdy things. Her work as a fashion stylist was a solid, sturdy thing, and her family was a solid, sturdy thing. So when it came to friends, she simply thought it better to wait for something solid and sturdy as well.

Jory, and Kate, too, at that time, worked in a little French bistro called The French Café. Jory knew there was something about Liz and she proceeded to, as Kate teased her, "friend stalk" Liz until she had no choice but to become their friend.

"Hi, I'm Jory," she'd finally said one evening, reaching out to shake her hand, which Liz took, her eyebrows furrowed. "This is Kate. We have decided we want you to be our third amigo. So what are we all doing tomorrow?"

The three had been solid, steady, and inseparable ever since, other than Jory's constant wanderlust.

The girls sipped their prosecco as they reminisced, but Liz looked over the brochure again and dug into her eggs Florentine that had just arrived. "Well, I love you and you know I support you. And god knows I'd kill to be on that boat." She pointed with her fork. "But girl, ain't no way in hell you have the money to be sailing around on a superyacht, and even if you do have some sort of Vanderbilt blood, you gave that up ages ago."

"And kept my soul intact," Jory teased. Money was never something Jory had had in large quantities, even though she could have. That was an adamant choice she'd made years ago. "You know how I feel about my father's money. And while I know you don't think my waitressing job at The French Café is a real job, Liz, I have managed to save heaps in the past eight months by picking up extra shifts. As long as I can eat all the food I want and drink all the wine I want, I'm fine to budget on other things. Like this. Look on page five at the big ferries that take people around to the islands. It's actually quite inexpensive."

Liz opened to page five. "Quite reasonable. I suppose I always thought Greece would be super expensive."

Jory finally bit into her omelet. "I know. I can't wait to eat all my favorite foods—feta, olives, delicious sun-ripened tomatoes. I'm not taking my phone or laptop or even a guidebook. I'm totally winging it."

"Jory—don't you think that's a bit tricky in this day and age?" Liz asked.

"When I first started traveling, I didn't even have a phone, and not only did I find my way just fine but they were some of my best trips," she replied. "Don't you remember that one time I was on the train?"

"Oh wait!" Kate interrupted. "I love that story. Is it the one where you hopped on the local train in Egypt to avoid paying the exorbitant tourist prices and hid in the bathroom just long enough that by the time the police found you, they couldn't throw you off but had to escort you all the way back to Cairo for fourteen hours—"

"Surrounding you only with women and children you had to babysit?" Liz finished. "That was a good one."

"Or was it the one when you had all your cash stolen from your bag on the way from Nice to Barcelona, and when you went to buy your next ticket, you realized it was gone? I wouldn't imagine that to be one of your best stories, come to think."

Jory grimaced. "No, it was the one—"

"Oh! The one in India where the tout took you back to that hotel that was really nice but ended up stealing the wine you'd smuggled in duty-free? That one was truly cruel," Kate said. Liz nodded emphatically.

They were all laughing then, as the waiter came and opened another bottle of prosecco. He stared for an exceptionally long time at Jory. Kate and Liz raised their eyebrows and gave Jory a kick under the table.

"Ow, what was that for?" she grumbled, making the waiter blush before he walked away. The girls rolled their eyes.

"Honestly, Jory, the waiter was totally into you. He was really cute," Liz said.

"I have absolutely no desire to be in a relationship, thank you. You know this!"

"I still don't understand why you're so adamant about that," said Kate. "I mean, I know you love your life, and it is an awesome lifestyle, but couldn't you have both?" she asked for the hundredth time.

"Could I still leave at the drop of a hat any time, whenever my instinct kicks in? Could I travel by myself for months at a time, nothing but freedom and letting myself explore and experience the world in just my way? Without thinking of anyone else or holding back at all?" Jory replied with too much passion.

"Well...no, not really," Kate said honestly. She brightened. "But what if you met like, the big one? What if you met—what does your mom call him, Jory?"

Liz answered with a grin. "The sizzler!"

Kate laughed. "That's right! The one who, as soon as you meet, and his skin touches yours—sizzle. So what if you meet *that* guy?"

"Then I will absolutely run the other way and get a ticket out of there. That one is danger incarnate!" Jory said dramatically.

Kate pretended to pout. "But your mom always says it with such lusty zeal, like it's a good thing."

Jory rolled her eyes. "You're talking about Cindy St. James here, ladies. It does not take much to make her sizzle when she meets a man, but it doesn't take long for that sizzle to fizzle either. St. James women have terrible luck in love. Now, Kate, just because *you* found your sizzler in Mark..."

Kate blushed but Liz squeezed her shoulder. "We tease because we are so happy for you, honey."

"Totally true," Jory said, squeezing Kate's other shoulder. "But back to the subject at hand, please? I happened to be talking about the train trip in England when I hopped on and stayed until the tracks ended and found myself in one of my favorite places in the world—a fairyland with a castle, where I had the most amazing summer. I'm telling you, I have a feeling about this."

Kate sighed. "You always have a feeling. But it isn't as if you're going somewhere unsafe. I mean, the Greek Islands."

Even Liz had the wherewithal to agree, albeit with more reservation. "I still think you should take a guidebook at least if you won't take a phone. When do you leave?"

"Next Wednesday. May twenty-eighth."

"But that's your birthday!" Kate cried.

"Yes, I know, so whatever surprise party you had planned for me, change it to the twenty-seventh, please. I'm sorry, but the ticket was on special for one day only, and it happens to be the twenty-eighth of my twenty-eighth year, so I figured it was kind of—"

"Fate," Kate and Liz answered simultaneously.

"You know I don't believe in fate," Jory said.

"Jory!" Liz sighed, rolling her eyes. "You believe in your St. James gifts, that home thing, that 'leave instinct' thing. That is all fate."

"No, there's a difference. Fate is like, something inevitable, that you have no control over. Like you have no choice in the matter. The other things like the gifts are innate, but you still choose what you're going to do with them. Does that make sense?" she asked, leaning forward.

"*No!*" Liz and Kate answered simultaneously.

"To fate!" Liz said, and they all laughed again, because after two bottles of prosecco on a Sunday morning before noon, everything was funny.

~

Okay, Liz, you were right. Not that I'll ever tell you that.

Jory sat in a very uncomfortable booth on the top floor of the largest ferry she had ever been on, realizing that she should have purchased a guidebook, or at the very least should have booked accommodation. The ferry had left Athens at three in the afternoon on what was meant to be a four-hour journey to Naxos, an island in the Cyclades. It was the middle of the night when the ferry finally pulled into port.

Okay, Marjory, what's the worst that can happen? You sleep on a bench somewhere. You're in Greece, it will be nice and warm.

But it was not nice and warm. In fact, at one o'clock in the morning, even though it was early June, it was exceptionally windy and cold. As they departed the ferry, however, Jory was pleased to see that the port was not all empty as there were a few locals loading and unloading goods.

She couldn't make out the town as the moon was not bright enough. It was all very dark and quiet. Starting to worry just a little bit, she watched as, one by one, they left with their boxes or packages that had been sent over from Athens. A young woman was one of the last, sifting through the pile, and though Jory spoke not a word of Greek, she was pretty certain she was cursing.

"Aha!" the woman said, picking up an overly large box.

Jory approached her. "Excuse me, I'm sorry to interrupt."

The woman turned, her dark eyes heavy-lidded, her mouth full, her long black hair in a braid down her back.

"Yes?"

"Oh good," Jory breathed, "you speak English. Did you need help? That box is very large."

"Thank you, but it is not heavy. Seeds and bulbs for my garden. You are a tourist?" the woman asked.

"Yes. I'm sorry, but I wondered if you knew anywhere in town that might be open for accommodation. A guesthouse or something?"

"You have not booked?"

"No," Jory said, resigned. "I didn't realize we'd be arriving so late. There was a storm." She was incredibly embarrassed, and yet despite that, increasingly cold and desperate.

"Storm, no storm, the ferry is always late." The woman looked at Jory for a long time, biting her lower lip as though she was debating with herself. Finally, she took a deep, woeful breath that sounded somehow familiar, as if Jory had heard it before. "I have a guesthouse, you may come with me," she said with a single nod.

"Really, you have a guesthouse? How lucky I came to talk to you."

"Lucky," the woman murmured, more to herself.

"Where is your guesthouse? Is it quite far?"

"Potamia. Up there." She pointed into the black distance. "My village."

"Oh." Jory had not expected to leave the main town. "And, um…how much?"

"Does it matter? It is me or a park bench, yes?" Her voice sounded amused, though she didn't smile.

"How did you…?"

"A park bench? Not a person on the island would see a woman sleep on a park bench, silly girl. I make fun of you."

This was one of the stranger encounters she'd had since she left, yet not unpleasant. Jory smiled. "In that case, thank you. I'm Marjory St. James. But everyone calls me Jory." She reached out her hand.

"Cressida Thermopolis. Pleased to meet you," she said, shaking Jory's hand. "Okay, shall we go?"

"Oh, right, okay." Jory pulled her pack up onto her shoulders, following Cressida to the parking lot where a dusty little pickup truck waited. She threw her bag in the back and hopped in beside Cressida.

They began to drive up the main road, past the village, then up and up what seemed to be the start of a mountain. Cressida didn't speak and Jory was beginning to wonder if this was a mistake. They climbed further still. Jory looked behind her in the rearview mirror, watching the great ferry pulling out into the blackness of the sea. It looked calm from this perspective, but she remembered the waves crashing over the top of what was, in essence, a four-story building. She shivered.

"It is colder up here than below," Cressida said, "but once we are in Potamia there is not much wind. You'll be the only tourist in town at the moment," she added.

At least she was speaking to her now. "Is it very far from the main town of Naxos?"

"Only nine kilometers."

Nine kilometers from the town? Jory didn't know if Cressida necessarily understood "guesthouse." She could mean her couch. Which at this stage would be fine for just one night, tired as Jory was beginning to feel. Cressida didn't seem like someone who was used to having guests—she'd barely spoken a word since they met and seemed uncomfortable. Jory glanced over to her again. She looked tired too. Perhaps that was it. It was, after all, the middle of the night.

"Have you always lived in Potamia?" Jory asked.

"I am from here and have lived here most of my life, yes," she replied. "Ah, here we are."

They entered a small whitewashed town. No lights were on, but the moon had come from behind the clouds and highlighted the village enough for Jory to see that it was quite pretty. They turned down a cobbled street and Cressida pulled up in front of a sign that read "Guesthouse." The large house was beautiful, white with purple bougainvillea climbing up the sides. They had obviously arrived from the back, but it sat precariously on a hill and Jory wondered what the view would be like from the best rooms in the morning.

"There are six rooms. I think room two will suit you as you are here on your own. It is on the ground floor but very nice. You will be comfortable. Thirty euro for the night."

Jory followed her down a winding little path through to a garden. Thirty euro? That was a great price, even if it was miles away from the main town and even if it was terrible. Cressida opened the door to room two. It was not terrible, not at all. The ceilings were low and rounded and plastered white, with the trimmings painted a lovely shade of turquoise. The floor was made of intricate mosaic tiles and a comfortable-looking double bed graced the middle of the room. There was no TV or phone and the room was small, but it had a lovely bathroom with a great big shower, and there was a sliding door on one side to her own private garden area with a chaise lounge and a little table and chair. There was a small fridge inside. It was beautiful. And it was *hers*. Something familiar hit Jory walking into this room. It felt like home.

"Do you like the room?" Cressida asked, a note in her voice Jory could not quite place. Almost…hopeful.

"It's beautiful and I love it. Thank you, Cressida. This is amazing."

She nodded and exhaled. "Be careful with the bathroom door—do not close it too hard or it jams. I will bring you breakfast tomorrow morning. Goodnight."

And she left.

Jory made to unpack her bag, but instead, she crawled between the crisp white sheets on the gloriously soft bed and did not wake until morning.

Two

Cressida woke in the morning with an uncanny urge to bake. She knew the feeling was dangerous when it was this strong, when nothing but using her hands to mold a cake or knead a loaf of bread would ease the deep longing inside her, but it had been so long since she'd felt it kick in like this that she could not resist.

Donning an apron over her blue dress, she walked down to the garden with a few big trays and her pruning clippers in hand. The olives were a daily job, in the tiny grove that had been on this land for hundreds of years. She walked past her herb garden, which was thriving from the rains they'd had in May. Now the days were mostly long and sunny and her vegetables were suddenly ripe and vibrant. The tomatoes that had been growing for a month were round and red, and cherry tomatoes littered the ground. The cucumbers were twice the size they'd been a week before, and her eggplant would be ready in another week or two.

But today, her figs were finally ripe. Weeks ago, she had covered the growing clusters with netting to keep the birds from sucking the juice out of her favorite fruit. She turned her figs into jams, pastes, syrups; she dried them and roasted them, but most of all she loved them fresh. She filled her tray with the purple delights, humming, and brought them back up to her kitchen.

She had already dropped Jory's breakfast on her porch without waiting for her to wake. Cressida needed to bake, and there was only one thing she could even think to make now that her figs were ready—her classic honey cake. It was a simple dessert, but it was still one of her favorites, perhaps because it had been Leo's favorite. She pulled out a large bowl and added eggs and sugar, beating them until they were creamy and thick. She looked down at the premium electric hand mixer Leo had specially bought her from America and she could not help but smile. He had loved his gadgets. And he had loved her.

At the sound of a door opening, Cressida peeked out the window, where she saw Marjory come out into the garden to eat her breakfast. A little flutter beat in her chest. Her first guest. She had her very first guest. Leo would be so pleased. He would also be grateful that despite not knowing why, Cressida had kept the rooms in pristine condition all this time. What would he be doing now if he were alive?

Certainly not hiding and being slightly rude to her.

No, he most certainly would not be doing either of those things. Leo was a charmer. He would be driving Jory around, taking her to all the tourist sites, making tea in the afternoon, introducing her around town. He would certainly be flirting with her, Cressida thought with a small smile. Leonidas was a born flirt. When her auntie on the other side of the island had first met him, she had tsked her disapproval with a blush she could not suppress.

"No woman should be marrying a boy who flirts like you do, Leonidas. She will have her heart broken," Auntie had warned him.

"Ah, but, Auntie, I was born to flirt! Why, even a baby likes to flirt with me." He had grinned, lifting his thick black eyebrows.

Cressida chuckled at the memory. It was true. Not a soul who met Leo had been safe from his charm. He was so happy, so personable, that everyone who met him loved him. No, he would not be avoiding his first guest.

First, or only?

She added in the flour next, and once blended, began to add in the rest of the ingredients one at a time, mixing now by hand with a large spoon she had inherited from her mother, who had also been a gifted baker before she passed away when Cressida was only twelve. She barely remembered her now, but when she used the spoon, it was as if some magic memory brought her back to her mother, to some part inside of herself that was not of her, but outside of her, and inside at the same time.

She stirred in the honey from Tomas's beekeeping station in Filoti, a village not far from Potamia. And though most recipes used lemon, Cressida preferred to use the zest and juice of an orange from her own tree. Lastly, she folded in her mizithra cheese, soft and delicate, and hand-stirred until the entire mixture was creamy enough to make you want to dip your finger in and eat it as it was. She then poured the mixture into a ceramic baking dish to cook in the oven. In the thirty minutes the cake took to bake, she drenched her figs in honey and walnuts.

As Cressida cleaned, she found the letter from the Resurgence Hotel Group again. She was two months late on her mortgage already, and the offer from the Resurgence Group could be a godsend. Should she sell to them and leave this guesthouse with no guests, the taverna she had never cooked in, and the memories that surrounded her every day, and begin a new life?

But there is one guest now. And one person you can cook for. What would it be like to have more?

The timer on the oven went off. She should not be thinking of such things. Cressida wiped her hands on her apron and took the perfectly golden honey cake from the oven to cool. But why shouldn't she think of them? She had a decision to make soon. She would no longer be able to afford to keep this place without having paying guests. Perhaps she should sell and go away from here. Live out her widowhood somewhere remote and far away from this almost life that never was.

When the cake was nearly cool, she added extra sugar and cinnamon before topping it with the honey-coated figs and walnuts. It looked perfect, so perfect she could not wait to invite Jory, her first or perhaps only guest, to taste it. Her heart began to race with something vaguely familiar. She almost felt... giddy. Shaking herself free of such thoughts, Cressida took a very small bite to check it was right.

"*Ohi re gamoto!*" she exclaimed. "*Skata!*"

And she promptly left the cake on the bench to throw out later, slamming the door behind her.

~

Jory set out on foot that morning after her delicious breakfast of tomato and cucumber salad with olives and a feta-type of cheese, though it was unlike any other feta she'd had before. She was going to explore her little village of Potamia—her little village, that was what she was calling it in her head.

"Good morning!" A woman in her sixties with a long braid of black and silver stepped out of the house next door.

"Oh, good morning." It was lovely to be greeted pleasantly after not having seen Cressida at all. "I'm Marjory St. James, but please call me Jory. Everyone does."

"Jory, it is lovely to have you here in Potamia. I am Mago, Cressida's neighbor. Are you off to explore the village?"

"Yes, I thought I'd meander and get a little bit lost," she said, smiling. "It's my favorite thing to do in a new place."

"Well, you won't have any trouble getting lost in the village. It was very badly designed." She chuckled. "Do you drink wine?"

"That may be an understatement." Jory laughed. "But usually not so early."

"You're cheeky, I like you. Wait here, I will call Arie. He has the most famous vineyard in our region and he is an excellent host. I will arrange for him to take you on a tour this afternoon. Then this evening you must come share some wine with me and tell me all about your day."

~

Potamia was comprised of three small villages set between flowing rivers. At first, Jory tried to follow the map Mago had given her but realized very soon that the streets and alleyways twisted and turned and almost always turned into a dead end. No matter how many times she knew she'd gone another way, she always ended up at the same stream.

It was a beautiful place, almost like she'd walked through a doorway into another world. The sounds and smells of the streets faded away, sunlight filtered through the trees and a sense of ease washed over her. Just a moment before, she'd been frustrated that she was lost, and then there she was at the stream again. It happened all morning, so finally Jory decided to give in and stay at the stream for a while. She tried to memorize the hand-drawn map, but instead fell asleep. When she woke, she was so surprised, she reached her hands into the stream and splashed the cold water on her face, which suddenly made her thirsty. She knew she wasn't supposed to drink from a stream—it could be filled with parasites. But this one was so clean, it was like glacier water. She drank from her hand until her thirst was quenched and finally went back to the village, and she didn't get lost again that day.

As Cressida promised, Jory was the only tourist around, though she passed many locals who looked at her with great curiosity. They were friendly, said hello, tipped their hats; the small children waved, but once she passed she could feel their eyes linger on her. Eventually she ended up in the town square of Ano Potamia, where an old water fountain stood next to the chapel of Agios Ioannis Theologos.

"Glorious, isn't it? Built in 1799 by the Venetians," said a man standing next to her. He was quite old, dressed in a three-piece suit and a Panama hat.

"It is. Are you on your way to a service?" she asked.

"No, miss, the only service in this church is our town meetings, though it's open to the public in summer," he said.

"Oh, I thought perhaps—you see, I was commenting on your fine attire," Jory said, smiling.

"This old thing?" He chuckled. "You are a sweet girl. I am Georgios," he said, shaking her hand. "We are so glad you have come, Miss Marjory, and we look forward to seeing you at the next town meeting."

He tipped his hat and walked on. How on earth did he know her name?

Now only half an hour from meeting Arie, she walked down the main road out of town. The buildings began to spread out a bit more, and finally at the end she saw the little petrol station Mago had told her to look for, the last in Potamia before the road headed toward Filoti and the rest of the island towns out of Chora.

She immediately spotted the road she was meant to walk down to meet Arie, but something stopped her. Mopeds for rent sat outside the service station, at a very reasonable price. Twenty-five euro for the day. Jory loved riding a moped when traveling and surely it would make travel around the island so much easier?

She walked into the service station, where a woman sat behind the counter, scrolling through her phone. She looked different from the other Greek women Jory had met so far. Her hair was not quite blonde, but a shimmery gold. Her skin, too, was golden, her eyes the strangest shade of hazel which made Jory wonder whether they were contacts or real. Her nose was long and curved slightly, but above her full mouth it only enhanced how pretty she was. She was also fully made up, down to a matte red lipstick that matched her red nails, and hair so perfect it must have been done in a salon.

The woman looked up and raised one eyebrow. "Yes?"

"Hello," Jory said quickly, realizing she had been staring. "I'm looking at renting one of the mopeds you have outside."

The woman stared longer than necessary, her expression cautious. "Nico!" she finally yelled toward the back of the service station. "Customer—moped." And she went back to her phone.

The Nico that came out also looked nothing like Jory imagined. He too had fair hair, worn longer over his collar, but it suited him.

"Hello, miss!" he said in stilted English. "You are wanting to rent a moped? Excellent idea! I shall take you for a ride around."

Nico walked her outside and took the sign off one of the mopeds, explaining the instructions of how to ride it. When Jory was helmeted and ready to go, he hopped on the motorcycle by its side and indicated for her to follow him around. They rode for ten minutes before coming back to the station.

"Excellent! You are a natural, Miss Marjory!" he said.

Jory took her helmet off. "How do you know my name?"

It was the woman who answered, coming out and snatching Jory's helmet. "We all know your name."

Jory was taken aback. "And yet I don't know any of yours."

"I am Nefeli. This is Nico, my *husband*," she said, emphasizing the word.

She turned and practically hissed something to him in Greek. He replied, still smiling through clenched teeth. Nefeli stomped away to the back of the shop, muttering in angry Greek the whole time, getting louder when she flung her hands around.

Nico followed his wife with his eyes before turning back to Jory with a shamefaced grin. "Tomorrow morning, Miss Marjory," and he returned to the back of the shop, where Jory could hear them yelling at one another.

She didn't want to witness a private argument, so she meandered down the little path to where Arie would pick her up. Unfortunately, that little path came right around the back of the shop, where she saw Nefeli pushed through the outside door. She turned and pushed Nico back. Jory hid behind the tree, not knowing whether to intervene. But then the strangest thing happened. Nico began to kiss Nefeli's neck, ravenously, passionately, and she started moaning and reaching for him.

"Get off me," Nefeli hissed between kisses.

"No. Move back into our room. A man and a wife belong together, sleeping in the same bed," he hissed back, kissing her neck and turning her around.

"No. You know why I won't share your bed anymore!"

The moans grew louder and when Jory heard a "zip," she ran as fast as she could down the path, her breath pounding. She realized her little village was certainly turning out to be filled with more stories than she could have imagined.

~

Arie was a man in his late sixties, his silver hair intertwined with a few black strands still holding their own. He had the tanned, creased face of someone who had worked outside his entire life, and black eyes that were in a perpetual smile, even when his lips were not. Jory immediately liked him when he picked her up at the gate of a large farm with an orchard and a small vineyard. They drove through the orchard in a ride-on mower until they reached a water mill with an old barn beside it.

"Welcome to Vineyard Diamantés—that means diamonds in English. I named it for the tartrates that are sometimes found in wines. They are called wine diamonds. Do you like Greek wine?" Arie asked her gently. Everything he did and said was gentle. She had never had Greek wine, she told Arie. "Here in Naxos, our patron god was Dionysus—the god of wine—so we have been making and drinking wine as long as there have been humans on the island. My own family has been making wine for over two hundred years."

Arie took her for a walk through the vineyard of about ten acres, pointing out grape varietals she had never heard of, like fokiano, monemvasia, savatiano, aidani, and finally one she recognized, muscat.

"We mostly here make a white blend, very crisp and dry, despite the addition of the muscat. We also make an 'almost red,' or better known to you as a rosé."

"You mentioned that the vineyard was only a small part of the farm, Arie. I noticed we drove through a citrus grove on the way in. Is that your main business? Citrus fruit?"

"Ah, and now you have a proper Greek drink—though you will only really find it in Naxos now. Kitron is our traditional drink here on the island. It is made of the leaves of the citron tree, which is harvested when the aroma peaks. Then we distil it, sometimes two, three times, adding new leaves, or other secret ingredients like I do. We make three different types of Kitron here—a dry, strong liqueur, a mid-strength, and then our most famous, a much sweeter one, with extra sugar and orange zest, that we sip as an aromatic or digestive. This is what I am most famous for. Here, I will pack you one specially for my Mago, if you please can pass it on to her?"

My Mago?

"Of course, and thank you so much for such a wonderful day. Mago and I will enjoy this immensely tonight."

"My absolute pleasure, Miss Marjory. And when Cressida decides to open her taverna, you tell her to come to me for the wine."

Jory didn't know what he was talking about or what to say, so she said nothing.

Arie reached and took her hand and kissed it, saying, "Pass that onto Mago too."

"Okay, so tell me, are you and Arie…?" Jory asked Mago a few hours later when she dropped the Kitron to her. Mago invited her in, and they sat on the porch together as Mago poured them both a drink.

"He is my lover, yes," Mago said, taking a sip, looking completely at ease and unabashed.

"Wow," Jory said, impressed. "Nice. He's a good-looking man, that one."

Mago looked pleased. "Yes, I know. So tell me, how was your exploration of the village? Did you get 'lost' as you'd hoped?"

Jory threw her head back and raised her arms. "Every damned street!"

Mago chuckled and sipped the Kitron.

"No matter which street I took, or which of the three little villages I was in, I ended up at the same stream. For hours."

Mago looked up, startled. "The village took you to the stream? Hmm. It never does that, it usually hides it. Did you drink from it?"

"What do you mean the village hides the stream? You make it sound like it has a soul or something."

"Perhaps it does, who is to say it doesn't? The stream has quite a vivid history. It is said that the women of the village—which was, amazingly, even smaller then—drank from the stream and interesting things began to happen around the village. They say the descendants of those women have particular gifts," Mago said in a spooky voice, raising her eyebrows and grinning.

Jory laughed. "Is that why you asked me if I drank from it? Or was it because it's filled with parasites like most streams?"

"You won't get giardia from that stream, don't worry," she said, patting Jory's hand. "The mayor is trying to turn it into a tourist destination. The debates are wonderfully lively. I'll bring you to the next town meeting. They're a hoot."

Jory lit up. "I heard about the town meetings! I was invited by an older gentleman in a suit named Georgios. He said he was looking forward to seeing me at the next town meeting. And he knew my name before I introduced myself," she said, confused again. "He wasn't the only one either. I stopped at a petrol station to look at a moped and this woman, Nefeli, she knew who I was too. She said everyone did. Is that true?"

"Ahhh," Mago sighed, closing her eyes. "You have met the great Nefeli and Nico, yes? Nefeli, the most beautiful and wealthy girl in the village. Nicolas, the golden boy from the wrong family. A terrible match. Two people so beautiful should never be together. Something messes with the gene pool."

Jory leaned forward, whispering. "They seemed a very… passionate couple." Her face went bright red.

"Yes, they have great passion. I remember the year they met—little embers started lighting my fireplace in the heart of summer. Happened to everyone."

"What do you mean little fires? Starting from a passionate couple? That sounds impossible!" Jory exclaimed.

"You may find that our village has a few seemingly impossible things in it," Mago said. "But Nico and Nefeli, ah. Sometimes I think they have great love, but who is to know what is true behind another's closed door?" Mago looked out to the moon, pensive, but a moment later, she was leaning forward as if she'd never turned away. "So you will rent Nico's moped then? What is he charging you?"

"Twenty-five euro per day, but he'll give it to me for one hundred and forty for the whole week."

"He's a fair man, Nico. You are staying a week?" Mago asked, looking intrigued. "That is a long time for a girl like yourself to stay here in Potamia, or even Naxos. Most people come through and island-hop around the Cyclades."

"I like it here," Jory said. "Though I don't understand why Cressida seems to dislike me. She avoided me this morning and didn't even say hello when I was having breakfast, though I know she saw me."

"Cressida does not dislike you, my dear. She has had a very bad week at the end of a very bad year. Give her time."

Jory was feeling a bit tipsy from the Kitron and quite hungry as she made her way down the garden to room two. Just as she was about to go inside, the most amazing aroma hit her, awakening her every sense. *What was that?*

And then she saw it. Just an arm's length from Jory's terrace sat a cake. She looked to the main house but Cressida's lights were out. Suddenly she felt quite touched. Cressida must have left this for her, as an apology of sorts for not speaking to her all day. She brought the cake inside her room and took a bite.

"Oh my god…"

And just at that moment, little shooting stars rocketed around the Aegean Sea, aligning in a way even they never saw coming.

Three

Cressida had not slept at all. Finally, at five o'clock in the morning, she gave up and wandered into the kitchen. How could she have allowed herself a moment of happiness yesterday? And to have inadvertently baked that feeling in her honey cake? Somewhere in the night, she cursed her mother for inheriting the Callas gift of being able to bake her emotions into her food, prayed for forgiveness for that happy moment yesterday that she could not control, followed by the reminder that Leo was dead and she had no right whatsoever to live life happily without him. She slept perhaps a few minutes at a time. Something kept waking her. A beat, strong in her heart, as if it were screaming, *I'm alive, let me live!* That one moment of life sparked into her, because this girl Marjory was suddenly here, a guest in her guesthouse. It was too much. Mago often said Cressida needed to move on, to live again. She could not do that to Leo. She would never do that.

Somewhere around three o'clock as she lay staring at the ceiling, she realized Marjory had to leave. This thing that was sparking in Cressida, that was inspiring her and forcing her to bake again—it must be squelched.

Marjory's presence gave her a renewed sense of energy and purpose. To nurture and care, to make people happy through her gift of food, something she had not had since Leo passed. She *missed* cooking for someone. She could feel that in her heart when she baked the honey cake yesterday. She took a breath now. She would not make that mistake again, baking and tasting her happiness...it had tasted like betrayal. Betrayal of her love for Leo.

Sifting through the bottom drawer of her kitchen cabinet, she pulled out the Callas's leather-bound journal of recipes that had been in the family for nearly a hundred years. It had been written and rewritten in so many times it was hard to read, nearly impossible if you were not a Callas woman. They did not often talk of their gift, simply kneaded and stirred and whipped as if they were born to do it. But occasionally an event would happen or a person would come along and they would put a little star next to a recipe. Cressida knew exactly which one she was searching for. She flipped the pages until she found it.

Marathopita. The little stuffed flatbreads her grandmother made when Cressida was a small girl. Her favorite breakfast food. They were filled with olive and Halloumi, quite classic, but her grandmother had made notes: **Add fennel for keeping one complacent. To repel, switch to spinach and dill.* Cressida had spinach and dill in the garden. Once the dough was made, she finely chopped the dill and spinach and pressed them into perfect little stuffed breads and put them in the oven. Soon they were ready to take to Marjory for breakfast. She had to decide on her own to leave. Cressida could not be filled with even more guilt by asking her to leave.

Just before ten, she had the breakfast tray set, the coffee made. Perhaps she would just wait for Marjory to wake, Cressida thought, mid-knock on the door. But before she could turn around, her guest had stepped out into the garden, a welcoming smile on her face.

"Good morning, Cressida!" she said, fresh from the shower, dressed in jeans, a white T-shirt and sneakers. She smelled like apricots and lemons with just a hint of bay leaf, like the way home smelled before Leo died.

Cressida, stop it, you are thinking crazy. This is why you must make her leave.

"Good morning, Marjory," Cressida said.

"Please, call me Jory."

Cressida nodded. "I brought you a classic Greek breakfast. We grow everything here on Naxos, much of this from this very garden. In June the spinach is in season and filled with flavor. Are you hungry?"

"I am, yes. But first, I just wanted to say thank you."

Cressida sat across from Jory and placed the tray on the table. "Thank you? For what?"

"For the cake last night. I know I was silly not to make a booking and you weren't expecting a guest, and I truly apologize for that. I hadn't realized what an inconvenience it must be before you were prepared for the season. But that cake you made for me...oh my god, thank you. *Thank* you."

Cressida stood quickly, her heart racing. "Cake? What cake?"

Jory blushed. "The cake with the honey and figs you left me. I found it last night. It was for me, wasn't it? It was sitting just on the edge of the porch next to my room."

She had found the cake? And eaten it?

Jory was still talking. "I'm not sure what was in that cake, but I don't think I've eaten anything that has made me so happy. I don't know why, but every doubt I was feeling about coming here, every fear, even regret, was gone." She leaned to squeeze Cressida's hand. "Sincerely. Thank you."

Jory looked to the tray of marathopita. "I am so excited to taste what you've brought for me today!"

Cressida didn't realize her grip was so tight on the tray of food that her hands were shaking. But her heart was shaking even more. Her cake. Making that cake had brought her personal happiness, and that was wrong. It would never be okay. She was not allowed to be happy. But for the first time since Leo died, her cake had also brought joy to someone else. Was that not what she did? Bring joy to others through her food?

"When was the last time you had a guest at your bed and breakfast?" Jory asked innocently. "You said it wasn't tourist season yet."

As she said this, Jory reached out to take one of the marathopitas, startling Cressida out of her reverie in such a way that the tray fell out of her hands and the flatbreads fell to the ground.

"Oh my gosh, I'm so sorry!" Jory exclaimed, quickly bending to pick them up.

"It wasn't you," Cressida mumbled, kneeling as well.

But Jory continued and hadn't heard her. "I have been a waitress for ten years, and despite being clumsy at so many things I have never dropped a tray. I'm not sure what just happened!"

She went to continue but Cressida looked up and put her hand on Jory's arm. "It wasn't you," she said again.

Jory met her eyes and they shared a moment, neither knowing quite what that moment meant.

A tumble and faint "Oof!" sounded behind the garden wall. Mago.

"Good morning, little doves! I smelled Cressida's famous coffee. Yes, thank you very much, I will join."

Mago reached out to take one of the marothopita Cressida had cleaned up and put back on the tray, but Cressida's hand stopped her. "You do *not* want to eat that," Cressida said with meaning. Mago gave her a stern look and shook her head.

"Mago, this is Marjory St. James," Cressida introduced her. "She arrived on the ferry just the other night." She nudged Mago under the table. She did not want Jory to know she was the first guest. Mago kicked her back and refused to meet her eyes.

"We are already fine friends, Jory and I. Oh look, Jory, you can see the ferry coming in from here. It's quite a sight. Sometimes, when Cressida does not know it, I come sit at this very spot and watch the ferries come in."

"I will get new locks," Cressida mumbled as they all watched the great ferry come into the bay below.

"I can't believe I was on that ferry just the other night. It looks so small from here," Jory mused. "It felt like a floating skyscraper on the water when I was on it. Just look at it now. Perspective is really amazing, isn't it?"

All three looked down to the bay. Cressida got the same pang she always did, followed by a deep sadness. Leo would not be on that boat, either. She sighed. Leo. Leo would expect her to offer Jory a ride to town. He would also expect that she would have eaten by now, seeing as they were opening a bed and breakfast.

"Jory, I must go down to the town soon, if you would like a ride."

"Thank you, that would be lovely. I'll just grab my sweatshirt," Jory said.

"Do not rush. Enjoy your coffee while I prepare you a plate of fruit and yogurt to start your day. Mago, will you help me in the kitchen?"

Jory turned to Mago. "Thank you for introducing me to Arie and for the company last night. I hope we get to know more of one another over the next week."

Mago smiled at Jory as she watched her pour a cup of coffee and followed Cressida into the house.

"She is staying," Mago said, not as a question.

"I know, Mago," Cressida said tiredly.

"Cressida, he is dead. Leonidas is dead. You have your very first guest, a girl around your own age who seems lovely, who adores your food and would be a good friend if you let her. Please, my dear girl, join the living again."

"I don't know how."

~

Cressida dropped Jory at the end of the road in the main town of Naxos, which was properly called Chora Naxos, Mago had told her. She walked to the end of a peninsula to the famed Portara, the Temple of Apollo, or the Great Door of Naxos. It was truly a spectacular sight, this unfinished marble doorway looking out to the sea. She wished she could have seen it coming in on the ferry.

Jory had the same rush she always got looking at a piece of ancient history. It did not feel like history to her. A temple, a church, a structure—it was like bridging a gap between history and today somehow, making the past feel more real, and bringing her this unbelievably comforting feeling that the world had gone on for thousands of years before her, and would continue on for thousands of years after. The world may have phones and computers, but it did not produce structures like this anymore.

She sometimes wished she had studied history or archeology instead of philosophy, but her philosophy department had a competitive debating team that she fell in love with early on and she couldn't bear to leave. She was a good student with good grades, but even she had to admit that despite her passion for it, she often lost her debates. For her graduation present, her teammates had bought her a sweatshirt they'd designed. On the front under the university logo was Jory's favorite phrase to end her debates.

Does that make sense?

The text on the back was *NO!*

She pulled the sweatshirt on now, thinking of Kate, who was on the team with her.

Jory met Kate on their first day at the University of Maryland. She clearly remembered the day Kate and her parents arrived at the huge building called Cumberland Hall which would now be their new home.

Jory's mom, Cindy, had transformed their room as she always did. In the photos online the rooms were large but uninviting, with white walls, two single beds, and a side table with a closet. But their room looked nothing like that. Sheer linen curtains hung from the windows, and there were pictures and shelves on the walls and a wooden plaque on the wall that read "Life takes you to unexpected places to bring you HOME."

The beds were covered in thick creamy comforters with blue throw pillows and classic quilts at the end. The desk supplied by the school was replaced by a white and oak desk with two chairs, and a beautiful throw rug was in the middle of the room. When Kate opened the door, she and her parents stood looking like they had the wrong room.

"It wasn't me. Feel free to take anything down you don't like," Jory had said, inviting them in.

Kate looked exactly the opposite of Jory, who was willowy with frizzy blonde hair and a wide grin. Kate was smaller but with an hourglass figure, long brown hair that looked like it was brushed a hundred times a day, and a heart-shaped face with an expression that made her look genuinely kind.

"Sorry about my mom. She can't help it, honestly. I'm Jory," she had said, extending her hand. "Short for Marjory."

"But everybody calls you Jory," Kate had answered with a smile.

Thinking of her friends made her long for their company, so she started at a brisk pace walking and looking for a little shop where she could buy some postcards and perhaps a new book in English, as Cressida's guesthouse did not have the book exchange that she was accustomed to from other guesthouses during her travels.

She supposed Chora Naxos might have seemed a charming small town coming from Los Angeles, but compared to Potamia it was downright large. She heard some tourists coming down the steep street talking about something called "Kastro," so she started making mental notes about where she wanted to explore. But first, finding a bookshop.

After turning down countless alleyways, Jory finally found a shop with a "Books in English" sign on the window. She stepped into what appeared to be an art gallery. A young woman came from the back, a smile of greeting on her face. The woman was only a bit older than her, probably in her early thirties, with straight black hair and a thick fringe, wearing an off-the-shoulder red top and black capri pants with high striped heels.

"How can I help?" she said in lightly accented English.

"Well, I actually came in for a book and some postcards. I didn't realize it was an art gallery. Are you the artist?"

She raised one eyebrow. "No, this is a collection of pieces from artists all over the island. They are more high-end pieces, quite expensive. The books in English are in the back corner with a few other little souvenirs."

"Oh. Thank you." Jory loved art and longed to peruse the gallery but felt like an intruder in the high-end shop, dressed as she was. Instead, she quickly looked through postcards and picked her favorite five, all copies of the artists' work in the gallery. The old used books were two euro each so she grabbed three: a little pocket guide to Naxos in English, a history of Greece and its mythology, which she thought would be interesting while she explored the place, and a light novel for fun.

She went to the counter to pay and the woman put her books in a small bag, nodding and heading to the back of the shop. Jory looked down at her sweatshirt and shook her head. "Excuse me?"

The woman turned back to her, one eyebrow raised.

"Do you think perhaps you could tell me where you do your shopping?"

"My shopping?"

"Yes, for your clothes. You look very nice and I…" Jory glanced down and gave a shamefaced smile.

She seemed to be considering for a moment, then she nodded. "Meet me here on Friday after work. I will take you to a local shop the tourists do not know about."

Jory was surprised. "That's very kind of you. I didn't expect—"

"I make a commission," the woman said bluntly.

"Okay. Thank you. I think," Jory muttered, about to walk out when she heard the bell over the door.

If the woman behind the counter had looked striking before, she was like a supermodel now with her megawatt smile. "Shane!"

Jory turned to see a man in his early thirties, with curling brown hair and a short beard, his eyes blue and sparkling, his smile wide and cheeky. Jory's mouth went dry. He was dressed casually in tan khaki shorts and a button-down shirt rolled up to his elbows, yet somehow he looked as elegant as the woman in the shop.

"Tell me you've come to whisk me away?" the woman said, kissing each of his cheeks and holding his arms for what seemed like a long time.

"Only so you can break my heart? Why so cruel, Selene?" He gave her a grin worthy of a movie star and looked up, noticing Jory for the first time.

His smile made her more self-conscious than she had felt for a long time. Jory knew she was not unattractive, but today, in her baggy sweatshirt and in the company of a woman so put together, she felt unbelievably ratty.

"Shane, I will break your heart, time and again, if only you would let me," Selene sighed dramatically. But the man was still looking at Jory, who was now looking at the ceiling and blushing. Selene frowned. "I will go get your painting now."

He strolled over closer to where Jory stood. *Get yourself together, Marjory*, she told herself. *You're a grown woman, not a besotted teenager.* She turned to smile and found he was very close, so close she stepped back and nearly tripped.

"I'm sorry," he said. "I was trying to read your sweatshirt just to make sure. You're a Terp."

"What?" She went momentarily blank.

"The University of Maryland Terrapins, right? Everyone knows you as the Terps. Great basketball team. I'd say they were our rivals but it's hardly a rivalry if you lose every game." He laughed. "Penn State," he added, putting his hands in his pockets and shrugging.

She was finally catching on, looking down at her sweatshirt and smiling. *One win for you, sweatshirt.* "Ah yes, good school. Aside from their basketball team."

"So did you just graduate or something? Summer abroad in Europe?" he asked casually.

"I'll take that as a compliment and not a dis on my sweatshirt," Jory teased. "It may be seven years old but a good sweatshirt is hard to find these days."

"Here you are, Shane," said Selene, hurrying in from the back of the shop. "Your painting." She handed the wrapped canvas to him. "If you come back tomorrow, I will have the Certificate of Authenticity ready for you."

"Selene, every day you say if I come back tomorrow you will have the rest for me. I'm beginning to think you might be pulling a scam on me." Shane chuckled, winking at Jory. He reached out his hand to hers to shake. "Nice to meet you, Terp."

Jory lifted her hand, but the moment his skin touched hers it was as if an electrical current ran through her body. She wrenched her hand from his and stumbled back into a display of cardboard prints, sending them toppling.

"Whoa!" he said, reaching to catch the stand, but Jory jumped back again to avoid his touch and managed to take down yet another display.

She did not even want to look from sheer embarrassment.

"Are you okay?" he asked with concern, no hint of humor in his voice.

"I'm fine, thank you," she muttered, starting to collect the prints into a pile.

"Here, let me help," he said.

"*No!* I mean, no thank you," she amended, blushing even more.

But Jory was saved by Selene. "Shane, darling, please spare her the embarrassment. I will help her, and I'll see you soon with the documents."

"But—"

"Shoo, shoo," Selene said and Jory could hear the smile on her lips.

Finally Jory heard the door close and she slowly turned to see Selene, looking at her with an eyebrow raised, tapping one foot on the floor.

"I'm so sorry," said Jory. "I don't know what happened. I'll clean all this up, I promise."

But Selene raised both eyebrows then and pointed to the door.

Jory nodded, grabbed her things and headed for the exit.

"Friday at four, for the shopping," Selene said from behind her.

Jory turned. "You're actually still going to take me? After that?"

Selene rolled her eyes. "Commission, I told you. Plus, I owe you."

"Owe me?" Jory asked, confused. "For what?"

"Making me look even better than I already do."

Jory couldn't help but smile and wave to Selene, who rolled her eyes again.

Once outside, she walked down to the waterfront to grab a bite to eat, rubbing her hand that had touched Shane's.

It was sizzling.

Dear Liz & Kate

~~*Dear Liz & Kate*~~

~~*I think I met my sizzler. I'm freaking out and buying a plane ticket tomorrow…*~~

~~*Dear Liz & Kate*~~

~~*Everything is so wonderful here! I'm having the best time of my life and it is completely conducive to exactly how I want to live my life and why I want to live it the way I do. I mean, I'm a traveler! I am completely open to all situations that life can throw at me!*~~

This is officially two ruined postcards! Damnit.

Dear Liz & Kate

You will be delighted to know that I am finally going to retire my debate team sweatshirt, though to be fair, in its last hurrah, it did begin a conversation with a gorgeous man, even if it did have him call me "Terp." Now don't get all excited, I will never see him again as we're both American tourists. I met him in an art gallery on the island of Naxos. Actually, I am staying in a very small village nine kilometers (about six miles) from the main tourist town called Potamia, at a lovely little no-name guesthouse run by a woman named Cressida. She doesn't seem to like me much, truth be told, but I am determined. I have met a few of the locals in Potamia—Mago, her neighbor, is great company. More details to come. I think I'll stay a little while on the island. Something about it feels like home. And it has nothing to do with the gorgeous stranger, so stop all thoughts of that at once. Miss you like a rogue limb.

X Jory

There, she thought. Honest enough but without the detail about the sizzle. She simply couldn't deal with Liz and Kate going on about that again.

Jory had had her fill of Chora Naxos by the late afternoon. She had a big lunch of whole fish, fries and Greek salad at one of the restaurants on the main waterfront strip on Naxos Quay. The food was fresh and the ingredients local, but the meal was obviously catering to tourists who wanted to sit on the water for a view. She was of course one of them, but after that cake yesterday, she felt there was something perhaps a bit special about Cressida's cooking, even if she never got to try the flatbreads this morning that looked and smelled divine. A sudden pang for Potamia and her room hit her, which was surprising. She was pretty certain Cressida didn't really like having a guest in her guesthouse and didn't want to be friends, and yet Jory still wanted to be there more than she wanted to be anywhere else. She had her new books and a bag of food, including olives, sliced meats and some local cheese, for dinner on her porch.

She got the last bus back to Potamia where it dropped her in front of her guesthouse around 5:30 p.m. She couldn't wait to pick up her moped the next morning and explore further afield, so she flipped through her new guidebook and earmarked some pages. Jory took a hot shower in the classic Greek bathroom—a sink and toilet on one side with an open shower that filled the entire bathroom floor before draining. She hadn't quite got used to the design yet, or the door that kept jamming from the expansive heat of the room. Finally, after mopping the water down the middle drain and wrapping a towel around herself, she kicked the door open.

Keep the door open, Jory, remember that!

After she dressed, Jory decided to take a chance on Cressida. Bringing the chilled bottle of wine she had bought, she knocked on the main door. She knocked twice more before Cressida finally opened the door, only an inch. Though it was still early, she was in what looked like pajamas and her face looked puffy and swollen.

"Yes, Jory, how can I help?" she asked politely.

"I bought a bottle of wine—I just wanted to see if you were interested in having a glass before you finished the day? It seemed too nice to waste on just me." Jory smiled.

Cressida did not smile, though she looked at her for a long moment. "That is very kind, Jory, and thank you. Perhaps another time. I am quite busy tonight." She went to close the door but remembered herself. "Sleep well, I will have breakfast for you at ten o'clock in the morning, unless you would like it earlier?"

Jory sighed. "Ten is perfect, thank you. Sleep well and goodnight."

The door closed.

"Psst. Jory." She looked around for the hissed voice. "Up here!" It was Mago, grinning at her from above the fence separating her house from Cressida's. "I heard you say you had wine. I'd be more than happy to share with you if you'd like." She winked.

Jory made her way to the road and around the fence to where Mago stood with the door open.

"Don't worry, she'll come around," she said softly, ushering Jory in.

Mago's house was narrow and much smaller than the guesthouse next door, but it was decorated with family photos and painted in bright colors, with a second story where she had a seating area and a terrace overlooking a small garden.

"Have a seat on the terrace," she said. Jory opened the wine as Mago brought two glasses and a little board of cheese and bread outside. "What did you get?"

"Oh, just a little bottle of something white and chilled that said it was from the island. I was limited to the wine shop in Chora," she said, pouring the wine. Jory took a sip. It was not exceptionally flavorful but felt cool and crisp in her mouth.

"It's certainly not as nice as any of Arie's wines—I should have bought more than just the one yesterday. But is it okay?"

Mago tasted and swirled in her mouth like a professional. "It's wine and has alcohol. Just fine then," she said, and Jory laughed.

Mago handed her a slice of bread with some soft cheese on top. It was delicious, but suddenly Jory felt an unbelievable sadness. She couldn't swallow and put the bread down.

"Sourdough?" Jory asked. Mago nodded. "It tastes perfect, so soft in the middle with a crunch on the crust, the cheese melding into it. And yet...I suddenly feel as though I'll cry if I take another bite. Which is so strange, because until this moment I had no intention of crying."

Mago sighed. "Yes, this is Cressida's great gift and curse. Her baking contains a piece of her soul. When her husband died and she baked for the funeral, the congregation was inconsolable for two solid hours, eating her grief."

"I didn't know she had a husband who died. She's so young," Jory said softly.

"Yes. Leonidas, just last year. He was a very charming young man from Athens who came to the island one day and fell in love straightaway with our Cressida. For years they lived in a little shoebox in Chora, saving money while working to buy the house next door, which they dreamed of turning into a guesthouse and taverna. They bought it about three years ago, renovating most of it themselves with the help of the village. The garden was cultivated to provide herbs and food for the taverna. Cressida is an exemplary cook. Leo sometimes took the ferry back to Athens to visit family and buy things for the guesthouse. Then one day we watched the boat come in, but it was only his body they were bringing back. Car accident. Very sudden."

Jory put the bread down, as she certainly didn't need to bring more tears of compassion to her eyes. Mago patted her knee and took another bite.

"Doesn't the bread affect you in the same way?" Jory asked.

"Oh, it does, but I too lost a husband and so the grief and sadness, it is familiar, like an old friend."

Four

Jory picked up the moped just after her breakfast of an omelet filled with peppers, tomatoes and a cheese Cressida said she made here at the house. She was not overly chatty but was friendlier than before. Jory decided she would try a little each day to befriend Cressida, the young woman whose husband had died so young, now catering to a guest she was obviously unprepared for, but she wouldn't push it.

"Here we are, Miss Marjory," Nico said with his friendly grin, handing her a helmet. "Yours for the week. Do you need some suggestions as to where to go?"

"Oh, that would be great! I have a list here," she said, pulling out the notes she'd jotted down from the guidebook. Though it was at least five years old, she assumed many if not all of the places would still be there. Nico took the list and the guidebook from her, opening to the map page and making a few notes. He handed it back to her.

"I can tell by the places you have picked to visit you like to explore off the beaten path, so I have circled a few more beaches and coves for you to find. You may get lost. Don't panic. If you are going down, you will end up at the water. If you are going up, you are headed back home. Got it?" he asked, winking.

She grinned and gave him a thumbs up. "Got it. Thanks, Nico! I'll have her back next Tuesday!"

Nico waved and headed back to the shop. Jory could hear the arguing begin.

"Why do you throw things at me, Nefeli? Are you jealous?"

"Jealous?! Of *what*?" she yelled.

"The life you could have had if you'd never married me! Like hers!"

Jory quickly pulled the helmet over her head and started the engine before she could hear any more.

See, Jory, how lucky are you that you never want to be in a relationship or fall in love? Mago said Nico and Nefeli had such sparks when they met that little fires would start in fireplaces around the village. Like Mom always says, you find the one that makes you sizzle and burn, your life will change forever.

What if it ended up like this? Giving up everything she knew and loved to stay. Like Nefeli did.

But she would not have that fate, she thought, pulling open the map and picking her first destination.

Life, Jory, not fate—stop thinking that word! You know there is no such thing as fate, damnit!

Because even if there was someone who made her skin light fire, her sizzler, she would not be tempted. And Shane would be off the island before she knew it. Not that he was anyone who made her feel anything other than silly. No, she felt nothing. Nothing at all.

Jory spent the next few days exploring the island on her little red moped. She loved the feel of the wind on her body, the world rushing past quickly, but not so quickly she couldn't see everything. It opened up the whole island to her. Naxos was the largest island in the Cyclades, at 430 square kilometers, and yet the majority of the population was in Chora Naxos, so even during the busiest tourist season you could find a road and a beach to yourself.

It was early June, and while the summer was officially here and school holidays had begun, the island still felt quiet. The wind had died down and the temperature sat at a steady twenty-six degrees Celsius every day—the perfect combination of humidity and sea breeze to keep it warm enough to want to swim but not so hot it was stifling. The height of the tourist season did not begin until July and peaked in August, so Jory often found herself the only person, or one of a few, in the secret little coves she would ride to.

She went to Mikri Vigla's dual beaches, the northern of the two named Parthenos, which was famous for the "Meltemi" winds she'd felt when she first arrived, where Jory took a windsurfing lesson. It was amazing. When the wind finally lifted her sail, it was as if she were flying, pulled at a speed that brought her on par with a sailboat. She was laughing joyfully until she faceplanted into the water, leaving her with a black eye the next day.

There was Orkos, which was more of an array of hidden little coves with crystal-clear water, and the following day, Alyko, which was surrounded by a forest of cedars. That was her favorite, with its rocky backdrop and big sand dunes—the soft white sand like powder under her feet. It was completely unspoiled, and Jory felt she'd arrived in paradise.

Once she'd explored the more well-known spots, she started on Nico's map, finding hidden coves and beaches where she was often the only person there. These she would circle on her map and show Mago in the evenings. They sometimes had a name and sometimes not. When they didn't, Jory would make one up as if it was the title of an episode of *Friends*. "The One Where I Fell off the Cliff." "The One with the Black Eye." "The One with the Monster Tide," and so on.

Every evening Jory came back to the guesthouse and knocked on Cressida's door with an offer of food or a drink. And every night Cressida opened the door slightly, smiled a smile that didn't reach her eyes, and said no, but thank you, closing the door behind her. And so Jory would end up at Mago's instead.

Every night they shared a Kitron or wine. They talked about seemingly everything, and Jory adored Mago. She had a feeling that Mago was hiding something, but she didn't know her well enough to pry. It was in the way she would look to the moon, as if in a trance sometimes. Or feel her forehead as if wondering if she was overly hot. Or the way she lapsed into silences sometimes after she spoke of Arie, like it made her sad to be so happy.

"So which secret cove did you discover today?" Mago asked.

Jory giggled. "Okay, I named this one, 'The One with the Boobies.'"

Mago laughed so hard, she coughed up her wine. "Could I even try to guess why?"

"No," said Jory, "so I'll tell you. I found this hidden cove, one of the ones on Nico's map. And it is *completely* hidden. So I go for a swim and meet these two lovely girls, and we are chatting and chatting, and finally a wave comes and they jump up and...!"

Mago was in stitches. "Topless! And we have one with the boobies."

"Now we do," she said, laughing.

"Oh, Jory honey, what a gift it is to have a fresh young person here in Potamia. It has been far too long, you know. Far, far too long. I almost wonder if Nefeli was right."

"Nefeli? What does she have to do with this?"

"Last town meeting, right before you came, she shared one of her portents. Change was coming, she said. In the form of a stranger who would feel familiar, somehow. Like home."

Jory was intrigued. "That sounds a bit kooky, and yet exactly like me. I'm a St. James—that is our gift." She paused. "Is it normal, for Nefeli to have, um…portents?"

"Oh yes," Mago said, "it is her gift. Many people brush off her words because who knows what she's looking up on that phone of hers. But I know Nefeli Castellanos. Not as well as Cressida, but well enough."

"Cressida and Nefeli?"

"The absolute best of friends, once upon a time, though I don't think they've spoken since Leo died."

"What happened?" Jory asked, leaning forward.

"How would I know?"

Jory laughed. "Because you know everything, Mago."

"True, but not if it's someone else's gossip."

Jory hesitated. "And what of your own gossip?"

Mago chuckled softly, glancing back up at the moon. "I'll let you know if I ever have any."

"Okay," Jory said, squeezing Mago's hand and letting it go. For now.

On Friday at four in the afternoon, Jory stood outside the art gallery as Selene closed and locked the door behind her. She turned and looked at Jory, who had ditched the sweatshirt but was still in jeans, a T-shirt and sneakers. Selene once again looked at her, her eyes narrowing when they settled on her hair.

"Is there honestly nothing you can do about that?" she asked, nodding at Jory's head.

"Not when I have a helmet on and off all day. It can't be that bad," Jory said, touching her head. "What do I look like, seriously?"

Selene pulled out a mirror from her bag and pointed it toward Jory, whose mouth dropped. "Oh my god! I cannot believe I've been walking around like this for three days!" The top part of her hair was flattened by the helmet, but the bottom part which she had not tied back had become so frizzy from the humidity, it was three times its normal thickness around her shoulders. She pulled it into a low bun but still looked ridiculous.

Selene's mouth quirked into an almost smile. "Come, Madam Dionysia's shop is this way. Her selection is divine. It gives hope to even the most dismal prospects," she said, looking pointedly at Jory, who blushed but followed quickly behind her.

Selene opened the door to Madam Dionysia's Boutique, leading Jory to a small sitting room. She walked through to the back studio and knocked three times, their signal when Selene brought a paying tourist. Madam, whose real name was Doris, came out from the back, dressed in a fine red pantsuit.

Selene remembered when she was younger and had no money, she would watch the rich tourists come in and out of this shop and admire Madam, swearing one day it would be her shopping here. Madam caught her once, shortly after Selene began to work in the gallery across the way, staring through the window of her shop before she opened.

"Have you ever heard the phrase 'fake it until you make it'?" Madam had said from behind her that day, five or six years ago. Selene had startled at the voice behind her, hating that she'd been caught looking longingly. She had put on her haughtiest expression. Madam had nodded approvingly. "I see you have then. Come in, I've been watching you these past few weeks."

Swallowing her pride, as she so desperately wanted to go into Madam Dionysia's Boutique more than anything, she followed the elegant woman inside. Madam showed her through the empty sitting room out front with a table for champagne and cheese, and one fitting room draped in gold. There were no clothes in sight but for those on a couple of mannequins, and a trellis of hats, scarves and jewelry.

"Where are all the clothes?" she asked. Selene had expected beautiful rows of satins and silks, organized perhaps by designer.

"Follow me," she said, and so Selene did, out to the back where there were rows of freestanding clothing racks with hundreds of glamorous pieces. Her mouth watered in envy, and she suddenly wanted to leave right then, so jealous was she of what she didn't have. She turned, but Madam stopped her and went to a rack, finding an off-the-shoulder black top and matching tailored cigarette pants. She then went further into a closet and came back with a pair of shoes. She handed it all to Selene.

"Go to your gallery, wear this, and pretend that you are just as good as everyone else who walks through that door. And when they ask you where you get your designer clothes, you bring them to me. For every five thousand euro you help me sell, I will give you one new outfit—that will be your commission. And in time, you will gain the life you want, and no one will ever know it wasn't yours to begin with."

That was years ago and Selene was well on her way. She saved her salary, which was not bad, to buy the finest shoes, to go to nice restaurants where eligible men might offer to buy her drinks, and to have a nice apartment she decorated well. But she still earned Madam's best commissions and they had, over the years, become friends.

"Selene," Doris said, kissing both her cheeks. "Thank you, my dear, for another customer. You truly have excelled in your role here." She looked out into the shop where Jory stood awkwardly twisting her hands. "You're right, she definitely needs a new wardrobe. I never know why these wealthy Americans play down their looks this way. A woman should take pride in the way she dresses!"

Selene nodded, turning her head to avoid Madam's eyes. She knew very well Jory could not afford anything in this shop, but a little fib never hurt anyone. She brought a girl who wanted new clothes, that was her job. She knew it wasn't right to involve Madam in her scheme, but Jory needed to know who was on the playing field against her.

"Come, I'll introduce you. Just the top-end pieces, remember?" Selene said, and Madam followed her out with a rack of her finest garments.

Jory immediately felt embarrassed when Madam Dionysia brought her the selection to try on. She should have known, based on Selene's attire and the setup of the shop, that they would be well out of her price range. She'd been in a store like this in Beverly Hills once and she'd never forgotten it.

There was no doubt the clothes were worth the price tag, hand-stitched and made with the highest quality fabrics. And they were beautiful. When Madam brought out an emerald-green jumpsuit with a high collar and open sleeves that she adored and fit her perfectly, she thought she might even consider the splurge. But when she saw that splurge would have set her back two thousand euro, she gasped. That was her budget for a month of traveling!

"That's a lovely color on you, Jory," Selene said. And Jory, turning to glance suspiciously at the sweetness of her voice, did not miss the amusement in her eyes.

Selene knew she could not afford these pieces and brought her anyway. It was a type of sabotage and Jory wondered if Selene simply did not like her for some reason, or if that reason might be that guy, Shane—the one she had not thought of once, not at all. Selene had flirted with him with great enthusiasm.

She didn't know whether to be embarrassed, hurt or amused. She was amused by Selene, but not amused that she had to now deal with a situation that would embarrass Madam, who had taken so much time with Jory and was incredibly passionate about her clothes.

In the end she decided to simply be honest, and stopped Madam as she was bringing another beautiful dress.

"Madam, these pieces you have selected are unbelievably beautiful and I would love to purchase them. But I am afraid I have wasted your time and yours, Selene," she said, looking at her. "I didn't realize how far out of my price range they would be, though I should have, considering how beautiful Selene's clothes are. But I am afraid I simply cannot afford them."

Madam looked at Selene, confused, but to Jory she smiled. "Of course, miss," she said professionally, nodding her head and going to the back of the shop again.

Jory turned back to Selene, who had her right eyebrow raised and was staring at Jory with mock innocence. "I am so sorry to have embarrassed you. This is where *I* shop, of course, so I assumed it would suit your budget as well."

Jory realized then that this was definitely about the guy. Selene was going out of her way to prove that she was somehow better than Jory, and that was always because of a man. "Did you think I was interested in that guy at the shop or something? Is that what this is about?" Jory asked.

Selene looked up in surprise but did not meet Jory's eyes. "Shane? Good lord, no. I'm holding out for a rich man to sweep me off my feet. Shane, he is attractive, but he's a passerby. He'll be off this island in a few days and back to whatever it is he does. Do you know what he does?"

Jory shrugged. "Not a clue. I only met him that once. He's leaving soon, you said?"

Selene nodded.

"Great, that's a relief."

Selene looked confused when just then, Madam came back out, radiant and holding up a yellow dress. "This one!" she declared.

Jory's eyes lit up at the simple floral sundress that buttoned up in the front, with short puffed sleeves and a cinched waist.

"Oh, thank you! I'll go try it on!"

"What are you doing, Madam?" Selene hissed. "And where did you even get that dress? It's not even stylish."

"Selene, Selene, you do what you do, and I do what I do. You've had your fun, now let me have mine. She said she's not interested in the guy, so leave it. I always have a rack of less expensive items for the budget crowd, otherwise I wouldn't be able to cater to everyone. And I think that dress is very charming. It will suit her."

Jory came out in the yellow sundress. Suddenly the room smelled like the banana milkshakes Selene and her mother used to make every Sunday night as a special girls' treat after her dad left them for a rich tourist when she was six. The days were filled with bitter resentment when she was in high school, all but for Sunday milkshake nights, when the world felt a safe and hopeful place. So much did she feel that right now, her throat closed up and she nodded tightly, trying to keep a tear from falling.

She nodded and Jory smiled. "Thanks."

Selene almost smiled back.

In the few days she'd been exploring the island, Jory nearly always finished in Chora, so she'd become very familiar with the main town on the island. She loved exploring the Naxos Kastro, the thirteenth century Venetian castle that contained both the Archeological and the Venetian Museums. It was a beacon at the top of the hillside town where all roads led. The Naxos Promenade along the waterfront was touristy but still a beautiful stroll next to the crystal-clear blue of the Aegean Sea. Her little village of Potamia was far superior in her heart and she felt at home there, but she did love Chora Naxos.

Mago had told her of a very good restaurant a bit off the beaten path where Cressida used to work, and Jory was so curious to know more of Cressida's past. She wanted to ask about her husband, about Nefeli, her cooking, why her guesthouse had never had a guest before her. So many things she wanted to know, so she came here to perhaps pick up a good conversation starter that might engage Cressida that evening.

Jory made her way to the old part of town, past the water-front restaurants filled with tourists, and turned down a little alley until she got to the place Mago had recommended, Rigani. It was very busy, but most of the diners looked Greek and not like tourists. Small tables covered with red and white checked tablecloths spilled out of the compact space and onto the side-walk. A waiter noticed Jory hovering and pointed to a table outside, told her to have a seat and he'd be right with her.

A moment later he was handing Jory a menu. "Good evening, miss. May I start you with a drink?" he asked.

"Yes, please. A glass of your house white wine, thanks."

"I shall bring it right over."

Jory perused the menu, which was slightly pricier than some of the other restaurants she'd been to, but the dishes seemed original and unique. She loved food and dining out, discovering new dishes. She looked up, right at the very moment that man, Shane, was walking toward the restaurant.

"Shit!" she hissed, looking around for an escape route, instead lifting the menu in front of her face so that she was hidden behind it. *Shit, shit, shit. Surely he won't be coming here. He's just passing by.*

"Do find a table, sir. I will be with you shortly," her waiter said, his voice drawing near.

"Your wine, miss?" he said, glancing down at her with a confused look.

"Oh, yes, thank you," she whispered.

He looked around, wondering what to do. Finally he leaned in and whispered back, "Would you like to hear the specials?"

She peeped over her menu, seeing Shane looking for a table. The one just a few down from her was free but it hadn't been cleared yet after the previous diners. He went to stand near it, though he didn't sit down.

"Miss?" her waiter whispered again.

"Oh, um. I'll just take your house specialty. Whatever you recommend."

He nodded. "In that case I must recommend the pasta with fresh locally caught tuna and capers. It is our signature dish."

"Perfect," she whispered with a smile.

"Excellent, miss. Your menu, please?" he said, reaching out his hand.

"Oh, um, no, I'm fine, thank you," she said, holding the menu up higher as she saw Shane glancing over curiously.

"Miss, your menu, if you please. I'm afraid we are a bit short tonight," the waiter said, his patience waning.

"Okay," she said reluctantly, handing him the menu, just as the waiter thankfully stepped in front of Shane's line of sight as he went to clean the table. Jory had just enough time to scootch her chair around so she was facing the other way before he could see her.

Nice one, Jory. She gave herself a small hurrah.

"Terp!" she heard behind her and jumped in her seat.

"Damnit," she muttered. She turned, looking up, her mouth going dry the same way it did when she first saw him a few days before. He was extraordinarily good-looking. Seeing him close up, she realized his eyes were the clearest shade of blue. His light brown hair curled slightly and he wore a neat beard. He was dressed in a similar outfit as the other day, but in jeans instead of shorts, the sleeves of his cream linen shirt rolled up over his forearms, which Jory noticed were beautifully sculpted.

Despite the new dress and few other bits she'd purchased from Madam's budget rack the other day, she was back in her University of Maryland sweatshirt and jeans.

It doesn't matter what you look like, Jory. Because you are not at all interested. Not even a little bit. And his touch does nothing for you…

"Under the assumption that you likely have a name that is not actually Terp, allow me to introduce myself," he said. "I'm Shane." He held out his hand.

Jory stared at it, her heart aflutter. She couldn't shake his hand. Because even though she was not at all, not even a little bit interested in him, she could not deny that his touch made her skin tingle with electricity. *Sizzle.*

She continued to stare at his hand. Eventually he pulled it back, his expression confused.

"Jory. Short for Marjory, but everyone calls me Jory," she muttered out of habit, feeling embarrassed at her rudeness but unable to bring herself to touch his hand.

"Jory, I like that. Though I was getting quite fond of calling you Terp in my head," he said.

"You…thought about me?" she said, hating the way her voice sounded the tiniest bit breathless.

This time he smiled fully, and Jory noticed he had perfect white teeth and a slightly lopsided grin. Her skin was tingling with his presence. She felt herself drawn toward him like a magnet, so she quickly shook herself out of it and leaned back in her seat.

"Are you dining alone? Would you like some company?"

"No!" she practically yelled. "Sorry," she said, lowering her voice. "I mean no, thank you. I'm, um, busy. Journaling," she said, pointing to her little book on the table.

"Oh, okay," he said, obviously disappointed. But he brightened and pulled a journal from his back pocket. Jory recognized it as a sketch journal. She'd done a sketch journaling tour in Paris and had loved the concept but was a terrible artist. "I love journaling when I travel too."

Stop making me feel the crazy desire to see into your soul! What have you drawn in that book?

"I'll let you get to your table and to your sketch journal then," she said as coolly as possible, lowering her gaze and opening her own diary. "Nice to meet you," she said as though an afterthought, proffering a smile that was meant to be polite but didn't quite reach her eyes.

He started to walk away and Jory relaxed, releasing a breath, until he turned around and came closer to her again, reaching to touch her shoulder.

Jory flailed about, knocking her wine glass clear off the table. It shattered on the floor as Jory squealed an inelegant "Eek!" People were staring as the waiter rushed over and quickly cleaned the glass at her feet.

"Christ, are you okay?" Shane asked, reaching out again with a concerned look. Jory recoiled, mortified, speechless, and he turned away, frowning. "Fine, I'll leave you be then."

"Thank you," she breathed with obvious relief, which elicited a look of hurt on his handsome face. Jory felt her stomach twist in guilt.

Shane finally went to sit at his own table. The waiter brought Jory a replacement glass of wine, and she turned her chair around even more so that her back was completely to Shane. She pretended to write in her journal even as her meal arrived.

"Our house specialty, miss. Handmade pasta with locally caught tuna and capers, and fresh seasonal tomatoes. Enjoy."

And for a brief moment, she did, focusing only on the food and jotting notes down in her journal. But she could feel the same electric tingling that she had when Shane was near, and kept rubbing the back of her neck. He was looking at her, she could *feel* it. But why? She turned around to look at him, but he was working furiously in his sketch journal. Had she been imagining that feeling? Of his eyes on her, making her skin feverish? The burning continued. Her food was truly delicious but she was finding it difficult to concentrate.

She began shifting her seat gradually to the side so she could see if he stared at her. That felt better. Her skin still felt warm, but like she was sunbathing, not on fire. Every time she glanced up, certain he was looking at her, he was always focused on something else. When she finished her meal, she crossed her arms and stared at him, waiting to catch him in the act. A minute passed before he finally looked up and caught her gaze, looking so startled she immediately jumped up from the table in embarrassment and turned to slam straight into her waiter.

He did not look amused.

"I'm so sorry," Jory said. "I'm leaving, I promise."

She practically ran to the counter to pay, apologizing again and leaving a tip the same amount as her actual bill, which she hoped would placate the waiter. She hurried out and up the street, and just as she arrived at the corner, she turned one last time to see Shane staring right at her, this time with a smirk. He waved and went back to his journal, whistling, and Jory had a feeling he could read her every thought.

Thank god Selene said he was leaving soon or she'd end up breaking everything in Naxos. With a touch like his, she'd take the Portara down next.

Five

At four o'clock in the morning, Mago gave up trying to sleep and turned on her light, pulled on her robe and went out to her balcony, opening the Kitron Jory had brought from Arie. It smelled of orange sweetness and a little bit of Arie, making her heart flutter. She took a sip straight from the bottle, like a secret honeyed kiss from her lover.

Marjory had blushed like a schoolgirl when Mago had proudly called him that. Young people, they think the older the person, the less human they are when it comes to sex and love, but that certainly was not the case. She and Arie had a very physical relationship, but it was more than that. Arie loved her and had for years, and he was not in any way shy about it. He loved her, and he wanted more, and he let her know that whenever she was ready, he was all hers, for the rest of their lives together.

She slid her feet into her slippers, as she walked outside her balcony to face him, the man in the moon, who was watching her, waiting for her. She was not ready. Her chest began to ache with anxiety. "Leave me alone," she whispered to the moon.

Mago's mother and her grandmother had both lost their lives to breast cancer when they turned sixty-eight, the exact age Mago was now. When she was younger, she had thought she was invincible. That she was a different kind of Samaras who would escape that fate. But a month ago, just after her own sixty-eighth birthday, she felt a lump under her arm, just above her left breast.

After that, Mago told Arie that she would never marry again. She knew he'd been waiting for the right time to ask her, and recently she'd even been thinking she'd say yes when he did. But not now. She could not bear to say the words "till death parts us," as if by not voicing them out loud, perhaps they could cheat this possible cancer.

"That doesn't mean we can't spend the rest of our lives together," he'd said.

"I never said it didn't," she replied with a small kiss, never saying why that phrase broke her soul, for she was living in joy with her Arie, and the fact that the rest of her life may be ending very soon was enough to leave her so devastated she could barely breathe.

She thought about Cressida's honey happiness cake and all the advice Mago was constantly giving her—to live, to come into the world again and allow herself the happiness she deserved. But what of Mago? Did not she too deserve the same happiness? Her children were grown, and her husband had been gone for eighteen years.

Without knowing why, she rummaged through her closet until she came across a blue jersey dress she'd made years ago, for someone in particular, though she wouldn't know who that particular someone was until the moment they needed it. And suddenly, she knew that Cressida needed it, and needed it now. It needed some stitching and finishing, so she went to her machine and began to finish the dress started so long ago now, she did not even remember when.

Mago learned about her particular gift when she was twelve years old. She went into her first day of home economics class, which all girls were required to take through their secondary years, and they were told to design a dress for their little dolls. None of them yet knew how to sew, but for the buttons and mending they had all been doing since their hands were old enough to thread a needle. But what she could see, very clearly, was something the other girls could not. She could see the colors, all around her, and feel the difference between the satin and the silk, the cotton and the linen, the wool and the poly blend, and know how they were meant to go together to be perfect. She did not draw anything. She just started cutting and sewing. And her doll's dress was a thing of great beauty that made her immediately popular with the other girls.

She tried to explain to her teacher what she saw. "Well, I could see the fibers of the materials all had different waves." It was the only way she could think to describe the way they shimmered. There were sound waves, right? Couldn't there be color waves as well? "And the colors, they started talking to each other," which was the only way she could describe the way they naturally radiated toward one another. It seemed so obvious to her that she was sure everyone else saw it the same way. "And then they just all came together and I could see it perfectly. The dress that was meant for Holly...my dolly," she concluded.

And so it was greatly unexpected that she was taken to the front of the room and had her hands slapped repeatedly with the meter stick for being an immoral liar and somehow, without proof, a cheat.

"I wasn't lying, Mama," she said later that night, as her mother gently iced her bruised hands.

"I know you weren't, darling. You are a Samaras, and we women have a gift that was given from the sacred spring many years ago. It was passed down to me from my mother, and now it is passed down to you. How it will grow in you and how you will use it is up to you. But it is best not to talk about the colors that way. People will think you are quite mad." And her mother had smiled at her.

Despite that she never again told the truth about her work, it continued on just the same, for all of her life. Mago and her friends became grown girls. It went from dolls' dresses to dresses for dances, and as they became women, to wedding gowns. If Mago made something for you to wear to a specific occasion, it was meant to be, for it was perfect.

What Mago's gift gave to her friends was a sense of rightness. What it gave Mago was the finances, independence and confidence to adventure off on her own and travel around Europe when she was old enough. When her mother became ill and she came home a year later, she married Kristopher.

Kristopher had been much older than her, already nearly thirty when they married, while Mago was just nineteen years old. Theirs was not quite an arranged marriage, but as close as you could get in those days. Kris had worked with her father, and he was from a good family with a solid job and was financially stable. He was the perfect match for her, her father said. Mago had rebelled at first. She was a Samaras woman, strong-willed and vivacious, she had traveled, and she had a great gift. She was young, and she wanted to *live*.

But being a Samaras woman still meant being a Greek Orthodox woman in the 1970s. The time before divorce was legal, the time when an arranged marriage was still what a woman in her village was meant to accept. And so she married Kristopher. He was kind and gentle, and they had a good marriage, and a good friendship, and they had two boys they both adored. It was a heart attack that took him when he was sixty years old. Mago had been only fifty.

She had mourned for him, greatly. After over thirty years together, he was her family, her friend, the father of her children. He had not been her great romantic adventure, but she had a happy life.

She met Arie…well, she met Arie *again*, about five years later—a man she had known most of her life. They had been friends as children and gone to school together. But it was as though they were meeting for the first time, and while they took their time embracing what they felt for one another, once they did, there was no doubt that it was true and genuine love and care for one another.

She took another sip of the Kitron he had made specially for her and hugged the bottle to her chest. She wanted to marry Arie. She wanted to embrace the second chance she had found at love, the joy he brought her. She wanted to heed every word she'd told Cressida and let herself live again. But she could not do that to Arie. She could not give him the hope of a life together when it would be so short-lived. When she could be dying. She knew she should go see her doctor but she was too afraid to know. And too afraid to not know.

Her legs became restless, her foot tapping endlessly. She finally got up and put on a jacket over her pajamas instead of her robe, pulled on her walking shoes and went out for a stroll. The town was black, the man in the moon hiding behind a cloud. She walked not far, but just far enough to try to release the energy in her legs, in her heart, the tireless thoughts in her mind. At the end of the path, just before she turned around, the scent of jasmine affronted her senses. Her favorite smell in the world. She loved the way the first bloom grew rampant over walls and gardens, and how for just a few weeks of the year in June, the whole world smelled like heaven should smell. Change was coming.

Suddenly, a light went on at the house beside Mago's. It came from Jory's room in the guesthouse. She heard her stumble around and mumble "damned bathroom door!"

Another light went on. Cressida's. She heard the pots and pans move around. Cressida was about to start baking. And then another light down the village went on, and another, and another. Yes, change was coming.

No, Mago thought, glancing up again and pulling her coat tightly around her. Change was here.

Cressida woke the following morning for the second time at 7:49 a.m. on the floor of her kitchen, covered in flour. She had made a rosemary focaccia at 5 a.m., before she could bake anything dangerous into her bread. While waiting for the bread to cook, she'd dried five trays of figs, then pulled the loaf out of the oven and fallen asleep on the floor. Cressida jumped up now and ran for the shower, realizing how late she was.

She did not make Jory her breakfast at this early hour. Cressida knew she had not been a very good person of late, not as a hostess or friend. Things were happening inside her head, the way she felt, the way she was yearning to live a more proper life. When her honey cake tasted happy, she'd cursed the gods and thrown it out, getting down on her knees and praying to Leo to forgive her for forgetting for just one moment that he was dead and that meant she was too. But then a voice in her head stopped her. A voice that said to her, *Cressida, you cannot go on this way—he is dead and you are not.* She did not know if it was Mago's voice, or Leo's from the heavens, or her own, or even one greater than herself. But she knew she needed to do something.

Nothing in her wardrobe was quite appropriate, but that morning she'd discovered a box at her front door from Mago. As soon as she put on the blue jersey dress, she felt like she was a competent business owner and not a defeated Greek housewife with a pipe dream that was never fulfilled because her husband had died too young. Today, she wanted to be a woman of strength.

She drove the pickup truck to Chora Naxos where a man named Michael Smythe wanted to meet. It was Michael Smythe's name that was signed on the letter from the Resurgence Hotel Group, and his email that had followed asking her for a meeting today. It did not take her long to find the restaurant on the Promenade that was popular with tourists. Naxos was becoming a destination for culinary travelers around the world, and she and Leo had planned to be at the forefront of that movement before he'd died last year. Still, the most popular restaurants along the waterfront continued to serve the same Americanized dishes. Calamari, deep-fried instead of gently sautéed. The most beautiful fresh fish of the Aegean Sea, flash-fried for speed instead of roasted whole in the combi oven with butter and herbs that would allow the freshness of the sea to come through. Greek salad with imported hard feta from the mainland instead of the beautiful local cheese, olives out of a can instead of from one of the local groves. And fries, frozen fries everywhere.

"Mrs. Thermopolis?" A man called from a table at a cafe near the water.

As she walked over, his eyes widened and she felt eternally grateful to Mago for the dress. He had obviously been expecting someone quite different.

"Mr. Smythe?"

He nodded. "I appreciate you coming down to meet me." He waved for the waiter to bring another cup of coffee. "And my apologies for the location—this is the only cafe open this early. I usually go to Fidel's."

Cressida was surprised. "That is a local place. I didn't know any tourists knew about it. They certainly have the best coffee. I never understood why he doesn't open earlier."

Michael Smythe agreed with a nod. He was younger than she'd expected, probably in his mid-thirties, with glasses and a kind smile.

"I actually live here in Chora Naxos most of the year," he said. "My grandmother lives here. I started spending my summer holidays here when I was nine and haven't seemed to stop since." He smiled.

He was not the lawyer type she had been expecting and it threw Cressida off slightly. The waiter brought her coffee and she took a sip to regain balance.

"May I talk a little about the ethos of the Resurgence Group?"

He continued after she nodded. "The Resurgence Hotel Group is a chain of bed and breakfasts and boutique hotels. We don't have any large hotels—we're not like the big chains. It started very small. The CEO worked at a guesthouse that was about to go under financially. He bought it, and with his financial support it became very successful. From there, we have selected some of the finest properties in places around the world to join the group, and we have had remarkable results. Have you looked at our website? You can see that all of our properties are flourishing."

Cressida had looked at the website, and some of the hotels looked charming and beautiful, like she could imagine her guesthouse. And yet there was something about them that felt a little too polished. In the photos, the receptionists were smiling, professional, but they were not family. They were not a local who knew every village secret and every little quirk of the town. They would not drive in a pickup truck telling you stories of the strange gifts of Potamia. They would not be sitting on your porch with you in the late afternoons, with Mago hopping over the balustrade to share a cheeky glass of wine.

The restaurants attached to the Resurgence properties each shared common themes that she could appreciate—a small, locally skilled staff and food that appeared passable. But none of them looked like her kitchen. None of them had her mother's recipes or her own gifted hand. They were pleasing menus, but they could be any menu down on the Promenade right now. None of them were *hers*.

"Tell me, Mr. Smythe—"

"Call me Michael."

"Mr. Smythe," she repeated, "if I *were* to sell, what exactly would become of my guesthouse and taverna? What would be your plan?"

He smiled, relaxing in his seat, and began to speak about the kind of hotel they would run—an out-of-the-way getaway with world-class food and accommodation, outside of the normal tourist haunts. It would be beautiful, charming, rustic.

"And what of me?" she asked when he finally stopped speaking.

It was Michael's turn to look confused. "I don't understand."

"Would I be required to stay on?"

"I can assure you Mrs. Thermopolis that you can walk away with no responsibility whatsoever," he replied confidently.

"I see." It was too much for her to wrap her brain around at the moment. To be truly left with nothing from her life there. But she did have one last question. "And if I don't sell?"

Michael's eyes widened. "Mrs. Thermopolis, we can't force you to sell. But as you can likely imagine, the properties we place an offer on are usually in dire need of financiers. Yours is one of them. We assumed, considering you have never had a guest and never properly opened the taverna, that we would be offering you a chance to make money from all your hard work preparing it. Mrs. Thermopolis," he finished gently, "we are aware of your financial situation. The bank will foreclose if you cannot pay your mortgage soon."

Not one word he had said was unkind or untrue, and yet she felt so infinitesimal, so insignificant, as though she had failed everything and was worth nothing. She stood up to leave and suddenly, for no reason whatsoever, thought of Marjory. Over the year she had almost become content in her grief, knowing that her home and their dream was alive somehow. But the day Cressida got the letter from Resurgence, it was as though Leonidas had died all over again, along with their dream. She had wept, and prayed, and begged for a sign, any sign, that would tell her what to do. And then quite unexpectedly, on what now seemed a fated night, Marjory had arrived. Alone, yet not lonely; lost, and yet found; unaware and yet unafraid. Cressida had not felt the tingling gift of her Callas baking since Leo's funeral, until the day Marjory arrived. And she had baked happiness. Joy. For Marjory...Jory, she said she was always called. Her *guest*.

An enigmatic cloak of strength and confidence enveloped Cressida then, and she stood tall. "I do have a guest." And she turned on her heel and walked away.

⁓

When Cressida pulled back up to the house in her truck, she immediately went into a panic to see what looked like the majority of the town lined up outside the door to Jory's room. She left the truck in the middle of the road and ran out.

"What has happened?!" she cried, running through the crowd.

Mago stopped Cressida when she was near. "Jory was locked in the bathroom for the past five hours. It was only an hour ago I heard her yelling and went to get Nico with his tools. Unfortunately, the whole town followed."

Cressida ran to room two, where Nico was on his knees with a set of tools, taking all the hinges off the bathroom door. "Not a worry, Miss Marjory, you are almost out."

"That goddamned door!" Cressida yelled. "Leo was a charmer but he could not fix a flat tire if someone had paid him a million dollars to do it. I asked him to fix that door for a year. A year! And now look—our only guest ever has been trapped for hours!"

Cressida could feel the silence of the town behind her, could feel their surprise at her outburst. She turned to them. "What? You all know it's true! I loved my husband more than anything in the world," she cried, her breath ragged, "and then he went and died—before he could fix the damned door!" Anger was coursing through her and she had no idea why.

Suddenly Mago's hand was on her back, gently soothing. "It's okay, my girl, breathe. The anger is good," she whispered gently so no one else could hear. "He was a good man, but a fallible one. If you can be angry with him, soon you will also be able to say his name and smile, and laugh, and miss him properly. Living in grief too long makes us forget about the life before death. Let it go now."

"I can't," Cressida sobbed. "I don't know how."

"Yes, you do. You already are."

"I've got all the hinges off, Miss Marjory. I'm just going to pull the door off now!" Nico called, standing and slowly removing the bathroom door as a shell-shocked Jory walked out, blinking in the sunlight.

Cressida ran to her, grasping her shoulders, then taking her chin. Jory looked up and met her eyes.

"Jory, I'm so sorry," Cressida sighed, pulling her in close. She had not touched another human like this in over a year, and suddenly she began to cry softly. "Come, let us go up to my house and have something to eat. You must be hungry." She left her arm around Jory's shoulder as if protecting her from the looming crowd. "Oh, go away, you people," she shooed.

"What did I say? I said things would be changing. Did I not say?" Nefeli muttered, shaking her head and walking away. "No one ever listens to me."

Although everyone knew that Nefeli got her portents from the horoscopes, no one could say a word against her now. Instead, they looked at Jory anew, even in her Tyrannosaurus Rex pajamas, and even as they were all shooed away by Cressida, who, arm around Jory, took her into her home.

"My Leonidas, he was actually an accident, you know," Cressida said later that night as they opened their second bottle of wine. It had been hours now and they had not stopped talking.

Jory was feeling a little light-headed in the best kind of way. It felt good after this morning. Now all of the sudden everything seemed a bit funny. She was enjoying Cressida being a human being—one that she really, really liked. "How was he an accident?" she asked.

"I had gone to Athens to spend the summer with family. I was young, only about eighteen. I didn't like the city very much, but still, for an island girl from Potamia, it was an exciting change. I met a boy there. He was very handsome, and very rich too. He came from a big Athenian family that owned the restaurant I was working in as a pastry chef. Nothing ever happened. He came in, he flirted with me each day. I was smitten.

"I came back home at the end of the summer and started working at a restaurant in Chora Naxos. One day, Nefeli comes in and says to me, 'there is a boy here from Athens, and he is so good-looking.' I was so sure it was him, that my spirits lifted to another level of joy, expectation, desire. I was baking bread at that moment and put every ounce of my desire into that bread." She stopped and looked at Jory. "Do you know about my baking?"

"That you can bake your emotions or something into your food?"

She nodded. "I am a Callas—since my great-grandmother we have had a gift with food. All of our food is made with a certain flair and feeling, but when we bake, when we use our hands to knead and press—then we sometimes create something magical," Cressida said, leaning forward. "So I filled my bread with desire and I sent it out, and ten minutes after, this boy comes into the kitchen and stands in front of me and says, 'I am going to marry you.'"

She paused before continuing. "It wasn't him. It was this boy called Leonidas and I'd never seen him before in my life. He was attractive and charming, but I said he was sorely mistaken. And yet, one year later we were married."

Cressida laughed. "I never knew I could love anyone like I loved Leonidas. Leo, that is what we called him. He was the best accident that a girl could ever, ever hope for."

She went silent then.

"Mago told me you were just about to open this guesthouse and a taverna when Leo passed away," Jory said after a time.

"Yes. Leo thought my magical cooking could make us rich and famous." She giggled, then hiccupped.

Cressida drunkenly giggling was a glorious sight to Jory. She suddenly seemed much younger and approachable.

"I said I could not cook fame and fortune into anything—it doesn't work that way—but I could cook other things. Leo, he was the ideas man. He had the whole design in his head, and he was going to be the front man and take the little truck we bought down to the docks and bring people up to the best little Greek taverna in the whole of the Cyclades that no one knew about, until everyone knew about us and then we would be filled to capacity all summer. He was such a dreamer."

"You could still do all those things. You could still open this little Greek taverna," Jory insisted.

Cressida finished her glass and poured herself the rest of the second bottle. "I miss cooking. Having you here has made me see the idea come to life, but I *can't* do it! I can cook but nothing else. I cannot be a waitress; I can't find people to come up to the restaurant…I don't even know how to decorate it. I can do nothing but cook. The rest was all Leo. And Leo is gone. Gone…" she trailed off.

Jory leaned forward and touched Cressida's hand. "I know he's gone. But you're *not*. You are living, and you must accept that sooner rather than later or you'll waste your life away. I'm here. I have worked in hospitality for ten years as a waitress. Where I've been for the past seven years, The French Café, I help with functions, wine pairings, ordering and managing when I'm needed. I have all the experience to help you get started. We can open your taverna together!"

"You can't stay here, you are traveling the world. You would feel stuck, trapped."

Jory scoffed. "You just had me locked in your bathroom for five hours and I'm still here. Can't get more trapped than that."

At that, they both laughed until they were crying, and cried until they were hugging, and then laughed again until they realized they desperately needed to get some sleep.

" 'The life you have led doesn't have to be the only one you lead,' Cress," Jory said as she turned to go back to her own room. "That was the quote that first inspired me to travel, to start a new life."

"Did you just call me Cress?" she asked, slurring slightly.

"I did. A new nickname for a new life."

Cressida scrunched her brows together and tilted her head. "But cress is a herb."

Jory started laughing again. "Well, I like it. It suits you. See you in the morning, my dear new herb...I mean, friend."

Jory hugged Cressida again then left, smiling as she closed the door.

Cressida smiled and leaned her head back on the wall. "Friend," she whispered, falling asleep against the wall.

Six

There was no breakfast tray awaiting Jory in the morning, and for a moment, in her slight headachy haze, she wondered if Cressida would revert back to her standoffish self. And then she saw the lunch basket. A note was stapled to it.

My dear friend,

Take this basket and your scooter to hike Mount Zas. As I was making your lunch today, it seemed to make itself for Zas— you know I do not know why.

Tonight I make us dinner. I think dresses are in order—Mago, who will join us, agrees. Please if you would like, be at my door at six in the evening. Oh, and please find the key to your new room. The bathroom door works fine.

Cress

Jory couldn't help but smile. Cressida was trying on her nickname, like a Leonidas who is Leo and a Marjory who is Jory. She was now a Cressida who is Cress. Jory reckoned she quite liked it.

Jory stopped by the petrol station to fill up her tank. Nico was absent so she did it herself, but Nefeli was there to take her money, phone in hand. She didn't scowl this time, though her expression was not quite friendly either.

"Where are we off to today?" she asked, scrolling all the while.

"I'm going to hike Mount Zas—it was Cressida's idea," Jory replied. "Also while I'm here, I'd like to find out how much to rent the moped for the next six weeks or so."

Nefeli nearly choked on her gum. "Six weeks?!"

There was something quite enjoyable about surprising Nefeli out of her frosty persona.

"Yes, I reckon through to the end of July at this stage. If you and Nico could put a price together, that would be great," she said, turning and starting her bike.

"But why? Why are you staying?" Nefeli called from behind her.

"I'm helping out a friend," Jory called back.

Nefeli watched the Marjory girl sloppily ride the little moped away. She started to smile. *Ah, Cressida, what are you up to, my girl?* Quickly she opened the latest horoscope, an expression of complete surprise forming on her face.

~

The drive to the base took a good hour, and once Jory arrived she locked her helmet under the seat, propping her bike next to the only other, much nicer motorcycle. Someone else must be on the track already, so she kept an eye out, especially the one time she had to scoot behind a tree to pee.

Jory had not brought proper hiking boots with her, just a pair of sneakers which she wore with black leggings and a T-shirt, her sweatshirt around her waist—not that she needed it. As the days passed further into June, the island was warming up, and today was hot. Jory was sweating in no time.

The hike was harder than she'd anticipated. The trail was clearly marked but not as well trodden as it would be at the end of the season. At this time of the year, flowers and plants grew over the path, making it harder to see, and branches of trees reaching out to catch the sun now banded together to block the way forward.

It took Jory a solid three hours before she finally arrived at the summit, feeling remarkably proud of herself as she took in the entire view of the north part of the island. She was here. She was in Greece, doing exactly what she loved—exploring the world, letting life happen, experiencing the freedom. She had not expected to find Potamia, or to make a new friend like Cress who was some sort of magic baker, who seemed so lost for someone so young. Jory felt found, content, happy, and so unbelievably grateful for the freedom she had to do as she pleased and to help where she could. This life called to her. She could not imagine another one.

"Hello."

Jory nearly jumped out of her skin. She'd forgotten about the other motorbike at the bottom of the mountain. She turned quickly...to see Shane sitting on a rock behind her. Of course, *of course*, it would be him. Her face, already red from the climb, flushed an even brighter shade.

He didn't smile, nor did he get up from his rock. Instead, he looked at her warily. Which was not surprising. Jory had had a lot of time to think when she was locked in the bathroom the night after their last run-in at the restaurant in Chora Naxos. She'd played the evening over and over in her mind, cringing every time she remembered smashing the glass of wine. She felt undeniably guilty when she replayed the look on his face, the hurt look. She'd been so rude to him. And while Jory knew she was doing the right thing by suppressing her attraction to him, she did not have to be unkind. She was never unkind.

"Um, hello," Jory managed. "Shane, right?"

This made his blue eyes crinkle as he nodded, as if in on his own joke, though he still did not smile. She took a deep breath and ventured a step toward him.

He put his hand in front of him. "Whoa, stay back. Don't come any closer."

"What?" Jory said, stopping, her eyes wide. "Why?" Did he really dislike her so much after her antics the other night?

"Because," he said, standing, "it's a slippery walk and I don't know if you've noticed, but you have a tendency to fall down a lot," he said, deadpan.

Jory laughed, relaxing for the first time around him. He grinned and joined her at the viewpoint. "It's so beautiful here," she said.

"Wait until you see the view from the top," he said.

"Is this not it?" she asked, looking around in confusion. "I don't see more of the trail."

"It's just a little further up. You have to scramble a bit and I actually wasn't teasing about it being slippery," he said. "Did you want me to help you up there? It's a bit scary doing it for the first time on your own."

Jory bit her lower lip. What if he had to help her and she reacted to his touch like before—she'd likely end up falling off the cliff! Or, she thought, what if she stopped being so overdramatic? What if she just decided right now that she and Shane could be friends. Travel buddies. She always met like-minded people traveling. Sure, he might be a sizzler, but she could overcome that. Maybe the spark was only so strong because she was so adamantly trying to avoid it.

Hmm...good point, Jory, she thought, nodding with a self-satisfied smile. *That makes perfect sense.*

"I'm dying to know what you're thinking right now," he said.

Embarrassed, Jory shook her head and saluted him. "Lead the way!"

He pulled on his day pack. She followed his lead, trying not to be distracted by his tanned, muscular calves below his shorts, or the way when he stopped and turned, lifting his white T-shirt to wipe the sweat from his forehead, she could see his taut, muscled chest and abdomen, the hair on his chest, brown and gold like his head. Her mouth went dry and her stomach twisted with longing.

The climb was difficult, and when he turned to check on her, she stumbled inelegantly under his gaze. Thankfully it was only a few more minutes to what seemed to be a huge rock on top of the mountain, but he was right about the view. The summit of Mount Zas offered 360-degree views of the entire island, which was saying something. From here you could see water in every direction.

They stood side by side, both panting.

"Wow," she breathed, at a loss for any other word.

Shane nodded. "Wow."

They stood this way for a few minutes as they caught their breath from the hike, too distracted by the view to pay much attention to one another. Finally, Shane turned to look at her.

"Shall we eat our lunch just there?" he asked, pointing to a flat section of the rock.

Jory nodded, and they sat side by side. Shane grabbed his sandwich and started to eat, while Jory pulled out the baguette that Cressida had packed for her, the smells of what she now considered "home" wafting out of the paper.

Shane stopped chewing and closed his eyes. "What *is* that smell?"

"Oh," Jory said, surprised. "That's my sandwich. Can you smell it too?"

"I never thought I could be so tempted by a mere sandwich, but I am." He looked down at his ham and cheese, frowning.

She laughed, tearing her baguette in two and handing him half.

"It was made by my friend Cressida, who's a wonderful cook, so I imagine it will taste as divine as it smells." She took a bite and sighed. "Ah, Cress, who can make even a sandwich taste like heaven." She tried to discern the flavors. "Let's see...the bread is baked with rosemary, and something else, I'm not sure. See, Cress is the most amazing baker. You can usually tell what kind of mood she's in based on the bread that morning. I don't know exactly how it works, but she seems to bake her soul, or at least her emotions, into her bread."

Shane was staring between her and the baguette. "Are you serious?"

"Very. Does it sound crazy to you? But it doesn't take long on an island like this to believe in magic. For instance, I got locked in my bathroom for five hours the other night, and when I was finally rescued by the entire village, Nefeli told everyone that I was the sign they'd been waiting for. Apparently, even though she gets her predictions from the horoscopes the town couldn't deny what she'd said."

He laughed. Jory took a large bite of her baguette and sighed with pleasure. And it truly was pleasure. Suddenly she felt giddy, and at ease, and for some strange reason wanted to tell this handsome man every single secret about herself and know every one of his.

Shane took a bite too. "What is your story, Jory?"

"My story? I have a lot of stories…"

She told him some of her travel tales. Those were the kind of stories Jory was used to telling, used to sharing.

He was howling with laughter when she finished the story about getting robbed by a baboon in Zambia at Victoria Falls, and she could barely contain herself when he described having to walk back to a boat on the Lycian Way in Turkey in only socks and underwear when his backpack was taken during the night.

"Okay, but now tell me your real story. Why it makes sense that you ended up in a magical village," he said. "Yes," he added with a wink, "I've been listening."

"My real story?" she asked, swallowing nervously.

"Yeah. You know, the one that sort of changed your life path somehow. The one you never tell anyone," he said.

And even though they were both joking just a bit, neither of them really knew where the jokes ended and the reality began, and so Jory told her most secret story.

~

Jory's inner compass had not always been so steady when she was young. Nowadays, she always knew when it was time to leave and when it was time to stay. Back then, she'd often felt torn in two, somewhere between lost and found, unsure if her compass was pointing her in the right direction.

She'd assumed that her unsteadiness was because she didn't have her father in her life, and that if she had, it would have been a life of constancy and always knowing what to expect—a world that did not alter off a planned course. But she also knew that her sense of feeling found and steady was *because* of her mother and their transient lifestyle. Cindy St. James had a knack for decorating and she worked as a designer for showroom homes, so every few months they'd pack up and move to a house just a few blocks down, or a town not too far, a new neighborhood, a school district just slightly different than the last.

"We're like nomads," Cindy would say, winking as they packed their few bags. The furniture belonged to the company, so they never had to pack much. Jory loved feeling like a nomad. One day, she thought, she was going to travel for real, like her mom had, until she'd met Jory's father and unexpectedly gotten pregnant. Jory would take up where her mother left off and travel the world.

Within hours, Cindy could create a fully decorated space that felt like home. Jory made friends easily as they moved from place to place—sometimes so quickly she had not even said hello when new friends would be around her. For little did Jory know she was bringing home with her in curious little ways. When her room was peppermint pink with white trimming when she was eight, she brought the smell of candy canes and Christmas with her, and her new friends felt like she was where they belonged. When they lived in the little apartment right on Chesapeake Bay, and Cindy decorated it in pale blues and greens with shabby chic white wooden and wicker furniture, Jory smelled like Hawaiian Tropic and sun, even in the middle of winter.

And so Jory always had a lot of friends, but nothing ever lasted longer than the time they lived in one place, and so when Jory was sixteen and in high school, despite her St. James blood and wafting scents of home, she was like any other teenager. She looked around at all her friends, who had real homes and wore BFF 4-EVER! bracelets, who had more money and nicer things and went on holidays to Europe or on cruises over the summer, and she felt jealous. But she knew she *could* have all those things—all those things and more, if she embraced her father and his family.

So the next time she walked in the door and saw her mom packing up the house Jory had really grown attached to, in the middle of her junior year, she made a decision. "I'm moving in with my father."

Cindy was a great beauty in her day, and when Christopher Buchanan met her painting on the streets of Paris on his year abroad learning his father's business overseas, he fell head over heels with the beautiful bohemian artist. Not only her curling blonde hair and green eyes, but her freedom, the way she drifted and felt like home wherever she was, made him feel at home like he never did back in South Carolina. She moved into his apartment before the summer even began. He came back one afternoon and she'd filled the room with used books and the musty smell of the only part of his childhood he loved—the library. He felt home, and never wanted to leave the place that would only smell that way because of Cindy. Cindy told him he made her sizzle, and they made love day and night, while she painted and he went to his father's company office as little as necessary.

His absence did not go unnoticed, and eventually Christopher's parents showed up unannounced at the apartment. He introduced

Cindy, but they turned from her greeting and asked her to take her things and leave. Christopher was to stay, but he left instead, and went to Cindy in her shared bohemian flat.

"Chris, sweetheart, only this means anything," she said, touching her stomach.

Chris was young, but he was determined to give it a go and they spent a summer in Paris, his parents cutting them both off. It never bothered Cindy, the lack of money, but he woke up every night at the same time, panicking. What would he do? For his family? A child? He was too young to have a child! Were his parents right?

Then, in the middle of the night, he left, with only a note for Cindy.

Cin,

I am going back home to my parents. I know you think you don't want this, but we can have our baby together in South Carolina where we can have a safe, steady life. You can still paint. You can be free. So long as you stay. Come with me tomorrow. I'll be waiting for you.

Chris

But Cindy did not meet Christopher at the airport the next day, and had her daughter in France, naming her Marjory St. James, not Buchanan, and calling her Jory.

So Jory lived with her mom and only saw her father and his family on a few holidays through the year. Jory didn't like spending time with them—her grandparents were always telling her to sit up straighter, making snide comments about her mother, who was her best friend. Her father never defended her, just sat, quietly. His wife didn't seem to like Jory at all. But he always said Jory could come live with him, if she wanted. That she was his daughter, and every opportunity was available to her if she wanted it.

Jory loved her mother, more than anyone in the world, but she was sixteen. She wanted to live the kind of life that looked like an Abercrombie & Fitch ad, living in *one* house for longer than a year, having real friends and not just transient ones. She called her father and asked if she could come live with him, and amazingly enough, he said yes. There was a clenching in Jory's stomach that felt all wrong. Her inner compass was going awry. She ignored it, packed her bags with help from her mother and turned up at the Buchanan mansion.

"Which one is my room?" she asked her father, hoping that somewhere in the massive expanse of this ancestral home, there would be some place she could feel was hers, was home.

He shrugged. "Pick whichever guest room you'd like. When school starts in August, you'll be there most of the year, and I imagine you'll want to see your mother on the holidays."

"What do you mean, I'll be at school most of the year?"

"Boarding school, of course—you'll be living in a dormitory with your new friends," he replied.

"I won't live here? I don't want to live at a boarding school. When I called and asked if I could stay here, why did you say yes if that's not what you really meant?"

"Marjory, this is what 'here' entails. You'll have the Buchanan name if you decide you want to change your surname, which will afford you all that money can buy. And I promise, money can buy anything in this world."

Cindy picked Jory up from the bus stop an hour later. Jory felt a fool, but more than that, she felt guilty for every moment she'd put her mother through agony by suggesting that she was not enough. That their life had not been good enough. That money could have made Jory happy. It only took a moment in that house to know that money made people miserable.

Cindy stroked Jory's hair off her face. "Oh honey, money isn't evil. Money pays our bills, puts a roof over our head. Money is part of the world we live in, and you have to accept that. Sometimes great wealth can distort our view of money. Your dad... Ah Jory, he is a good man, he just doesn't know any other way. You do. Take this as a lesson—your life is your own. It's not mine or your dad's or anyone else's. Make your own path. You'll find your feet, sweetheart. You're a St. James, and do you know what it means to be a St. James?"

"No."

"It means you always know where you are because you are always home. And you will bring that wherever you go, and other people will feel home with you near. It is our great gift. Why do you think you make friends everywhere you go, without ever trying?" Her mother grasped her hands. "The way I can decorate so well and make you feel home? Jory, what we have is not something to be ignored, but embraced! Once you embrace who you are, you'll never feel lost again. I promise you, darling," she said, kissing her cheeks. And Jory believed her.

"I can't believe I just told you all that. What did Cressida bake into this bread?" Jory said as Shane smiled, leaning back.

"I like your stories. So, as a St. James, you are home wherever you are? Is that how it works?" he asked. She nodded. "It sounds like you came to a place where you really fit in, like the other women you've met."

"I guess it was like, once I knew my purpose, I could truly embrace who I was and stop searching for a missing piece. I always felt where I was meant to be, and I could *share* that. That's when I realized how I could embrace this feeling I get sometimes—I call it my 'leave instinct.' I know it sounds silly, but when I get my leave instinct, it's almost like I'm called somewhere, and then when I arrive, I feel found again, because I always feel home. I suppose that's why travel suits me so well."

Jory stopped. What on earth was making her speak like this to a stranger? Not only a stranger, but the only person she'd ever met who made her sizzle. She'd never even voiced these thoughts to Liz and Kate. She may not have ever voiced these thoughts to herself.

She glanced at Shane—he looked as though he was thinking intently as well.

"Do you want to hear something even stranger?" he said. "I get the same thing sometimes, but it's the opposite of wanting or needing to leave. It's more that occasionally I arrive at a place, or I'm about to leave, and I get this 'stay' instinct. Like there's more to do before I go. It's actually how I've run my entire... life," he finished, as if he'd been struggling to find the last word of the sentence.

They were quiet again, not looking at one another. Finally, Shane broke the silence. "What *did* your friend bake into that bread?"

"I'm going with truth serum," Jory said, forcing a laugh. This was getting far too personal, and the moment she heard Shane use the word "stay" she felt her leave instinct kick into gear. She looked down to her wristwatch and jumped up. "Oh my gosh, look at the time! How long do you think it'll take to get back down?"

Shane took a breath, saying, "Half the time, if we move quickly."

He started down the path at a brisk pace, checking back on her occasionally. He tried to make small talk but Jory left her answers at "yes" or "no" or sometimes a mumble. She was questioning her own sanity at telling him that stupid story. I mean, her family! Her fears, her life, every insecurity she'd just told Shane, a stranger and yet not, because when he talked about his own instincts, even though it was the opposite of hers, she related to him and he related to her. He had finally stopped trying to make small talk and did not speak to her the rest of the way down. She had officially ruined any chance. That is what she'd wanted.

So why did she feel almost…bereft?

"Not much further," she heard Shane say.

"Mm-hmm," she murmured just as her toe caught on a tree root and she tripped and started sliding down the bank. "Argh!"

Shane tried to catch her, but she knocked him off balance and they both tumbled down the last few feet together, thankfully landing on a patch of moss.

"Are you okay?" he asked breathlessly, his arms around her, pulling her up.

Jory was so stunned, she didn't realize at first that she was finally still for the first time in days. No restless electricity, just this ambient feeling of warmth, like sunbathing. And then she looked up to see that she was wrapped in Shane's arms. She wanted to stay there forever, so good did it feel.

She managed to pull herself from his grasp somehow and find her footing, checking her ankles and knees. When she looked back at Shane, the intensity in his eyes made her stomach flip. So he felt it too, did he? The knowledge made it even harder to step back.

"I'm okay," she finally managed. "Thank you."

When they reached the carpark she walked to her moped, feeling his eyes on her, every part of her wanting to turn back. But she stayed her course, got out her helmet.

"Have you ever heard of the Kouros of Apollonas?" he asked quickly.

"The Kouros of what?" she said, turning.

He looked embarrassed, putting his hands in his pockets. "Apollonas—it's a ruin on the other side of the island. I thought if you hadn't seen it, I could take you there on Thursday. It's a long ride so my bike would be better, and it seats two. You really shouldn't come to Naxos without seeing it."

Yes, yes, a thousand times yes! her body screamed.

"I . . . thank you," she said, "but I can't." She went to put her helmet on but turned to him. "Thank you for today. Truly. Goodbye, Shane."

"I'm going," he called over the sound of her engine.

"What?"

"On Thursday!" he yelled. "To the Kouros at 10 a.m. I'm going to be at the parking lot near Grotta Beach then. I hope you change your mind."

She went to reply but he saluted her instead, racing away on his motorbike before she could even think of something remotely clever to say. Instead, she let out a sigh and drove back to Cressida's slowly, trying to calm her racing heart and mind.

Seven

At exactly six that evening, Jory walked fourteen steps to knock on Cressida's door. Mago answered, looking very different from how Jory had ever seen her. Her silvery black hair was pulled back into a bun and sparkling earrings dangled from her ears. Her dress was a sequined flapper style, and she wore heels to match and a long iridescent shawl—she looked like she just came off a 1920s movie set. Jory smiled, kissing Mago's cheeks, one after the other.

"Oh Mago, you look magnificent. I feel highly underdressed!"

"No, you are perfect. I am highly overdressed, but once you get to know me, you'll understand that I don't know why I have to wear a certain thing, I just do. Oh, and of course why I left those little yellow clog heels in front of your door." She looked down and smiled to see they went perfectly with Jory's dress, though she'd had no idea what the dress would look like. "Welcome to the party. You look sensational, my dear."

Jory smiled. "Thank you, I didn't know it was you who put them there. I suppose you are my fairy godmother."

She followed Mago out to the garden, where an ornate white cast-iron table she had never seen before was set with a small plate upon a large one, and full cutlery on either side. In the middle of the table was a single candle.

"Wow, look at this." Jory smiled. "We're in for a proper treat. What on earth made Cressida do all this?" she asked Mago.

Mago sat at the table, getting an inkling as to why Cressida had asked them to dress up so. "Here, let me pour us some wine. Cressida asked us to start with this one—the white blend from Arie's vineyard. So tell me, how was your day? Cressida said you hiked Mount Zas?"

Jory blushed. "I did, yes. It was interesting."

"Oi skamata!" they heard Cressida yell from the kitchen.

They both looked curiously to where Cressida's voice had come from. "What do you think is going on in there?" Jory asked.

Mago was staring at the door intently. "I have an idea."

They were quiet for a time, sipping on their wine. Mago looked contemplative. Finally, Jory reached out her hand to Mago's. "Mago, I have to ask. Is something wrong?"

"Wrong?" she asked, chuckling but not meeting Jory's eyes. "Whatever would be wrong?"

"I don't know, and forgive me for being intrusive, I just—"

At that moment, Cressida came outside, and Jory had never seen her look so sure of herself. Her dress was bright red, the sleeves short and puffy and slightly off the shoulder, the bodice pulled tight and the skirt flaring from the hips. A short apron was tied around her waist. In her arms was a tray of something that smelled so magnificent, Jory and Mago both leaned forward to take in more.

"Piperies yemistes me feta," she announced, walking slowly to the table in her red flats.

"Peppers stuffed with feta cheese," Mago whispered to Jory.

"Jory, these are Greek peppers, called florinas, and are different from your American bell peppers. They grow on a farm on the other side of the island. Inside is not your traditional feta cheese, but one I make, called Lefko Tyri. Sometimes I use the mizithra in its place, but tonight I wanted something stronger to match Arie's wine, to match the day, the occasion. This will whet your appetite, make you want something more, make you desire the next bite even more than the last."

Cressida turned away then, very quickly, while Mago stared after her, her suspicion confirmed. She smiled.

"Should we eat?" Jory asked Mago.

Mago nodded. "Most certainly we should. We are, after all, the little taverna's first guests."

And just as Mago finally understood, so did Jory. Cressida had unofficially opened her taverna.

"Anginares me koukia," Cressida said, bringing out the next dish about twenty minutes after they had finished their stuffed pepper and glass of wine.

The dish was a spring salad like Jory had never had before. Fava beans paired with freshly peeled artichokes soaked in lemon water and fried gently with onion, salt and pepper. It was served at room temperature and garnished with dill and mint. The flavors and tastes seemed to bring forth the life of the whole island that thrived in the hands of the farmers and pickers and growers. Every bite was like tasting a collective truth.

Later, Jory poured the one bottle of the complex and full-bodied red wine that Arie had sent her home with. She hadn't known what she could pair it with, until yesterday, when Cressida had asked her for the bottle for cooking. She'd assured her she would only use the smallest amount and give them the rest for dinner. Neither Jory nor Mago were normally red wine drinkers but Cressida insisted. "Pour it when I say. It will be perfect."

And so when the last course—*kouneli stifado*—came out, Jory poured them two large glasses, saving one for Cressida. It was a rabbit stew made with tomatoes and red wine seasoned with allspice berries and cinnamon. As the rabbit fell off the bone and matched so perfectly with the very rich red wine, it was as though all the imperfect things in the imperfect world suddenly made sense, like they were made for each other.

It was almost too much to take, until the little cup of coffee with tiny little sliver of baklava came out and in one bite brought the meal to a close. Cressida joined them then, and the three women sat in the garden into the late hours of the night. Cressida told stories about her mother, her baking, lighting up as she realized that sitting here meant her dream was finally going to come true. When the sun was nearly up, they finally parted ways, their embraces just a little longer, their smiles just a little more meaningful. For tonight was the start of a summer of new beginnings. They could feel it.

Arie was always up with the first rays of sun, had been since he was a boy working on the vineyard with his father. He did not need an alarm as his window faced east and the first sunlight poured through not much later than it came up over the Aegean Sea. He stretched in his bed, feeling the achy parts in his knees and back, reminding him that he was not as young as he once was. He found the silence of that time of the morning both comforting and lonely. Comforting in knowing today was another day to get up and work and live, and lonely because he was in love with Mago Samaras and he knew she was in love with him, and yet she was not there to share his mornings.

The first time he'd known he was in love with Mago, he was ten years old. It was a Saturday when the Samaras family came down to the vineyard. His father greeted them with deference so Arie knew they were important guests. They had brought a young girl who he knew from school, Mago Samaras. She was okay for a girl; she was cheeky sometimes and made him laugh in class.

His parents told Arie to take Mago on a tour of the vineyard. She had rolled her eyes as they were shooed off by the grown-ups who were talking "business."

"So what do you do here all day anyway?" Mago had asked him.

He did not know why he felt so intimidated. "Pick grapes, work the farm. Sometimes take the tractor around and make sure everything is working as it should," he lied. But that got her attention.

"You have a tractor? And *you* drive it?"

The way she said "you" really irritated Arie then, enough to make him keep lying.

"Yes, *me*. And it's fast too. The fastest on the island. My dad says it's a John Deere model from America and nobody else in Naxos has one."

This was all true. One morning, one of their pickers, an English boy with ginger hair named Ben, had taken Arie out on a ride where they hit nearly thirty kilometers per hour on the flat. Arie didn't know what that meant but he did know that they were going faster than he had ever gone and flying through the vineyard with absolute joy.

That said, his claim of being able to drive it was indeed a lie.

But it was worth it to see Mago's face light up, and her black eyes went a little wild. "Let's take it out. They'll be hours up there. I can tell Dad's on business. Take me on the buggy, Arie!"

It was her saying his name that did it. He was emboldened by her sense of adventure, something that he did not really have too much of himself. He was his father's son—pragmatic, a worker, loyal. But she made him want to have a true adventure. They snuck around the back of the barn where the tractor was parked. The keys were inside. Most of the pickers were still out at this time of the morning, so it was theirs for the taking. Ben had taught him how to turn it on and put it in drive. He figured it wouldn't be much harder than riding a bike after that, really.

Arie turned the key and the engine roared. Mago's face gleamed. So did Arie's, though he had an increasing guilt that he could not quite shake. But he really, really wanted to show Mago that he could drive. So he put it into gear. Turned out it wasn't like riding a bike, not at all. He started and stopped a few times going forward. Though Arie was tall for ten years old, he was not quite tall enough to reach the pedals without compromising his range of vision as to where he was going. But Mago squinted at him, and that was all it took before he growled and put his foot down and they were off, faster even than when Ben took him out. He could barely see where he was going, so he was thankful for Mago yelling, "Left! Right! Left! Right! Ahhh!"

It ended with them taking down a whole row of vines, scaring a herd of cattle, and in the end, crashing into a tree, though they had slowed enough at that point to not destroy the entire thing. They both began to breathe heavily as the voices of the farmers and their own parents were heard as they ran down the hill after them. Arie was terrified, but at the same time, he was flying. He turned his head, shocked and shaking, and Mago turned her head to him. Then she started laughing.

"That was the best moment of my life," she breathed.

"Mine too," Arie said.

And from that day, he knew that in some way he would love Mago Samaras until the day he died.

Over fifty years later, Arie was at the ripe age of sixty-eight, and he still loved Mago Samaras. Of course, she had been Mago Nomikos for over thirty years, but to him, she would always be a Samaras.

He did not eat breakfast until he assessed the day's work ahead. He took his tractor through the vineyards, a much newer

John Deere version than the one of he and Mago's adventure back in the late 1960s. The grapes were looking good, the citrus fruit nearly ready. Already he had acquired a good deal of staff for the harvest. Many came from other parts of Europe and worked in exchange for accommodation and lifestyle on the island.

When Arie came back from his first round, he made the only breakfast he knew how to make, which was bacon and eggs on toast. Sometimes the butcher gave him some sausages but most often it was just bacon and eggs. It was all part of the usual morning routine he had followed for many years, until he looked over and saw something slightly unexpected. One of his wine bottles, the red. He never sold the red. Only this bottle was not here in the kitchen earlier when he made his coffee, and it certainly wasn't empty as it was now. There seemed to be something written on it. As he came closer he saw that Mago had signed the bottle, as had Marjory and Cressida, along with a note which said, *Your wine has found its match.*

"The red one?" he said aloud to himself. "Nobody buys the red in summer. It is too full and rich for most palates in the heat." The red was Arie's favorite no matter the time of year. It simply needed the right match.

"The red was perfect last night," a voice said from behind him.

"Mago," he whispered. And then smiled. "What on earth could have been so delicious that my strong red wine met its match?"

"*Kouneli stifado*. The earthy game of the rabbit stew mixed with the strength of the red wine…it was perfect."

"I must be coming to your home for dinner on the wrong nights." Arie laughed, his eyes crinkling. Mago hated to cook.

"Cressida, she is going to open the taverna," Mago said softly, walking through the room. Finally she turned back to Arie. "Why did you never marry?"

Arie knew this question well enough by now. "You know why," he replied.

His answer seemed to bother Mago lately, make her restless, rub her hand over the back of her neck, around to the front and ending on her chest. "I did marry. And I lost a husband. What if…?"

Arie put his hand up. "Never in my life did I think Mago Samaras would let fear rule her life."

"I'm not afraid!" she said defiantly.

Arie took the hand that still rested on her chest and took it into his own. "You are afraid of something. I don't know what. But when you figure it out, I will be here. I always have, I always will."

Eight

reakfast the next morning was a loaf of brioche dipped in spices and cheese and baked afterward. Jory and Cressida sat outside her room on the balcony. Jory sipped the coffee and eyed the bread, not eating. Cressida hadn't noticed yet and Jory realized why when her eyes followed Cressida's. Mago was pacing back and forth between her house and her own porch, her face drawn, whispering on the telephone.

"Something is wrong with Mago," Cressida said anxiously. "I have known her for a long time and I've never seen her like this. She is hiding something. Has she spoken to you? I know you spend a lot of time together." She turned back to Jory.

"No, she hasn't mentioned anything, but though I haven't known her long, in the times she thinks I'm not looking, I can see something making her anxious. I thought perhaps I was imagining it as she's so open and cheerful and full of quirky tales and cheeky advice," Jory said with a fond smile.

"Perhaps we can ask her together and see if she opens up to us," Cressida said. "I wonder what I could make…" she said, her words trailing as she looked pensive.

Aha! She did bake something into my bread yesterday. How do I get her to confess?

"So, um," Jory started, swallowing her embarrassment. "You know how you told me about your baking? I thought maybe you might teach me what you do. Give me a sort of Callas cooking class. I'd love to know, if, um, you know, you *always* bake something into your bread?"

Cressida turned to Jory, staring at her. Jory did not meet her eyes, so she leaned in until Jory had no choice but to look at her. "Why aren't you eating my brioche? Still full from last night?" She leaned back in her chair crossing her arms and waited. "Well?" she demanded.

"Okay!" Jory admitted. "I'm scared to eat your bread because I don't know if you baked truth serum in—like my sandwich yesterday!"

Cressida leaned in again. "Marjory St. James, I cannot believe you think I baked truth serum into my brioche. That is simply insulting."

"I'm sorry, I didn't mean to insult you. It's nonsense."

"Psh, of course it's not nonsense, brioche is simply the wrong dough for that. I would bake that into something much more traditional, like a rosemary focaccia."

"So you did bake it into my rosemary bread yesterday? I knew it!"

"Jory! What on earth happened yesterday? You are intentionally hiding something from me. And no, I did not bake a truth serum into your bread yesterday for your hike by yourself. That would really have been a waste of my efforts. But you obviously thought I did, so why? Spill the green beans."

Jory blushed as her eyes fought to find anything to look at other than Cressida, her fingers twisted in knots.

"Oh my gosh, how silly of me not to have figured it out earlier," murmured Cressida. "You met someone. A man. Only a man would make a woman act so flustered."

Her guess was confirmed as Jory dropped her head in her hands and let out a sigh so woeful Cressida had to laugh.

Jory told her about meeting Shane in town, and her ridiculous reaction to him. And then again at the restaurant. "You should have seen me, Cress," she moaned. "Honestly, he is always put together, and confident, and then there's me," she said. "A clumsy clod who stumbles or breaks something every time this guy touches her. And I'm always just such a mess," she sighed, pointing to her hair.

Cressida chuckled and took a sip of coffee. "You are a bit, aren't you?" Even Jory laughed at that. "But it's part of your charm. What happened next?"

She began telling Cressida about everything that happened at Mount Zas and explained why she thought Cressida had put a truth serum into the bread. Even Cressida had to admit it looked suspicious. The more Jory spoke about her day and the way she felt when he touched her, when she finally gave into it, the more it was clear to Cressida that Jory really, truly liked this man and that it frightened her. But she did not understand why.

"Isn't meeting a man you like a good thing? A timely thing? It must feel wanting at your age to not be married or have a boyfriend."

Cressida had wondered about it often since Jory had arrived, that she never mentioned a boyfriend or even any particular desire to have one. When Jory talked of her life, and told stories of some of her travels, and broadcast into her future, it was all very solitary.

Jory put her coffee down and pulled her chair around so she was facing Cressida, sitting up tall with her ankles crossed, like she learned in debate class back in school. Jory knew Cressida would say something exactly like that, so she had prepared what she considered an excellent argument in her favor that she would surely win. Why she was debating Cress in this matter she wasn't sure.

"Okay, meeting a man I truly like is the one thing I've been hoping to avoid for the past five years. I love my life. You know how you are a Callas? And that comes with a gift, a history? Well I am a St. James, and St. James women have a great gift too. But I can only have this life and use this gift, follow my purpose, if I am not in a relationship," she said, looking to Cressida to see if she was listening.

She nodded for Jory to continue, her face expressionless.

"I mean can you imagine traveling around the world and leaving for a place whenever I want, this kind of freedom, this perfect life I have, if I were in a relationship? No!" she said, answering her own question when Cressida's mouth opened. "Eventually there would be two options—I stay. Stay for some guy because I'm crazy about him and then no more traveling the world for Jory! Option two—I don't stay, and we break up, and then I'm heartbroken because I've gone and been stupid and actually went to the dumb Kouros of Apo-whatever when I knew he was my sizzler!" Jory's voice was getting louder as she stood and began to pace. This was why she often lost her arguments. She became overly emotional. But she couldn't seem to help herself.

"Your...what? What is a sizzler? Is it an American word I don't know?" Cressida asked.

"It's a ridiculous Cindy St. James word about the one guy in the whole world whose touch makes you feel like you've been electrocuted!" Jory cried, raising her hands and turning around in circles.

Cressida looked confused. "My English is sometimes not so great. Electrocuted, like…" She shook herself in a pained way. "Like it's very bad and could kill you?"

Jory threw her head back with a hurrah, then grabbed Cressida's shoulders. "*Yes*! I knew you'd understand! Very bad! Like being burned alive with so much desire and aching longing that you have never wanted anything so badly in your whole life and you want to die without having it! *That* is why I can never see him again! Does that make sense?" Her eyes were wide, and she felt slightly crazed as she waited for Cressida to answer.

"No!" Cressida insisted, standing and pulling Jory's hands off her shoulders. "That was the worst argument I've ever heard in my entire life," she continued, laughing so hard she could barely get the words out. "I thought you told me you were on the debate team in college?"

Jory opened her mouth to say something, then closed it, and finally, rolled her eyes with a self-deprecating smile. "Well, I didn't say I was very good," she mumbled and Cressida howled with laughter again. Jory could not resist and began to laugh herself. Eventually she sighed and sat back down. "Oh, all right already, that's enough."

Cressida wiped her eyes and sat down across from her.

"Do you know what I think?" she said. "I think you're scared. You, this brave and independent woman who relishes freedom. You are frightened that something might threaten that freedom so you stubbornly hold on. But this Shane, he takes you out of your comfort zone. He makes you feel so many wonderful things and that scares you. But let me tell you something—falling in love is not comfortable. Being in love is not comfortable. And that is why it is so beautiful." She paused for a moment. "Your truth is out now, so eat the damned brioche," Cressida finally said.

Jory pulled the brioche apart and cautiously took a bite. She could feel the effect almost immediately as the taste filtered through and she sighed with pleasure.

They were both quiet for a moment. "Do you still believe that love is so beautiful?" Jory asked her. "After everything that's happened to you?"

Cressida thought about that. "For a long time after Leo died last year, I did not think so. I thought, like you, that perhaps it was better to stay in my comfort zone, to not allow the unknown to happen." Her voice strengthened. "But I cannot believe that anymore. I have been living in my comfort zone of grief for over a year, and it is time now to move on. Your friendship has allowed me to come out of hiding and explore the unknown again. And even though I will love Leo until the day I die, the answer is yes. It was worth every moment."

~

"You are not a morning person at all, are you?" Cressida asked, opening the door to Jory in her oversized sweatshirt and jeans, her hair in a frizzy ponytail.

"I do not consider it morning until the sun comes up, and then usually a few hours after that," Jory grumbled, stumbling into the kitchen. "Oh, good, coffee." She poured herself a hefty cup. "Did we have to start this early?"

"I told you—baking is best done in the morning, before you get too many thoughts to focus on. Baking in the evening after a long day of thinking is dangerous."

"You're wasting your time trying to teach me. There is a reason I don't cook. It's always a disaster. I try to bake a cake and there's a hole in the middle. I make cookies and they all end up flattening into a tray of hard sugar."

Cressida laughed.

"I'm not kidding," Jory insisted. "I made blueberry muffins once and when Liz threw one at me it broke a window. Seriously. You do not want to see me cook."

"Yesterday, you thought it was a great idea to learn my magical baking skills," Cressida teased.

"Yes, when I was trying to catch you baking truth serum into my bread," Jory retorted. "Ugh, it's just *sooo* early!"

"You should have majored in drama," Cressida said, chuckling. "Okay, let's get started. I was going to get everything ready and measured for you but somehow that felt like cheating, so I've pulled out the recipe and all the ingredients you will need, and I will read them out to you and explain what to do. Today, we make olive bread. It is very simple, and it uses olives from here in the garden, so you will use the fruits of the land in what you bake. I also chose this because we make it in two stages. This morning we make the dough and let it rise. In a few hours we knead it again. It's an excellent recipe for seeing how your baking changes through the day. Plus, it will give us a few hours to talk about the taverna and allow me to show you around the rest of the property."

She began by instructing Jory to put sugar, yeast, and warm water into a bowl, measuring the rest while the fresh yeast activated and bubbled. She then mixed in the flour, salt, and olive oil. "We mix first with a spoon. Because I am teaching you to make my kind of bread, I will offer you my mother's wooden spoon. She used to call it something. I don't remember the word, but I called it the 'you can do it' spoon because it sounded something like that."

"Do you mean a conduit?" Jory asked, hiding a smile.

"Yes! Like a conduit to the dough. Now you take the spoon and mix."

Jory did as she was told, and Cressida had to admit that she had not been lying about her ineptitude. She did nothing with precision or finesse, but she was trying so hard it was impossible to correct her.

"Is this right?" Jory asked.

"Yes, yes, it's fine. Now it is time to knead. It takes a little while to get used to the motion if you've never baked bread before. This is why this part of the baking is most important to do in the morning. You will find that over the next ten minutes while you knead, you will almost go into a trance—being not fully awake is important. I find that if I'm too overly alert, I bake very personal things into my bread. It is not always like that, but for me personally, I find being a little sleepy keeps my focus on the baking."

"What makes you think I will have any ability to do what it is you do with your baking?" Jory asked her.

Cressida laughed. "I don't. But you wanted to learn what I do, and I will teach you to bake the way that I was taught to bake. Because while I have no reason to believe you will have the same gift, I also have no reason to believe you won't. You and I, we are connected, our gifts seem to be intertwined. Also, Mago told me you drank from the stream. I must at least take precautions." She winked at Jory.

She instructed Jory through the kneading process, and she did finally get into a flow after about three minutes. Folding, then kneading, and folding again, and kneading again.

"Good lord, this is exhausting," Jory declared.

"I haven't thought about it like that for a long time. Or perhaps I have. It is like working out, really. Look, I have very strong arms and hands." She flexed her muscles. "Perhaps if I must eventually sell, I will go become a famous arm-wrestler."

Jory stopped kneading. "Sell? What do you mean, sell?"

How on earth could she have let that slip? Cressida was not ready to tell Jory about the offer on her place, not when she was desperate to give it everything she had to actually open and see what might come of it. Cressida needed Jory. She needed her friendship and her companionship, and she needed her strength. She could not tell her, not yet. Not until they'd seen the opening through.

Now, she had one thing to do, something she knew she must, and that was to open her taverna. Michael Smythe was correct. She would likely have to sell. But she had the summer left to see through their dream and just perhaps, at the end of it, something even greater than she could have imagined would come out of it. She loved her little home more than anything in the world and she was not willing to give it up without a fight. A fight to make it hers.

"It's not good to stop kneading, you must keep going, no matter what else happens, otherwise the bread will not rise. And it will stick—terrible for countertops."

Jory went back to the kneading, quiet for a few minutes. "But you did say sell. Are you planning to sell?"

"I'm planning to open. Finally. Now knead, stronger, it is not fluffing up fast enough. The harder you work, the shorter time it takes to get it right."

Jory's look made her question how much of that statement was for the bread, and how much of it was for her life.

"Now we wait," Cressida said. She covered the large bowl of dough with a slightly damp towel and placed it near the window in the kitchen. "Dough must rise in a warm place but direct sun can kill the yeast. It is a warm day, so the countertop near the window works best. In the winter I might use the hot water cylinder in the pantry or put it in the oven," she explained. "Come, I have much to show you."

~

"*This* is your office?" Jory exclaimed.

Cressida had a nice Microsoft laptop hooked up to a modern printer. There was also a machine for taking credit cards, and an iPad mini that was still in the box.

"Leo." She smiled indulgently, shaking her head at the room. "He loved electronics and wanted the most up-to-date systems in place for us. Me—I like to keep things simple, he wanted to be modern. With simple food. He never tried to mess with my food. Please, feel free to use this office whenever you want to send emails or get in touch with your friends back home." She placed a key into Jory's hand.

"Thank you." Jory took the key and put it in her pocket. They walked through the office, which was spacious but felt smaller than it was because of the massive desk and all the office accessories. "Tell me more about the dream you and Leo had for here. What you had envisioned."

Cressida closed her eyes, allowed herself for one moment to live in a different world where Leo still existed. To try to remember what their dream was. "Leo, he was the charmer, the waiter, the maître d'. He wanted to do the advertising, he wanted to go collect guests at the port. He wanted the guesthouse. He wanted this to be the most famous taverna in the Cyclades. He wanted bookings.com and to be splashed all over social media. He wanted everything for us. He was a big, big dreamer, my Leo."

"But Leo is no longer here. What do *you* want? What do you envision now?"

What did she want? She wanted to cook, to find the joy and soul in bringing food and deliciousness to other people.

She wanted to see her taverna open, and to be a part of it. She looked around at the beautiful guesthouse. It was truly beautiful, and the rooms were delightful. Leo had collected magazines and found designs he liked. He went to Athens to find furniture to bring back, and she and Leo would make up the rooms like in the magazines, laughing and throwing paint on each other and making love in each of the rooms, loving their shared dream. But while the taverna was hers, the kitchen was hers, the guesthouse was not. The guesthouse was their dream together, or rather it was Leo's dream that she was a part of.

"I will host the guesthouse and you will cook, and we will create magic," he had said.

She wondered again if this place would not be better off becoming something that it was always meant to be, that she could not give it. Could the Resurgence Group do that for her guesthouse? Could they be the ones to make it what it was destined to be? But then she would have nothing. No kitchen, no food to cook.

"Cress?" Jory repeated, her voice soft. "Are you okay?"

Was she okay? She took a deep breath. She would always love her Leonidas and she would always miss him and mourn for him, but that could no longer be the center of her being. Her will to live was beginning to outweigh her will to not live. "I am okay."

Jory smiled, taking her hand. "Damned right you are."

"Come now, let's finish your bread, and we will talk through our ideas."

⌒

Jory could not believe it. Her dough had actually risen, like she'd seen in the pictures in recipe books all the other times she'd tried to bake and failed. It was a big ball of fluffy dough now, double its original size. She jumped and squealed, turning to Cressida. "Look at it! I did it!"

Cressida was laughing. "You are only halfway there. Now that you are awake you get to finish the bread—to take the dough and make it into something it has only just begun to dream itself to be. It is now yours to mold. From this dough you could make nearly anything. But today we make olive bread. Come."

Jory worked harder than she ever had, patting the olives dry, measuring out the spoonfuls of oregano and onion that Cressida herself had dried.

"Now, it is time to knead again. This time you will add in the fresh olives and oregano until they are evenly distributed. Have some flour on the side. The olives will make it wet and it might start to stick. If it starts to stick to the counter, you need to add a sprinkle of flour. But not too much. You add a little at a time, kneading, and then a little more, until it does not stick. Okay?"

"Got it," Jory said, kneading the bread like earlier today. It was even harder now.

"Yesterday in your, uh, frenzied argument, shall we call it?" said Cressida. "You mentioned going to the 'Kouros of Apo-whatever' with your man. Did you mean the Kouros de Apollonas?" she asked innocently.

Jory swatted her shoulder playfully. "He's not my man. And I think so. But I'm not going, remember?" Her face began to heat and a pool of warmth spread in her belly just thinking of Shane and seeing him again.

"That is a shame. It is a lovely spot, filled with history. And nice and far away, plenty of time to have your arms wrapped around him on his motorcycle," she taunted.

"Cress!" Jory squawked. "I'm trying to knead! Stop distracting me with thoughts of Shane."

"Would you like me to pack you a nice lunch? I can bake anything you want into the bread. Remember the first loaf I baked for Leonidas, thinking he was the boy I loved back in Athens? Came in and wanted to marry me and had never even seen me before." She grinned, then said in a witchlike croak, "We can make Shane fall under your spell."

"Oh heck no, you're not baking anything that I'm giving to Shane, I don't trust you at all."

"Such a lack of faith in your good friend!" Cressida said, her hand to her heart in mock offense. She leaned forward then and said in a loud fake whisper, "I can also bake virility into the bread, just to let you know."

"Cressida Thermopolis, you are diabolical!" Jory laughed. "Now be serious, is this the part that I bake something into it? The magic part?"

"Ah, my whimsical friend, believing in magic even in your old age," she said. "What would you want to bake into your bread?"

What would she want to bake into her bread? If she could do what Cressida did—which she was certain was actually some sort of magic—what would she want to convey? She wanted to bake something that would mean the taverna would be a success for Cressida. She nodded and began to knead, but the more she kneaded, the more her mind began to stray and she could think of nothing, nothing at all, but wrapping her arms around Shane on his motorcycle. She saw his eyes crinkle, the way he made her feel so lost that she wanted to be found by him, when that made no sense at all. But more than anything she could not stop thinking about the desire that was like electricity every time he touched her.

"Are you thinking about it? You are in a frenzy with your kneading, you must be thinking of some truly wonderful things."

Jory blushed. Oh god, would Cressida be able to see right through her, know into her deepest desires when they ate the bread?

"Are you feeling your fingers tingle now? That is what happens to me, when I know my intent is working."

Jory stopped. No, no tingling. That was a relief. Okay. Focus. Focus on success. On the taverna. Focus on anything other than the hardness of his torso as she fell into his arms, his warm breath so close to hers...so close...if only she could lean in...

Suddenly Cressida was behind her, and for just one moment, she touched Jory's shoulder as she lifted herself up to check her kneading. A pleasing warmth went down Jory's arm, and her fingers began to tingle as she kneaded the bread.

And then it was gone.

"Good, Jory. That looks very good. We can put the bread in a tray now and brush it with olive oil. Then top with the rest of the dried herbs, and into the oven. It looks like it will taste very nice."

Jory's hands were shaking when she placed the baking tin in the oven, the tingling gone, but the frenzied feeling like she'd had too much coffee remained.

~

Mago had been listening to the girls next door laugh for the past hour, and the sound made her happy, almost as happy as she had been seeing Arie the day before. That was the great thing about life. Sometimes it takes a long time to live joyfully. But when you finally do, change fills the air, and it smells like the first day of spring, when the morning frost has turned to a soft dew that makes the grass smell like grass and the flowers bloom. For winter is past. Warmth bathes your skin in the longer days of sunshine. Hope reigns, happiness looms.

Mago could feel all that now. In herself, and especially radiating from the house next door that had lived in winter for so long, for too long. Now it was bathed in laughter and hope. She brought her boiling pot of tea with her and went down the stairs to Cressida's, not bothering to knock.

"Hello?" she called.

"Mago! Come, we are in the garden," Cressida called, her voice light and airy, laughter making it tinkle. It brought Mago complete joy. She had not heard Cressida's true voice in many, many months. But this was it. A voice that sparkled with laughter.

"I brought tea to go with whatever it is you have made, Cressida. It smelled...desirable." Mago did not know what made her use that particular word, but whatever it was must have been correct as Cressida burst into a new peal of giggles, and actually snorted.

"Oh Mago, I think you hit the head with a snail."

It was Jory's turn to burst into laughter. "I think you meant 'hit the nail on the head,' Cress."

"What does that mean?" Cressida asked, and Jory laughed even harder.

"It means you got it right. What does hitting the head with a snail mean?"

"The same thing. But you know, you use a snail." She paused. "Oh, I see. There wasn't really a snail. No wonder it never made sense when Leo said it."

A renewed round of giggles began.

Mago poured tea, then took a slice of what looked like a perfectly delightful olive loaf. Before she took a bite, she stopped. "Did you girls put the pot in this bread?"

"Mago!" Jory admonished. "You aren't supposed to know what pot is. But no. There is nothing in this bread whatsoever. Nothing. Nothing *at all*." She gave a pointed look to Cressida, who grinned.

Mago took a delicate, hesitant bite, and suddenly could think of nothing but Arie's arms around her, her cheeks flaming, her stomach tight. "Good lord, Cressida, what on earth?"

"Jory baked this bread, don't blame me. She's the one who's gone all…what's the word?"

"Lusty," Mago said, putting the bread down.

"I am not lusty!" Jory argued. They both looked at her. "Okay, perhaps a little bit. But you haven't *met* this guy."

"Well, you certainly didn't need to bake it into the bread. Although," Mago took another small bite, her cheeks turning pink. "My goodness." Mago took one more bite before clearing her throat. "Girls, I would like you to come to dinner at my house tonight, if you haven't made other plans?"

Jory and Cressida glanced at one another at the change of tone in Mago's voice.

"We'd be delighted, Mago, thank you for asking," Cressida said.

"Good," she said with a nod. "Cressida, I do not want to put you out, but would you be so kind as to bake your famous moussaka for dinner? You do know that I am a terrible cook."

"Not as bad as Jory, I hear, but yes," Cressida agreed with a grin, "you are a terrible cook. I will happily bring dinner to save us all a sensationally bad meal."

Mago chuckled, standing and patting Cressida's shoulder, whispering, "I'm so glad to have you back, my girl."

Cressida's cheeks turned pink with pleasure.

"I'll see you both at seven. And Jory, bring some more of that olive bread of yours, will you? I'd like to share that with Arie next time I see him."

Jory sat up on the kitchen bench with a glass of wine in hand as Cressida pulled the tray from the oven, letting the smells of comfort wash over her, the smells of her childhood, of Sunday dinner with her parents, and later, with Leo.

"How did you learn to cook like this? The food you made Mago and me the other night was the best meal I've had in a long time. The flavors so fresh and so filling then so perfect. I am a foodie, and I've worked in restaurants and traveled and eaten my share of good food, but truly, Cress, that was spectacular. World-class, actually. And now," she pointed to the moussaka dish, "this."

Cressida wanted to scoff, to be modest, to shrug off what Jory was saying, but the truth was she could not, and no longer did she want to. Because what Jory was saying about her food was the truth. She had been born and raised by one woman who could cook magic, and she trained her through her life, like all Callas women before her.

"My mother taught me everything I know about food, Jory. She taught me how to cook and how to bake, yes, but she taught me so much more than that. To prepare a dish is more than throwing a piece of fish in a frying pan with butter and parsley. You can do that and make something tasty. But to truly be a cook is to appreciate that food is, from its beginning to its execution, a story within a story within a story. It is the story of the growers, the farmers, the fishermen. It is the story of the people as much as the product. The magic does not come from within, it comes from the whole story put together on a plate with appreciation and love of all the stories that came together to make it so. We, as cooks, are the storytellers. We weave and mend the flavors together into a novel. It isn't a skill that is learned. It is a gift of allowing the flavors to come through you, not from you."

Cressida paused. "Have you had moussaka before, Jory?" she asked.

"I think so," she said. "It's sort of a Greek version of lasagne, right?"

"I suppose that's the perfect way to describe it. I slice the courgettes and aubergine longways, like a pasta base. And then do a tomato-based meat sauce. Most places in Greece use lamb, which is very strong for this dish, but it is what is local and available. Here on Naxos we have excellent cattle, so I use beef for mine. Sometimes when I can find pork, I mince them together. The béchamel is very Roman, and then the fresh herbs are just from me. I have been wondering why Mago asked me specifically to cook this. Though aubergines are in season it is a heavy dish for this heat. I am thinking tonight she will tell us what has been on her mind."

"I was thinking the same thing," Jory said, jumping off the bench and grabbing two bottles of wine from the refrigerator as Cressida placed the lid over her casserole dish to keep it warm for their twenty-second walk. "I got two from Arie today, just in case."

Dinner was a quiet event. Mago ate slowly, savoring every mouthful of Cressida's moussaka, her eyes closing as she chewed and swallowed, and then she would open her eyes with a smile and take a sip of wine. Jory and Cressida glanced at one another often, waiting for Mago to finish her plate and finally speak.

"Jory," Mago said finally, "did you enjoy your moussaka?"

"Oh yes," she said, "it was delicious."

"I am sure Cressida is wondering why I asked her to make this dish in particular at this time of the year?" she said, glancing at Cressida, who gave a small nod.

"Moussaka is a quintessential family meal that brings comfort and warmth. My mother used to make this every Sunday, and sometimes on an occasional weekday if it had been a particularly difficult day, like the day I learned about my gift," she said. "My mother was a wonderful woman. I was devastated when she passed away from breast cancer when she was sixty-eight. Just as my grandmother before her had." She looked up and met their eyes. Both girls were holding their breath. "I am sixty-eight," she whispered, tears forming in her eyes.

"Mago," Cressida said, leaning forward and taking her hand. "What has happened? Have you found something?"

She nodded and touched her left breast. Jory and Cressida both gasped quietly. "Yes. And it has terrified me. Like my mother before me and my grandmother before her, I was not going to go to the doctor. You see, I thought...I'd rather not know." A lone tear slid down her cheek before she took a deep breath and pulled her shoulders back, wiping her eyes. "But I cannot live in fear any longer. This is my life and I want it, every single minute of it. The great ones, the thrilling ones, the boring ones, the charmed ones, the hard ones. I want it all, and I am afraid I will find out that I won't have it much longer. But fear cannot keep me from fighting. And so tomorrow I am going to Athens on the boat for the weekend. My sons are there, and they will take me to the oncologist for a biopsy. And no matter what the result, I will fight. And I just…I wanted you to know that."

Both Jory and Cressida, though they wanted to be strong for Mago, could not help the tears, nor could they help the anxiety they felt, both for Mago's fear and wishing they could somehow alleviate it, which Cressida knew she had, in a way, with her moussaka. But also their own fear of losing someone they had both grown to love. Cressida had had so much loss in her life already, and Mago was like both a mother and a friend.

As the next hour wore on, Mago relaxed a bit, making jokes and drinking extra wine until it almost felt like a normal night. Until they said goodnight, when their hugs held something a little more than just "goodnight" in them. They contained all the fear, love, and strength they could pass on in the gesture.

Cressida and Jory did not speak on the walk down the stairs nor did they hug one another when they parted ways. They both turned and met eyes, and knew that they could no longer live in fear either. Cressida had a taverna to open and a life to live. Even the hard parts. And Jory nodded and went to her room to get a good night's sleep. For tomorrow there was someone waiting for her, her great fear, her sizzler. And she was going to be there.

Nine

Jory's morning would have been a montage in a romantic comedy if it had been turned into a film. The contents of her backpack littered every corner of her room. She'd changed four times. From jeans and a T-shirt so that she was just being her normal self, not trying too hard, to her new sundress from Madam's. By the time Jory knocked on Cressida's door, she was in a frenzy.

"Coffee," she begged. "I need coffee."

Cressida, still in her robe and having been dragged from bed, slammed the door in Jory's face, muttering, "You do *not* need coffee."

But the second time Jory knocked, Cressida shooed her inside, sitting her down to deal with her unruly hair. "I'll do a fishtail braid," she said, nodding. "It will help your hair stay in place even with the helmet on."

She finished quickly and came around in front of Jory. "Why did you decide to go?" she asked.

Jory took a deep breath. "You already know the answer to that."

Cressida nodded. "Mago."

"Mago," Jory agreed. "It's just... I've never wanted to have a life of regret. So I've followed my instincts and my dreams to have this life. Because this is me, you know? Living life fully, no regrets. But... what if by not allowing myself this great terrifying adventure, I do regret it? What if I miss something big because I'm too afraid to change? Does that make sense?"

Cressida smiled softly and placed her hand on Jory's cheek. "That one makes perfect sense."

Jory was beyond nervous as she waited for Shane to arrive at the parking lot, which she did eventually find after a few misses back and forth. Her palms were sweating, and her stomach was tied in knots so tight she could only think of them as double knots, when she heard the growl of his beautiful red motorcycle pull up beside her. He took his helmet off and began to say hello but paused momentarily. Jory had finally decided on the sundress and a pair of white sneakers. Her hair was still neatly restrained in its braid and she'd even used some of Cressida's shiny pink lip gloss that complemented her coloring. She felt she looked rather pretty, and the look on Shane's face said that perhaps he thought she did too.

"Jory, you look…"

"Impractical? Laundry day. You're lucky I had this dress, otherwise you might have seen me in my knickers." She forced a laugh, her face flushing with embarrassment. "That was actually funny in my head."

Shane laughed genuinely. "It was funny out loud too, I promise. Not that I'd mind seeing you in your knickers," he teased, winking, but he was looking at her appreciatively. "But I was going to say lovely. You look lovely, Jory."

"Thank you," she finally managed. He was *not* helping with her sweaty palms.

"Are you ready to go?" When she nodded, he sat on the bike and told her where to sit. "Just behind me here. You can hold onto the handles to your side." He turned his head back to her. "Or you can hold your arms around me."

Jory didn't trust herself to hold onto him quite yet so she grasped the side handles, and they were off. The many twists and turns forced Jory to hold onto Shane a few times, much to her great pleasure. His body was firm and her skin tingled each time she touched him but instead of feeling electrocuted, her body was humming like a generator. When was the last time she had such a reaction to a man?

Eventually they arrived at the little seaside town of Apollonas. Jory stepped off the bike too quickly, her calf meeting the exhaust and burning her leg. She yelped, jumping forward and straight into Shane's arms.

"Are you okay?" he asked, catching her. His signature grin was missing, replaced by a slight flaring of his nostrils and a hardening of his body. She felt an unbelievable desire to lean in and kiss him. Instead, she broke the connection, stepping back.

"Yes. Just a slight burn. I'm a waitress. Slight burns are an everyday occurrence for me." She laughed through clenched teeth.

Shane ran his hand down her leg until he reached the small burn, about the size of her thumb. Jory had never been so grateful to be clumsy, her body lighting on fire as he touched her. Much to her embarrassment, her leg got sudden goosebumps under his touch.

"I've got salve for that in the back. Hold still a moment," he said, reaching into the console and squeezing the cream on his hand, which he then gently rubbed on the burn.

Oh my god, she thought, attempting to distract herself.

"So, how good is your Greek history?" she asked, running her fingers through her unruly hair, which had come out of the braid.

"Better than yours, I'm sure," he said.

"Well, wait a minute. Now I'm insulted."

"Don't be. I minored in archeology."

"Seriously?" she asked, waiting to see if he was joking, but he looked quite abashed.

"Seriously. I was a closet dork."

"If you minored in archeology, I think you were mightily out of the closet by that time," she teased.

He laughed, reaching in and pulling her close. "You're teasing me," he said. "Nobody ever seems to do that anymore. How's that burn?"

"Good. Really good," she said. His head was touching her forehead, his breath mingling with hers. She wanted to feel his lips on hers, but he closed his eyes instead, taking a deep breath and lightly touching her face. It was so intimate she almost lost her ability to stand upright.

"Come, it's just a short walk up the hill. I've been here a few times," he said, taking her hand in his.

Jory felt her brain was melting. She needed to focus on the conversation, not the feel of her hand in his.

"Actually, I was close to majoring in history or archeology myself at college," she finally said. "I just love the way I feel when I visit a historical place that resonates with me. I don't know if this makes sense, but instead of feeling like there's a gap between the past and the present, I feel more connected to it. Like, wow, these were people, just like me, you know?" Jory said as he guided her, hand in hand, up the hill to the quarry.

Shane beamed. "I more than know. Even though when I decided to minor in archeology, I had no idea I'd feel that way. I was a business major," he said, shrugging.

"Really? That's so practical. Why archeology then?"

"Because I wanted to be Indiana Jones."

She laughed. "I shouldn't have asked. Even I wanted to be Indiana Jones. I remember the first moment I glimpsed the Treasury in Petra, I felt like all my childhood dreams had just somehow come true."

"Jordan? You have traveled a bit then," he said, impressed.

She smiled. "Just a bit."

"The leave instinct," he said, obviously remembering their conversation at Zas. "You seem too young to have grown up with Indiana Jones."

"I could say the same about you! I guess with all the new versions these days it's a bit different, but *Last Crusade* was my favorite film as a child. My mother was very young when she had me, and seeing as we only had each other, that bridged the gap a bit between generations when it came to movies and music. I was born in the early nineties and she was born in the seventies. The eighties were sort of our compromise."

"Early nineties? That makes you…?"

"Twenty-eight. Just a few weeks ago actually, the day I arrived in Greece. It's my 'golden year' they call it." She shook her head with a smile. "Twenty-eight on the twenty-eighth. Plus the plane ticket was like, half-price for that day. It was weird."

"That is weird. Kind of like fate or something," he said.

"That's what my friends said too. But I don't believe in fate."

He scoffed. "So you believe in magical bread, gifts, the leave instinct, but not in fate? That's a contradiction if I ever heard one."

Jory rolled her eyes. "I've had this argument way too many times in the past few weeks and I'm giving up! But you know, I was thinking last night—can one go from not believing to believing in something? Or have we always believed but we're too afraid to accept that life is out of our control, that we're part of something bigger than ourselves?" Jory was surprised she'd said that out loud.

Shane looked deep in thought. "But we don't learn to believe, we learn to disbelieve. My twin sister, Sarah, has two kids. My nieces." He smiled, looking proud. "They still believe in Santa Claus. And every year I dress up and bring gifts and change my voice so that they can continue to believe in something so magical. And every year I wish I still believed that Santa was real. I wish I could believe in the magic I make for them."

"But you can't. You can't believe in something you know isn't real. You can't unlearn the truth," she said.

"How do you know what is truth? I could be Santa Claus. Hey, I *am* Santa Claus to two people in the world. That's the only reality they know."

"So you *are* a romantic," Jory finally said, smiling.

"And you are too, you just don't believe it yet," Shane said, taking her hand again. "Come, we're almost there."

Jory stood in awe of the 35-foot-long marble statue lying at the top of the hill, serenely, as though waiting in stillness to be found.

"This is Dionysus, the god of wine, the patron god of the island of Naxos," Shane told her, speaking quietly, almost reverently, as they gazed upon the statue. "It's a statue from the Archaic period of Greece, around the seventh century BCE. Archeologists originally thought it was Apollo, but realized he had a beard, so it must be Dionysius. It was never finished."

"Why?"

"The best explanation is simply that he was too big and heavy to transport. Even thousands of years ago, people were pragmatic," he said.

They spent the next hour exploring the ruins, every now and again accidentally touching one another and the air would sparkle. Once Shane knew of Jory's shared love of history, he was able to be himself completely, telling stories that had Jory sometimes in wonder, or in stitches, laughing. Finally, they made their way back down the hill to the seaside village.

"There's a lovely little restaurant just on the waterfront if you'd like to eat before we head home. I'm sure it won't serve food as magical as your friend's, but the seafood is fresh and the people who own it are lovely. I don't think you'll be disappointed."

"I'd love that, thank you."

The owners recognized Shane immediately, kissing his cheeks and welcoming him in Greek, and then did the same for Jory, but in English. They sat them at a table outside and sent a few mezze-style dishes to start—an eggplant and tomato dip, fried calamari followed by small fried fish with a Greek salad on the side and Naxos potatoes.

"You said you were a waitress?" Shane asked during the meal.

Jory brightened. "Yes. I started waitressing in college for extra money and fell in love with it. When I moved to Los Angeles, it made sense to get a job in what I knew. I have a lot of friends working in hospitality, you know, while they're trying to be something else—actor, writer, musician. But me, I just love my job. I've always felt this need to have purpose and meaning in whatever I do, you know?"

He nodded. "Me too."

"So one day, someone comes up to me at work and says, 'what do you really do?' Like what I did was meaningless. I'd started traveling at that point so sometimes waitressing did feel like I was just there making money to do something else. But that day, I realized the answer to that question is that what I really want to do is to be a person of significance, even if it's just to one other person. What if I have the ability to do some real good in this world? And what if it's as simple as walking into my restaurant every day and getting the chance to be kind to a hundred strangers? I mean, how great is that, right?"

Shane nodded. "Oh man, I love the feeling of someone walking into the bar, pouring them a drink, and knowing their day just got so much better just by giving them your attention."

"You're in hospitality?" she asked brightly. Shane opened his mouth to reply but Jory continued. "Just like me, I love that. I was a little worried when you said you majored in business," she said. He gave her a sour look but she winked. "So a bartender, huh? You totally look like a bartender."

"I think you mean that as a compliment," he said. "So does that mean you have a thing for bartenders?"

Jory leaned forward and said conspiratorially, "I might have a thing for *this* bartender."

Shane took her hand, sliding his fingers down the inside of her wrist. She was losing all ability to think and therefore to eat. She swallowed, parted her mouth, and pulled her hand back to touch the back of her neck, which was overheating. Shane gave her a knowing smirk.

"So, uh," she managed. "Where do you work? You said your family was in Pittsburgh?"

He hesitated, but then said, "My last bartending job was in Mexico."

"What?" she exclaimed. "You lucky man. Hmm." Jory's gaze wandered dreamily. "Mexico. Maybe that should be my next trip. Can you believe I've never been?"

Shane's jaw dropped. "How is that possible? You who's been to the Middle East and India. You, the only person I know who has been robbed by a baboon in Africa—you have really never been to Mexico?"

"Tell me everything about it," she said excitedly.

"This is going to take a while," he said and called the waiter over. He ordered a carafe of white wine made locally and began talking to Jory about Mexico and his favorite places, the food, the language, in which he was fluent. They talked about friends and family, travels and passions. At some point during the meal, something changed between them. Jory could feel it. That moment where their interest, desire and connection made the rest of the world all fall into oblivion. When they were finished eating, they leaned toward each other, foreheads practically touching, hands held.

"Marjory…"

She drew back abruptly. "Oh no, you just said my full name. That's never a good thing."

"I have to go to Athens for about a week to do some work, possibly longer," he said.

"Very serious bartender work?" she teased.

"Oh right," he said, shaking his head. "I have a friend here on the island. He's asked me to help him out since I had been planning to head back to the mainland anyway. But I have some unfinished business here, on Naxos. Will you be here when I return?"

Her heart stopped, hoping the unfinished business was her. "Yes, I'll be here."

He relaxed back into his seat. "Good. I want to see you when I get back. Will you want to see me?"

Oh god yes, she thought, her whole body flaming. She nodded, licking her lips.

"Jesus, don't do that, or I might kiss you right here, right now."

"Would that be such a bad thing?"

"The right here right now part might be a bit much," he said, nodding to the audience around them. "The kissing part? That won't be a bad thing at all." He made eye contact with the waiter and indicated for the bill.

Just minutes later they were walking hand in hand to the beach. At the water's edge, Shane stopped and turned Jory to face him, and immediately his warm mouth was covering hers. She pressed into him, needing to be closer, to feel more of him, running her hands through his hair. His arms wrapped around her torso, his hands running down her back, her waist, her buttocks. She groaned in the back of her throat. She had never felt so much need or desire for a man, as if everything were dependent on this moment.

She wanted to kiss him forever, but after a while the sky started to turn a blazing orange and pink, indicating the sun would be setting within the hour.

"While I would rather stay here, we should probably be going," Shane murmured as they slowly pulled apart.

Jory looked at him expectantly.

"I have a four am ferry," he explained reluctantly.

"Ah, yes, Athens," she said, disappointed.

They hopped on Shane's bike and he drove them back to Chora, the sun setting around them. The ride back was not long enough. Jory had her arms wrapped around Shane's body, while his left arm—when not taking the turns on the road—reached back and grazed her hip, her thigh, any chance he could. She was on fire when they finally got back to the parking lot in Naxos.

Jory got off the bike, her legs shaking as Shane took her face in his hands, kissing her eyelids, her cheeks, then down to her neck as he was running his fingers through her hair.

"Oh god," she whispered, and they were kissing again.

It took them a long while to pull apart, but finally Shane put his hands on her shoulders. "I'll see you next week, hopefully, all things on track."

"Until next week then." She took her keys out of her bag.

"Wait."

Her heart beat wildly against her chest. Was he going to ask her to come home with him? Was she going to say yes? "Yes?" she managed, clearing her throat.

"How can I get in touch? You with the no phone, no laptop."

Sweet relief mingled with disappointment. "Contact information would be helpful, wouldn't it? Cressida told me I can use her computer, so I'll give you my email address." She fumbled in her bag for a pen. "Damnit, I can't find..."

Shane was chuckling and she looked up. He was holding up his phone, waiting. "It's all the rage these days. It's called 'create contact' and it's quite helpful. Always gets me out of situations when I forget my pen and paper."

She poked her tongue out at him, which made his eyes crinkle. "I do have one of those you know, I just decided not to bring it," she said, typing her email into his phone and creating a new contact for herself.

"See?" She handed him back the phone. "New contact created. Me. I even made myself an emoji."

Shane looked at Jory's emoji of a toothy blonde with frizzy hair. Shaking his head with a smile, he put the phone in his pocket and started his bike as she went to her moped, turning around one last time. He saluted her and grinned, riding away, leaving her filled with an empty longing, her equilibrium completely out of whack.

Ten

Cressida spent the weekend walking Jory through the property so she could understand it fully. They went through each room of the guesthouse, which were all furnished and had full guest supplies already, but Cressida wanted to leave the guesthouse alone and focus only on the taverna.

"The morning after Leo died, I got up and went through every room of the guesthouse, dusting, polishing, making sure every room was at its most impeccable. I have done this every morning since. For a long time, I didn't know why, but I think it was a way of keeping our dream alive," Cressida said to her. "But now I want to focus on the taverna, on my cooking."

"Who's going to clean the guesthouse now then?" Jory asked teasingly.

"You?" Cressida offered.

Jory was most excited to learn about Cressida's famous secret garden and desperately tried to remember the names of the different herbs, fruits and vegetables, but Jory could not tell a weed apart from a herb so they both decided that would definitely not be one of her jobs.

"All things food, except the eating of it, of course, are in your capable hands," Jory said, bowing to her.

They went to the markets and Cressida shopped using her little Callas recipe book and handwritten diary with recipes. She would tick things off and the girls would come home and talk about their plans for the taverna while Cressida cooked and Jory ate all the different dishes, making notes.

They would then go to Chora, pretending to be tourists while they checked out the menus of different restaurants in town.

"Oh, look, Betty," Jory said loudly to Cressida in a mock Southern accent, "this one here's got calamari. Ain't that yer favorite?"

Cressida giggled and came over to take a sneaky photo of the menu with her phone. "You are terrible with accents."

"I know. Did you get a photo?"

Cressida nodded so they moved on.

"As far as I can see," said Jory, "the only restaurant here that would even compare to the class of food you'll be doing is that place Rigani, the one where you used to work."

She smiled. "Yes, with Nefeli. That is where I baked my bread for Leo."

"You know, one day you're going to have to tell me whatever happened between you and Nefeli. Of course, it's impossible for me to even imagine you two as friends, you're so different," Jory mused.

Cressida nodded thoughtfully. "We were not always so different. But life happens to people and sometimes they get through together and sometimes they drift apart. I have been thinking of her though, especially since finding out about Mago. Speaking of Mago, I wonder how she is doing in Athens?"

"Has she called again?" Jory asked.

Cressida shook her head. "Not since she called to say she arrived safely." She bit her lower lip.

"I know, I'm anxious too. But I'm sure she's doing fine, just catching up with her sons. And it will take at least a few days to get her results back," Jory assured Cressida.

"You're right. We can only be patient and wait. Speaking of making contact, have you heard from Shane yet?" Cressida asked as they headed back to Potamia from town.

"I haven't had a chance to check my email, actually. Do you think I could use the office tomorrow morning?" Jory asked.

"You have a key, silly! You don't have to ask."

So the next morning when Cressida went into town, Jory let herself into the office and sat in front of the large computer. She realized how much she wanted to be in touch with her friends and family back home. Especially Liz and Kate. There was so much to tell them.

Jory thought about what Cressida had said to her the other day. Was she frightened that something might threaten her freedom? Was she frightened of change? Of love?

But it echoed what Jory's mother always said to her when she somehow found herself feeling lost without knowing why. Almost a sense of stagnation. It never made sense to Jory before.

"Remember, Jory, wherever you go, you are still there," her mom would say. "It's different for you because of your gift for feeling home wherever you are. Other people can travel the world and those very experiences help shape them into who they might not have been otherwise. You are different. When you arrive at a new place and experience new things, it is you simply being you. The adventure is not enough—you still must allow those adventures to help you grow, to change, to become the best version of yourself. Let life change you sometimes."

That was exactly what Cressida was telling her with regards to Shane, that Jory was letting life happen to her but not making choices to allow herself to change, or be changed, by someone else. To be bold and stray outside of this life that she loved.

But this life made her happy, so why allow anything to alter that?

Because, she answered herself, *I really, really like him. And if I really like him but am choosing to run from it, then I am frightened.* Maybe opening herself up to Shane shouldn't be so scary. Maybe it should be a little bit wonderful. She nodded and smiled. *Excellent argument, Jory.*

Just the thought of actually *choosing* to let Shane happen made her heart beat faster. She suddenly could not open her email fast enough. She quickly scanned her inbox, spotting emails from her mom and the girls and, surprisingly, one from her father. Her heart dropped when she saw nothing from Shane. *It has only been three days,* she thought. *He's busy, he's in Athens. And I am not going to be that woman. Needy, waiting for an email from a guy.*

She poured a large cup of coffee from the French press Cressida had left by the computer and opened the email from her father first, out of curiosity and to get it over with quickly. She had written a quick email from Athens when she'd first arrived, letting them all know she'd landed safely and was on her way to Naxos the next day. Even though he'd never asked for one, her mom insisted she include him in these emails.

"Jory, just because you and your father are not the best of friends does not mean he doesn't worry about you. He calls me sometimes when you're overseas to check to make sure you're okay," Cindy had told her once.

She'd been so shocked she put her dad on her "I'm here safe" mailing list. But he'd never written until now.

Marjory,
Thank you for letting me know you have arrived safely. I have
fond memories of Greece from when I was young and your mom
and I were living in Paris. You will enjoy it.
Dad

Jory had no idea how to even think about replying. This was probably the most intimate thing he had ever said to her—he never talked about Cindy or their past. Was her father trying to change that, somehow? Was he trying to connect with her? She had no idea how she felt about that.

Since that day when she was sixteen, Jory had let go of having a relationship with her father and his family with their old money and their conservative views.

Though there were a few Buchanan annual Christmas balls she'd attended at her grandparents' mansion in Charleston. She'd actually taken Kate and Liz to the last one a few years back.

"Wow," Kate had said, as they walked up to the old southern mansion. "You could have been like Scarlett O'Hara had you grown up here."

Liz nodded. "You're sure you don't want in on any of this, Jor?"

"Not worth my soul, I promise," she'd breathed, squeezing their hands as they walked in together.

That party had actually been a good deal of fun. They stood together at the bar, creating stories of the strangest people at the party.

"Oooh, that one," Jory said, nodding her head to an odd-looking man in his early thirties with a young woman on his side, equally odd-looking, and an older, regal woman that reminded Jory of her grandmother. "Here with his wife and his mistress, one on each arm."

"Which one is which?" Kate giggled, sipping her martini. "This game is getting more fun with every martini I have."

"Gramma's the mistress!" Liz decided, a little too loudly. Jory and Kate started laughing so hard, vodka was coming out of their noses.

"Girls," a male voice said sternly.

"Sorry, Mr. Buchanan," Liz said solemnly.

"Yes, sorry," Kate repeated, looking embarrassed.

Jory just stared at him and did not apologize. He looked at her for a moment and then turned away, but not before she saw a fleeting movement on his face that almost, just for a second, looked like a smile.

That had been one of the last times she'd seen him. She had no idea how to respond to his email so she marked it as unread and moved onto emailing her mom, giving her every detail of her trip so far. Normally Jory shared everything, but she stopped when it came to Shane. Jory had never felt for a man this way before and she wanted to...protect it. To just be hers. Not to be a St. James woman with a sizzler, but to simply be a girl with a crush on a boy. Nothing else. It was the first time in her life she'd omitted telling her mom something important. She felt momentarily guilty but hit send nonetheless.

She saved the email from Liz and Kate until last. They'd written it together, it seemed, based on the subject line "It's us, we're drunk and we miss you!"

Just as she was about to open it, another email arrived in her inbox. Her heart skipped a beat when she read the subject line. "Thinking of you, Terp."

"Holy shit," she said aloud, opening the email.

I am. Thinking of you, that is. I look forward to seeing you next week.

Shane

Bliss washed over her as she hit reply, but her mind was blank. It was joyful, but it was blank. She'd sit on it for the day, she thought. Email him later.

Her heart was racing as she started an email to Liz and Kate. To them, she gave the R-rated version. Every stupid decision (she even told Liz she'd been right about the phone), every detailed meeting with Shane, asking their opinions on every touch, every kiss. She wrote to them about Cressida, about opening the taverna, about Mago and Arie, about the strange gifts of the women of Potamia and the little quirks of the villagers, from Nefeli and Nico to the man in the suit, to the mayor whose watch didn't work though he was always looking at it for the time and was never late, nor ever early. She was laughing as she wrote, pausing to look out the window with an unbelievable fondness for this new place, this new part of her life. A place and a life she was not going to be afraid of. Not even a little bit.

Okay, girls, forgive me for sending you an email the length of the Bible, but I miss you! I wish you could both come to Greece and be here when the taverna opens, to meet Cressida and the townsfolk, and to meet Shane (if he actually does come back). Miss you like a rogue limb.

X Jory

"Jory, are you still here?" Cressida called, opening the door after a knock but not coming in.

"Hi! Come on in. Thanks for letting me use the computer."

"So, did Shane email yet?" Cressida asked excitedly, walking into the office and sitting in the spare chair.

Jory blushed. "He said he's thinking of me."

"Gah!" Cressida said, her face lighting up. "Young love, blooming romance. So what did you write back?"

"Nothing yet, I'm sitting on it," she replied. "Okay, I don't know what to say!" she said at Cressida's look.

"Fair enough. Did you catch up with your friends and family then?"

"Mostly, yes. Hey, I've got an idea," she said. "Why don't I take a few photos tonight when we try some of your new dishes. I did a photography class once and took some photos for The French Café. I'm actually not bad and I brought my camera with me. We'll need at least a few food photos before we open up."

Cressida took a deep breath, looking nervous, but nodded. "Okay, I'll pull out a few recipes. And we'll have three." She smiled. "Mago's home."

~

"Must you take photos while I'm rolling the dolmades? It's very distracting."

Jory rolled her eyes behind the lens of her Canon. "Do you have any idea how hard it is to photograph food? And I'm no professional photographer, so I have to try all the angles. Like now, your hands rolling the dolmades—it's an action shot. People see it and they think, 'oh, this is truly authentic.' Trust me." She took a few more photos.

"Let her distract us, Cress," Mago said. "It's much more fun than my weekend was, I promise."

"Mago, the only important thing to us is how you are. So, what happened after your sons picked you up from the ferry?" Cressida asked.

"My boys just said, 'let's get it out of the way, Mum,' so we did. Went direct to the hospital for the biopsy and then ignored it the rest of the weekend, like family usually do when it comes to the hard stuff." She chuckled.

Jory reached for Mago's hand. "When will the results come in?"

Mago sighed. "Sometime this week. So until then, let's distract me, okay?"

"I'll finish the photos of the dolmades while you prepare the next dish, Cress," Jory called. "And then I'll bring them over for us to nibble on. Mm, they do smell delicious. I don't know if I've ever eaten them warm before."

Cressida snorted. "They are meant to be eaten warm. Though to be fair, they are one of my favorite cold picnic snacks." She turned on the skillet and threw olive oil in, then dusted the calamari in flour. She transferred them into a sieve and shook until there was nearly no flour left on the calamari at all.

Jory finished photographing the dolmades, and when satisfied she had some good shots, placed the plate on the bench between them. She picked one up and popped it in her mouth. "Wow, that's delicious."

"Agreed," Mago said. "Oh, Cressida, your famous calamari

too? Jory, once you have had it the way Cressida makes it you will never have the same relationship with squid."

They watched Cressida throw some garlic into a pan of olive oil and sizzling butter and then toss in the calamari. "Fried calamari?" Jory asked, picking up her camera again. "I love that. Don't you normally deep-fry it?"

She took a few shots of Cressida tossing the calamari by moving the pan around. "This is called a shallow fry, more of a sauté. The calamari is not battered, it is simply dusted very lightly with flour. Too much flour and it will cake and burn. Just the right amount and it will crisp to perfection, so long as the heat is high enough and you don't cook it for long."

Jory took a few more photos. "I think we should target the locals first. Here in Potamia and around the island. Perhaps we can put some pictures outside with an opening date so all those passing by will see and know. Your friends will all want to come support you, Cress. Everyone who knows you knows your food, and others will remember you from Rigani. And so they should. You are a culinary genius," Jory said.

"They only know me because they feel sorry for me. The pathetic Potamian with a dead husband and an empty dream," Cressida said, sighing.

"You don't believe that," Jory disagreed. "You told me of your mother teaching you your gift for food. But I understand that you might be scared. That I do understand," she said with a meaningful look to Cressida.

"I just don't know how I can possibly get everything ready in such a short time, and doing this without Leo. It feels incredibly overwhelming," Cressida admitted.

"That's because it is incredibly overwhelming," Mago said. "But we work together one step at a time to make it ready, and the people will come. I know, we'll announce it at the next town meeting!" she added, brightening. "Jory, I did promise I'd take you to one. They are—"

"They are like a very bad reality television show that should never have existed in the first place," Cressida said, but when she shook her head, there was a fond smile on her face. "Though I suppose you are right, Mago. We'll have no support if we don't make it official at the meeting. I shall bake something special for it."

"Psh," Mago huffed, "they haven't eaten your bread since the funeral. They're terrified of it."

Jory turned to Cressida. "We'll announce it at the town meeting first, then. And after that you can start to get a Facebook page ready to go, and get on Google Maps, because everybody uses that these days. It's all free, so what's the harm? But you can't do those things without photos," she said, holding up her camera. "I'm hopeless at social media," Jory admitted. "But I'll do my best to help and we'll print out some flyers as well. If you're opening a restaurant, you have to advertise it."

Cressida nodded slowly. "Still, I'll be alone in the kitchen, cooking an entire menu on my own..."

"I know, you'll definitely need to hire someone to help in the kitchen at some point, but in the meantime, keep it nice and small. Limited menu, seating and opening hours to start. I had an idea that we do the soft open night as invitation-only, that people have to RSVP for, just local friends and families, where you get to have a trial run and see how you go. I mean, you're only one chef and I'm only one waitress, so it's not like we can do too much at once."

"That makes sense," Cressida said. "Yes, then I can prepare knowing exactly how many people are coming. I can shop for the food, cook the right amount of everything. Like a dinner party." She nodded. "I can do this. I will start putting a menu together. When will we schedule the soft open? August?"

Jory scoffed. "By that time, we'll miss the start of the tourist season. No way. I say first weekend of July. That gives us a solid two and a bit weeks. We can do the invitation-only on the Saturday night and close Sunday and Monday, then be ready to open to the public on the Tuesday."

"That's too soon! I can't be ready by then!"

Jory came behind Cressida and hugged her. "Yes you can. You can do this," she said in a reassuring voice.

"*We* can," Mago said, joining in.

Jory said good night to Mago, holding her tight for a moment before she went back to her home. Cressida was cleaning in the kitchen and refused help, so instead of heading to her room, Jory went to the little office. She'd spent the entire day thinking of Shane's email to her. He was thinking of her. And he'd had no hesitation to put it in writing.

She hit reply to his email, changing the subject line to "Baking."

> *I baked my first loaf of bread with Cressida the day before our date. It was an olive loaf, and for the first time in my culinary history, I was successful and my dough actually rose, which is magic in and of itself. But let me just say, Cressida and Mago could indeed tell by the taste of the loaf that my thoughts were all of you.*
> *Jory*

She didn't know if it was too intimate, or just intimate enough, but she pressed send and then went directly to bed. She could hardly sleep in anticipation for the reply that she was certain would be waiting for her in the morning.

⁓

Jory and Cressida soon realized it would take every second of the two weeks to be ready for a "soft opening," as Jory called it.

Their first job was to start pulling things out of the storage unit, starting with the furniture, unloading fourteen tables and stacks of chairs into the garden. They were in good condition for the most part, with just a few needing paint touch-ups to chips and scuff marks.

Once Jory had rid the tables of cobwebs and scrubbed them clean with a hard brush and soapy water, she asked Cressida if she had an idea of where they would be positioned.

"Leo had a map I can probably find," Cressida called from the garage. "The wrought-irons were meant for the garden, and the plastic tables for the covered porch. They're not very pretty, I know, but we were going to get tablecloths for them. Bright blue ones, or an assortment of cheery colors. Can you put that on the list?"

Jory wrote "tablecloths" on the ever-growing list. "And that would leave the wooden tables for inside?"

"Yes. Should I try to find Leo's map? It will be on the computer somewhere." Cressida emerged from the shed, her long black hair tied back and covered with a bandanna. She was wearing a man's shirt that was far too big, sleeves rolled up, and tucked into a pair of baggy jeans. She looked strong, vital and determined.

"It's up to you. Do you want to see your and Leo's dream through the way he saw it? Or do you want to take the dream into your own hands and do it the way you see it?"

She thought for a moment, and finally nodded. "Leo had wonderful ideas. But I cannot do his wonderful ideas without him. I can only do what I can do. Let's just get the tables ready to go and see how many people RSVP before preparing a seating chart."

"Sounds like a plan to me," Jory said. "Now, let's get going on the wooden tables. Ugh, I think they're going to need sanding. Do you know how to sand things?"

Cressida scoffed, retreating to the shed and returning with an electric sander, holding it up. "Will this do?"

"Let me guess. Leo and all his gadgets?"

"Ha!" Cressida laughed, plugging in the sander and adjusting the setting as she reached the first of the four wooden tables. "Leo's passion was for toys. You remember the bathroom door that locked you in? He was amazing with technology but not a handyman at all. Greek men, they live with their mothers and then they marry," she said, turning on the sander, and starting on one of the tables like a professional. "Handyman needs a new word in Greek—handywoman."

~

The following day, Cressida drove them into Chora Naxos for supplies. They went first to the hardware store to pick up paint and more sanding paper. The next stop was to the fabric shop where, instead of buying cheaply made tablecloths, Cressida picked out three different linens—one a solid turquoise, a staple in all Greek islands; one a bright buttermilk yellow and one a pale pink with darker red and maroon grapes. It was cheaper and more efficient if you bought the fabric in meters instead of individually cut, so she purchased in bulk and tucked it into a bag to bring home.

"Don't even think about asking me to help with that," Jory warned. "If you think my cooking is bad, wait until you see my sewing."

"My dear friend, please take no offense, but I would never have thought to ask if you could sew a tablecloth." Cressida laughed. "Mago is a gifted seamstress. If you think I can bake magic in my bread, wait until you see what kind of mood she can create when she sews. And I think it will be a good distraction for her this week. She's asked me to involve her as much as possible to help her take her mind off things. She will know what to do with the fabric."

After that, they visited the local markets, where Cressida perused the fresh fish, meat and vegetables to note what was seasonal and available so she could create her menu. She bought food and ticked the items off one by one, going back into her handwritten recipe book and making more notes.

On their way back, Cressida pointed out a familiar gallery. "Lucas runs the recycle center down at the port—his sister, Selene, works in that gallery and can give you his contact number. Perhaps you can check it out later in the week? I'm looking for a little deep-fryer and refuse to buy a new one if Lucas has a secondhand one for practically free."

"Selene and I have quite a history already," Jory said. "I'm not certain she'll be thrilled to see me again. I met Shane for the first time in Selene's gallery, and let's just say she was not too happy about it."

"Ah, your Shane must be very handsome to have Selene's attention," she said. "We went to school together. She desperately wants to get off this island and into a wealthy man's bed."

"Cressida!"

"Well, I say good on her. What woman wouldn't want to be the wife of a wealthy man?"

Jory shuddered. "Me! I never want to be rich. Rich people are not to be trusted." Her father had shown her that. "Love makes the world go round, not money. My mother taught me that."

Cressida smiled, taking Jory's hand. "Do you ever think perhaps you are telling yourself a story that may no longer be true? You go back home to Los Angeles and work as hard and as much as you can for nearly a year to save money to have this lifestyle of travel and seeing the world. Money allows you to do that, it is not the enemy. Why can't we have it all, I say—love and money and happiness."

"I suppose I could try that on for size," Jory conceded, thinking of Shane.

⁓

The next day, Jory left Mago measuring tables and Cressida working away in the kitchen and hopped on her scooter to Arie's vineyard, where she found him in the tasting room.

His eyes crinkled with a smile. "Ah, Marjory. Just the person I've been expecting. Please, sit."

"You've been expecting me?" she asked, surprised. She'd only just this morning come up with her idea and hadn't told anyone yet. Her eyes narrowed. "Wait a minute. Do you have some sort of weird ability to sense when people are coming? Honestly, this town…"

Arie chuckled. "Yes, a few of our lovely women of Potamia do have some interesting gifts, though unfortunately, they never seemed to pass onto any of us men. Quite occasionally, however, they seem to involve us somehow, even if inadvertently. This is about the taverna, yes? I was hoping you'd come today, and hoping as well that you would ask me if mine could be the lucky vineyard to provide wine for the new establishment."

"Of course that's why I'm here. This is the best winery on the island, and we do need wine." She smiled at him. But the truth was, it was only part of the reason for the visit. "There is something else."

She outlined her idea. Diamanté's vineyard was busier in the summer, not only making wine, but with tour groups. If Arie was going to be providing the wine for the restaurant, perhaps he could play a larger part in helping them. Cressida had been correct—there was only two of them so there was only so much they could do at once. Group bookings made sense. It also made sense to know about them in advance. For the taverna to succeed, it had to actually have customers, and no matter how many flyers Jory put up, they were in Potamia and not on the main tourist trail, and there were dozens of other restaurants just on the water-front to compete with. It was not going to be an easy venture, at least not at first, without partnering up with someone.

"In short," she finished, "I thought perhaps you could recommend the taverna in advance to your tour groups when they book. What do you think?"

Arie nodded, thoughtful, and then his face lit up, his smile wide. "I have an even better idea." He stood, putting on his wide-brimmed hat and grabbing his keys. "Come, let's go for a ride."

⁓

Jory was elated and excited as she ran up to the guesthouse to share her news with Cressida, but hushed voices stopped her from calling out, and she paused to listen at the open door.

"What have you decided?" she heard Mago ask.

"I told you, I have decided to open," said Cressida. "I want to open."

"Yes, but what of the hotel group trying to buy you out?"

"I have a little more time to start paying the mortgage before the bank forecloses. If I can start making small contributions to it in July, the bank may be more forgiving of my late payments."

"And what of Jory? She has a right to know."

"What more does she need to know?"

There was silence then. Jory coughed intentionally and fumbled with the lock on her door. She didn't want them to know she'd heard. Cressida appeared at the top of Mago's balcony next door, her brow furrowed.

"Jory, I did not hear you. Have you just returned?"

"Yup!" she said brightly to cover the pit in her stomach. "Just back now."

"Have you eaten? I can make you dinner."

"Oh, no, I'm fine, thank you. I had lunch in town and I'm not really that hungry."

Mago stood then behind Cressida. "Surely you are thirsty. Come, tell us about your day."

"I'll be up in just a moment."

Jory closed the door to her room behind her. Everything she'd just heard confirmed what Cressida had hinted at days before. Her dream was about to come to an end if she didn't do something to help. If her friend hadn't told her about the possibility of selling or being bought out, there was a reason. Cressida needed her. Obviously if she could not get people in, she would never be able to make her payments to the bank and then her dream would be gone, sold to some horrible big hotel group. Jory hated those kinds of people, who fed off those who couldn't support themselves, and made themselves rich while those desperate lost everything. No. She would not let this happen to Cress.

She walked over to Mago's where Cressida and Mago stood staring at the crescent moon, glasses of wine in hand. They both turned and smiled when Jory arrived, Mago handing her a glass of the same crisp white.

"So, Marjory, what have you been up to today?" Cressida asked. There was no guile. Cressida smiled at her with such warmth, in a way that let her know that her presence meant something. Whatever else was going on, it changed nothing between them.

"Well," she began, taking a sip of wine and sitting in one of the bench seats, "I went for a little ride into town with Arie, actually."

Mago blushed hearing her lover's name. Cressida caught it and winked at Jory. "Why were you with Arie? You didn't mention anything about it this morning."

"Because I had an idea of how to get the tourists to the taverna. I went to see Arie to ask if he'd be keen to recommend us to some of the tour groups that start coming from next week. He told me he gets three to four per week. He's ready and willing to help, seeing as he is going to be our only wine supplier." Mago's face lit up at this news. "But not only that—we drove into Chora and met with the two wine tour groups, and they are going to use us as their lunch stop after visiting the vineyard. *Only* us. All summer."

"Oh my goodness!" Mago exclaimed. "That is the most amazing news!"

Cressida sat upright, her eyes wide. She didn't look happy necessarily, more surprised. "But...what if I am not ready in time?"

"Nonsense," Mago said. "You've been ready for this for years. Come here, give me your hands." She took their hands, nodding for them to do the same. They stood in a circle together. "Sometimes in life, our stories collide, and when the right stories collide, whether by fate or accident, magic happens. Magic is happening here. Embrace it."

Cressida nodded, her eyes shining with unshed tears as she looked at the two friends who were helping change her life.

"Good," said Mago. "Now, can we please drink some wine? It's seven in the evening and I find myself much too sober to talk about such deep matters. Jory, how are things progressing with your lusty lover?" she pressed.

Jory glanced at Cressida with wide eyes, but Cressida shrugged innocently.

"Don't look at her," Mago said. "I eavesdrop. It's my god-given right," Mago said. "So?"

Cressida leaned forward. "You don't have to tell us if you don't want. But it has been a while since you've mentioned Shane. Is he coming back to the island soon?"

Shane's daily emails were Jory's most anticipated moment of her day, despite how much she enjoyed the work she was doing with Cressida and the progress they were making with the taverna. She and Shane never wrote more than a few short lines to one another, and yet each email was filled with insight into their person. She thought of the email from Shane that she had read just this morning.

I bought a fake leather wallet from a man on a street corner a few months ago, just down from my hotel. I knew the quality was not great, but I simply couldn't resist the man who still smiled so broadly with so few teeth. The wallet falls apart every few weeks and every time I'm in Athens, I take it to him. He grins, repairs it in a few hours, and charges me nothing. I don't know why I haven't bought a new wallet, but I've found myself strangely attached to this one, and the old man who repairs it. I asked him if I could sketch him today while he made the repairs. I've never shown anyone one of my sketches before, but I am sending this one to you.

The sketch was amazing, perfectly capturing the wallet man's smile, with his missing teeth, and Shane's obvious affection for him.

"We email daily," Jory said now. "Just snippets really. But reading them has become the highlight of my day," she admitted.

Cressida and Mago gave her wide smiles. "Will he be back soon?" Cressida asked.

"He's been delayed, but not for too much longer, he said. Hopefully I'll be able to introduce you both soon. But enough about me! Back to the taverna."

Jory trusted them implicitly, but she didn't trust herself enough to hide the fact that she was falling hard for Shane.

Eleven

They were nearing summer solstice and the longest day of the year. The sun was already up though it was only 6:30 a.m. when Cressida walked down into her garden in her slippers. Citrus grew rampant over the island so she was never short, but in her garden there was but one orange tree. She pulled a lone orange from among the leaves and was walking back up to her kitchen, when she was stopped by the sight of a very serene Mago leaning over her balcony, eyes closed, letting the morning sun bathe her face. Cressida looked at her for a long moment before quietly moving on, but Mago's voice stopped her.

"Benign," she said, her voice calm.

Cressida could hear the current of relief, the dare to hope, running through it.

"The cyst is benign."

"Oh Mago," she whispered, tears pooling in her eyes as she felt relief wash over her.

"What are you baking?" Mago asked.

"Revani," Cressida answered. "For the town meeting tonight."

Mago took a deep breath and nodded down at her. "You go and bake some hope into that one."

Cressida's smile widened.

"There's no time like the present to remember to live."

Cressida made the syrup first, bringing to boil the water, sugar and the peel from her freshly picked orange, until the sugar dissolved, then taking it from the heat to thicken and cool while she started the cake.

She mixed the sugar and eggs in a bowl until fluffy and light, before stirring the dry ingredients and vanilla together in a separate bowl. She poured the sugar and eggs into the dry mix and blended briefly with her high-speed mixer, before adding her homemade yogurt and the rest of the orange peel, and mixing by hand, thinking of hope, and joy, and a little bit of magic.

Magic was indeed happening, as all things were coming together for the little taverna to finally open. Mago sat in her favorite sunroom, sipping her coffee, surrounded by the lengths of fabric Cressida had given her. She knew not to overthink or try to plan things when she was sewing, whether it be a dress, a quilt, a scarf or a tablecloth, though to be fair, this was her first attempt at the latter. But like all the sewing she'd done her whole life, she knew it was best to wait for the fabric to talk to her before she made any cuts.

When Cressida had put the fabrics before her and asked for help, she had wanted to say no when she still thought she was dying. But even then, she could not. Even if she was dying, she would pull all of her strength together to make the taverna a success. But the material around her was silent. The colors were not playing with one another, not dancing.

"Please," she whispered, to herself or to the fabrics, she did not know. A bit of both, most likely. "Please let me see you."

For a long while, longer than comfortable, nothing happened. And then suddenly, even with her eyes closed, she could hear the change, a subtle switch in the energy of the room. The colors were dancing, but in different ways than Mago had imagined. In the full light of the sun the little motes of color and promise were singing and dancing together like a song. Mago nearly cried with relief and delight as she began to measure, cut and sew the way the colors told her to, to make a happy garden at the taverna.

A few kilometers down the road, Arie stood at the bottling line as the special label of the taverna went to print and one was bottled. He had three cases, one each of his rosé, blended white, and red, being labeled specially for Cressida's opening night.

"Is this what you want, Arie?"

His staff presented him with the specialized bottle. Everything was the same as every other bottle but for the photograph on the label. He looked at it now and felt the same pull he had when he took the shot. Arie was not a gifted photographer. In truth, he had never taken a proper photograph in his life. The one on the label was a complete accident that happened with his iPhone about a month ago. He was with Mago for dinner, and they went for a long, late night stroll, as Mago often did. He enjoyed these walks. They never said anything, but he often saw her glancing at the full moon irritably.

But this night, the night of the photograph, the moon had been quiet and still Mago had not been able to sleep. They went for a walk, and on the way back, Mago stopped as they neared Cressida's.

"Shh," Mago said, straining her ears.

He heard it then. The low echo of grief. It surrounded them both.

"My dear girl," Mago whispered. "In your secret garden of grief, alone. It will all change soon. I can feel it. I can see the colors swirling."

Arie never asked Mago what she meant when she whispered such strange things, just like he never asked what Cressida *did* bake into her bread every time something strange happened after he ate it. They were Potamia women, and they were strange and wonderful. But what he did see was the woman he loved walk down a small set of stairs into a garden that no one knew was there until they arrived. A secret garden, a special garden that grew the most wonderful olives and herbs on the whole island, and that Cressida, with her unique touch, had turned into something even more wonderful than the garden itself. The garden was her. And she it.

For one moment that night, when Cressida was crying an ocean of tears for Leonidas and the full moon was keeping Mago safe from the man in it, Arie took a sneaky photo of Mago entering the secret garden in the moonlight.

He had never shown anyone that photo. It was too personal. Too special. It meant something but he did not know what. Until the day before, when he woke up and for some strange reason, that photo was saved as the backdrop of his phone. He had not set it, and no matter how much he tried, he could not unset it. That was when he started printing the labels for the wines that would be sold in the taverna, though he hadn't yet been told it would. Still, he knew.

He looked at the bottle. The wording on the label was perfect. "Taverna Mysticos Kypos." He nodded to Michele. "I will take one to Cressida to be sure she is happy and then yes, we go to print. Thank you."

~

Cressida had loaned Jory a dress for the town meeting that evening. It was a simple cut and fell just below the knee, in a jade green that matched Jory's eyes perfectly.

"Jory!" Cressida exclaimed as she came through the door. "You look sensational. I must insist you keep that dress—it is as if it was made for you!"

"Thank you!" Jory enthused. She was growing quite fond of the dress and was already thinking of someone she'd love to wear it for. "I have to be honest, I am having trouble picturing you wearing it." Jory was taller and had a willowy figure that suited the dress, where Cressida had the perfect hourglass figure that suited her style.

Cressida laughed. "That is because I did not. Mago left it for me once and though it did not suit me, when Mago gives you something you hold onto it, for it will find the right moment eventually."

"I should have known." Jory rolled her eyes fondly. She looked down. "You're sure I'm not too dressed up? I mean, it's just a town meeting."

"Mayor Andreas takes our town meetings very seriously and insists people come in their Sunday best. It is in a church after all, he always says. Look, I am in my Sunday best too," Cressida said, stepping out the front door into the porch light.

Hers was a red and white cotton dress with short puffed sleeves and a tie at the waist, the skirt swinging playfully around her legs to just past her knees. Jory loved Cressida's 1950s style, as though she'd walked right out of an old movie and into this world. Even her hair was styled from the era, twisted at the sides to meet in a low, knotted ponytail at the nape of her neck.

"Are you girls ready?" they heard Mago call from the top of the steps. "Don't make us come down, we are old!"

"You will outlive us all, I am sure, Mago," Jory called up, winking at Cressida. "Mago sounds so happy now, doesn't she? And she said 'we.' That must mean she's with Arie."

"I know, I love having her back. I was so frightened for a while. But now it does feel true. Mago *will* outlast all of us."

They laughed happily as they went up the stairs to find Mago in a fine emerald-green dress with matching flats and a nice little cream jacket, her arm linked through Arie's in his button-down shirt. He was not wearing a jacket or tie, but with his nice pants and shoes, he was certainly looking his finest. Cressida had not been joking about suitable attire for the town meeting.

They walked together to the old church where at least forty people were already seated in the old wooden benches, all in their finest. Arie had taken the Revani cake from Cressida and carried it to the church, but she took it back now.

"Are you sure you want to start the meeting by silencing it before it even starts?" Mago asked. "They haven't eaten your cake since—"

"I know, I know—Leo's funeral," she said. "But yes, I'm sure. I like causing havoc in the meetings and I'm not speaking until the end, so everyone will be waiting expectantly, staring at my cake the whole time," she added with a giggle.

"Diabolical," Jory said.

Cressida grinned and walked slowly with her cake dish to the table in the corner where refreshments were laid out for after the meeting. As expected, by the time she reached it, the chatter had ceased and the only sound she heard was her own heels clicking on the wooden floor. She finally placed the cake plate down and removed the wrap, knowing the smell would waft out through the room.

She could hear the various reactions behind her now—the breathing in, some surprised or shocked gasps, some mouth-watered moans.

"It's almost sinful how good it smells," she heard one whisper.

"Do you think we can eat it?" said another.

"Can? It's *should* we. Remember the last time…"

And there was silence again as Cressida turned around and slowly walked back to Jory, Mago and Arie.

Just then, at exactly seven o'clock, Mayor Andreas walked briskly through the door, looking at his pocket watch, though everyone knew it had stopped working years ago. Still, he was never late, nor was he ever early. Just right on time.

He was a rather short man with a round protruding belly that looked like a basketball tucked under his fine shirt. He wore a lightweight jacket, and he touched his handkerchief to his forehead as he reached the podium.

"Good evening, folks," he began. "We have a few things to cover tonight so let's..." He paused, his eyebrows coming together in confusion as he looked around, sniffing the air with his eyes closed. Finally he took a deep breath, his eyebrows relaxing, his eyes opening. "What is that?"

In one movement, the entire congregation nodded silently to the table in the corner.

"Ah," he said, licking his lips and swallowing. "Perhaps we could put the lid back on until the end of the meeting, Cressida?" he asked, looking her way.

She shrugged innocently. "It was only plastic wrap and I threw it away."

The townsfolk all sighed, resigned to their longing. Jory elbowed Cressida. *See,* she said with her eyes, *they have been waiting for you. They will support you.*

"Oh well," the mayor sighed, taking one more glance at the table. "Let's make it a hasty one, then. Who is first?"

"I am!" a voice called from the front row.

"Oh Jory, you have come to a good one! Phaedra and Matthaeus are on!" Mago said with excitement, leaning forward. "I should have brought popcorn."

Cressida had not been to a town meeting for a long time, and she was excited too. Phaedra and Matthaeus had been her and Nefeli's favorites even when they were younger. She found herself looking around discreetly to the seats where Nefeli and Nico usually sat. Nico was there, sitting alone, his face drawn.

Cressida's brow furrowed as she turned back around. Something was wrong with Nefeli, she could feel it. At times like this, she missed their friendship with intense longing. And then she remembered why she and Nefeli no longer spoke and that intense longing usually turned into anger. But tonight, the anger was not there. She heard a chuckle beside her and turned her focus back to the meeting.

"Where are they now?" Cressida asked Jory.

"Phaedra has just asked the mayor to fine Matthaeus three hundred euros for her lost olives," Jory whispered excitedly. "This is better than television."

"I am not paying this crazy woman one euro!" Matthaeus cried, standing in his chair. "That olive tree grows just on the border of our fence and into *my* yard! What my goats eat on my side of the fence are my olives!"

"The tree is on my land! It is my tree and therefore every single olive on it is mine! If your goats want to eat my olives, you need to compensate me for them!" Phaedra yelled, more loudly.

"In that case, I plead with you, Mayor Andreas, to seek the council do an investigation as to who the tree belongs to and we can go from there," Matthaeus countered.

Mayor Andreas rolled his eyes. "The council, of course."

"Everyone, including Phaedra and Matthaeus," Mago said to Jory, "knows there is no council from Chora Naxos that will come up for such a silly issue. Still, every few months they are back at the pulpit, arguing the same thing."

"Sometimes they argue about other things," Arie said, "other than his goats eating her olives."

"True." Mago nodded. "But these are usually my favorite. It's a good thing Cressida baked. They wouldn't ever throw *that*."

"I will get the council right on that, thank you, Phaedra," Mayor Andreas said. Phaedra gave him a spiteful look but left the podium. "Next please?"

Georgios stood next, in his three-piece suit, nodding his head gently and making his way to the front with his cane in one hand and a young man on his other side, dressed identically. Both left their Panama hats on their seats.

"How old *is* Georgios now, Mago?" Cressida leaned over, asking in a whisper.

"No clue." She shrugged. "Got to be nearing a hundred though."

"Who's that boy with him?" Jory asked.

"Ahem," Georgios's soft voice called from the front. "I would like to tell you that my quince is ready for the season. And this is my grandson, Raki, who has just finished university in Athens and has come back here to work the land with me. You will probably remember him. Town, Raki. Raki, town."

Raki waved and then helped his grandfather back down to their seats, where they sat at the same time, placing their hats on their laps.

"I'll have to call Georgios," Cressida said to Jory. "His quince will be perfect for the opening."

"Anyone else, before we finish the meeting and can move to the lovely refreshments table?" Mayor Andreas asked, looking longingly at Cressida's cake.

Mago, Arie and Jory all nodded toward the front, then looked at Cressida, and finally, when she hadn't moved, Mago and Jory lifted her up between them and said, "Yes!"

They pushed her forward until she stopped, turning to Jory desperately. "Come with me?"

Jory, surprised and nervous, followed Cressida to the podium, standing just behind her. When she didn't speak for a moment, Jory gently touched her shoulder. The townsfolk were all leaning forward expectantly and, Jory could tell, hopefully. They'd been waiting for this moment for years. Jory smiled at the knowledge and felt filled with a sense of being just where she was meant to be in that moment. Cressida turned to her, questioning at first, and then smiling. She felt it too. She turned back to the crowd.

"I have brought a Revani," she said simply. "And I am opening my taverna. Invitations will be in your letterboxes shortly. I hope you will come. Enjoy the cake."

The room was silent. And suddenly every single person stood and walked as fast as they could toward the Revani cake. Only Mago and Arie were still at their seats, smiling broadly at Cressida.

Jory remained beside Cressida on the podium. She pulled Cressida in for a hug. "Oh yeah. This is going to be a raving success."

Twelve

I love what Mago did with the tablecloths," said Jory. "I'd never have thought of doing that."

Mago had made fourteen tablecloths with the fabrics Cressida had chosen. The cloth that covered the tabletops were of a solid fabric, equal numbers of the yellow, blue, and printed. But on the material which framed the edges of the table and flowed over the sides she had sewn an intricate patchwork of all of the fabrics. When Mago brought them over, she seemed to know exactly which table each was meant for and arranged the tables as such.

"I know you only saw tablecloths on the plastic patio tables, but they made themselves for all. No, that one belongs over there, Jory," Mago called for the hundredth time that day, forcing her to pick up one of the heaviest tables and place it exactly where she said.

Jory sighed. "What does it matter? Why can't we just move the tablecloths instead?"

Mago narrowed her eyes at Jory. "Don't ask me, I don't know why. The tablecloths know where they belong. Ask them."

"I am *not* asking the tablecloths," Jory muttered under her breath, falling into a chair next to Cressida. She was tilted over her notebook, writing intently. Curious, Jory looked over her shoulder. She had written about thirty different dishes, crossing some out, then going back and circling them, and writing something else in its place. "Are you working on the menu?" Jory asked. "You seem to be having some difficulty. Can I help?"

Cressida grimaced and looked down at her book as if it were causing her pain. "I am very stuck trying to write a menu."

"I can see that," Jory said pointedly. "But I don't understand. You've been going through that book and writing notes, buying products, cooking with such confidence—I thought your menu was sorted for the open?"

"The menu for that evening, yes, I am nearly finished. But you asked the other day about what our dream was and what I could do now without Leo. The guesthouse was meant to be the main focus, with the taverna serving the best food on the island for our guests," Cressida explained. "I would get to know these guests so I could create a personalized menu each day—for the newlyweds in room four, the arguing couple in room one, the solo artist writing a novel in room two."

"She will have finished an entire novel the evening she was locked in the bathroom," Jory teased, making Cressida relax her shoulders. "Go on," she urged.

"I am a cook who can present to people what I want them to eat. I don't know how to create a menu for people to tell me what *they* want to eat," Cressida finished, throwing her pen down on the table and closing her book.

Jory nodded thoughtfully. "Perhaps you don't have to. What if...what if what makes your taverna stand out is that there is only a limited selection that you yourself choose?"

Cressida tilted her face to Jory, her expression intrigued. "Can I do that?"

"I don't see why not, but we can chat about it later tonight. For now, let's take one thing at a time. First, let's get these invitations together. I'm going to get them printed and out this afternoon—that gives us a week going forward to get everything ready for the soft opening night." Jory squeezed Cressida's hand and winked, as Mago came over, huffing.

"I managed to finish myself," she said, falling into the chair beside Jory.

"Did you have to talk to the tables in the end?" Jory asked.

Mago squinted at her with a harassed look, but Jory could see she was smiling underneath. "Girls, when you have been as strange a duck as I have for as long as I have, you will find you can talk to anything, both animate and inanimate, and people will simply shrug and walk along."

Cressida leaned in to Mago then, showing her the bottle Arie had sent that afternoon.

Her jaw dropped as she reached for her glasses. "Oh my. *Taverna Mysticos Kypos*," Mago whispered, lovingly touching the label. "The Taverna of the Secret Garden."

"The taverna is opening?" Selene asked with surprise when Jory dropped her an invitation later that afternoon.

"It's just a soft opening, so don't go telling everyone just yet," Jory said. "After Saturday, you can tell anyone you like."

"Look at me," Selene said, clicking her tongue. "Do I not look like the epitome of discretion?"

Jory shook her head. "Definitely not—you look like the queen of gossip. Which is exactly why you're invited. We need to get the word out once we get through the opening night."

"Thank you, what a lovely thing to say." She nodded her head regally, making Jory smile. "I will say nothing," Selene said. And then she handed Jory a handwritten card. "As you requested the other day—the address of my brother's recycling place. You'll find much of what you need very cheap."

"Thank you, Selene. We truly appreciate it," Jory said sincerely, heading out the door.

The address Selene had given her took Jory to the deepest recesses of the wharf, past the fish markets and into an industrial area with some office buildings and a few larger warehouses. Finally she found what seemed like a big recycle center. There didn't seem to be anyone around, so Jory walked through, calling out, "Hello?"

While she waited for Selene's elusive younger brother to show up, Jory looked more closely at the treasures surrounding her. It was a trove of mismatched things and throwaways. Jory took photos of some nice dishes, cutlery and long wooden boards that looked worn but on closer inspection only needed a sand and a paint. That was only the beginning. Next, she found a little plug-in deep-fryer which was what Cressida had been looking for, and best of all—a large blackboard for the menu, which was exactly what *she* had been looking for. When she finally found Selene's brother, Lucas, he put everything aside for her to pick up with Cressida's truck the following day.

"But this," Jory said, pointing to the blackboard, "I must take now. It's a surprise."

As she walked outside, a familiar sight made Jory's stomach lurch. Shane's bike was parked across the road. She would recognize it anywhere. Her heart was suddenly beating faster.

It had been over two weeks since Jory had last seen Shane, though it didn't feel so long because of their daily correspondence. Jory felt she knew nothing and yet everything about him. She wasn't completely sure what kind of business he was doing in Athens, but she knew that his favorite country was Mexico, that his twin sister was named Sarah, that he loved Coldplay, and that if someone needed help, he was an easy target.

And he knew that although The Smiths were *her* favorite band, she sometimes preferred Mariah Carey ballads when no one was listening. He even knew that she and her mother had watched *Dirty Dancing* so many times when she was younger that they knew the whole dance routine by heart even now.

But for the past two days there had been silence. So when Shane walked out of an office building near where his bike was parked, Jory was so surprised, she jumped behind her own bike. She watched for a moment while Shane closed the door behind him. Jory read the sign on the door—"Port of Naxos Office." She wondered what business he had there. Where had he been these past two days when he hadn't written? Why hadn't he told her he was back on Naxos?

"Jory, here you are!" Lucas said loudly, coming out of the recycle center with the large blackboard wrapped in paper. "You forgot this!"

At the sound of her name, Shane looked over in her direction and his face broke into a huge grin.

"I thought that was you!" he yelled across the road.

"Oh, hi!" she called. Jory looked down at the blackboard and back to her bike. She hadn't actually considered the logistics of getting it home.

Shane headed toward her, smiling radiantly. "What have you got here and how on earth are you going to carry it on your moped?" he asked.

"Oh, this is a gift for Cressida," she said. "Clearly an impulse purchase, I was not quite prepared for how to get home." Jory glanced at his handsome face, feeling longing and hurt that he hadn't contacted her. "I hadn't heard from you. I wondered if you were coming back."

"I just got back yesterday. I'm so glad I ran into you," he said, ducking his head with a smile. "I was just about to email you. I would love to have the pleasure of escorting you on a very special night out tomorrow if you're free?" he asked, tilting her chin up and brushing his hand across her cheek.

"Yes," Jory whispered, savoring the intimate touch. "I can be free tomorrow."

Shane kissed her briefly on the inside of her wrist and Jory felt his lips there even after they were gone. "Tomorrow," he said. "In the meantime, how *are* you going to transport that package? Can I bring it to you?"

"No," she replied, pulling the wrapped blackboard toward her protectively. "I must get this home now to Cressida. I can't wait to see the look on her face when I give it to her. I'll manage—it's not far."

Shane shook his head, smiling. "Fine, stubborn girl, but at least let me tie it to your bike with some bungees." He walked across the street to his bike, lifted up the seat and returned with a few bungee cords. It took him only a minute to secure the package safely to her bike.

"Thank you," Jory said gratefully.

Shane met her eyes and took her chin in his hand. He kissed her softly once. Then twice. "Five o'clock at the parking lot from before. Do you remember?"

"Yes, I remember," she said. "I'll be there."

She started her scooter and gave him a wave before pulling out, trying to ignore the fact that she already missed him. It was going to be a long twenty-four hours until five o'clock tomorrow.

~

After dinner, Jory told Cressida, "I have a surprise for you. Close your eyes and I'll go get it." She retreated to her bedroom and hovered in the doorway, holding the bulky package behind her back.

"Are your eyes closed?" she asked Cressida.

"No."

"Well, you better close them or you're not getting your present!"

Cressida sighed, closing her eyes. She hated surprises. Still, she was smiling when she said, "Fine, come in then."

"Ta-da!"

Cressida opened her eyes. Jory had brought in a large package nearly as tall as her.

"Open it," Jory encouraged.

Cressida unwrapped the paper to expose a blackboard. How on earth had she gotten it back to Potamia on that little bike? "What is it for?"

"Stop trying to create a menu you don't want to do. You can go to the market in the mornings, decide your menu for the day just like you've always done with me, then write it up on the board, and there you go, *menu del dia*. You can erase it easily to change the menu daily or even weekly, whatever you want. You could keep doing things this way or decide on a more permanent menu once you know what sells and what you love to cook. What do you think?"

"I don't need to come up with a menu for all the time?"

"I don't see any need to, at least not to start. Blackboard menus are all the rage these days, and keeping it small and simple is better. Food today is all about farm to table—what is fresh, local. Things you already do naturally that will greatly appeal to tourists. Yours would be more like garden to table. Do you like it?"

Cressida smiled. "Yes. I like it very much. Thank you, my friend. This is a good solution."

Jory grinned happily.

"So, what is on for tomorrow then? We have so much to do and it's all finally coming together!" Cressida said.

Jory glanced at her nervously. "We do have much to do. And I will be on hand all day. But…well, tomorrow night, you see…"

Cressida squealed. "Sharre's back! I should have known. You're glowing, and you have been bouncing in your seat all evening. So tomorrow night?"

"Yes!" Jory exclaimed. "And I'm so nervous! Will you help me get ready?"

"Of course I will. He must be really special to be causing such emotions in you. I can't wait to meet him."

"If things go well tomorrow, you will," Jory promised.

"Come then," Cressida said, refilling their glasses. "I think we both know exactly what dress you are going to wear."

~

The following morning, Jory managed to deliver twenty different invitations to the locals of Potamia alone. Mayor Andreas received his invitation with silent appreciation, checking his watch. Georgios was where Jory had first met him, in front of the church in the square, pointing out the intricacies of the architecture to Raki. They smiled at Jory as she presented them with their invitations. There were many others to follow, locals who had become part of her daily life in Potamia, but her last stop was the most important one, of that she was certain.

Jory rode to the end of town to Nefeli and Nico's station. She walked inside, finding Nefeli as always, looking at her phone, but also far away as well.

"Do you need petrol for your bike?" Nefeli asked without looking up.

"No. I...well, here." Jory slid the invitation across the counter.

Nefeli stared at the envelope. "She is opening then? Truly?"

"I heard you were friends once. I thought you'd appreciate an invitation."

"We were friends. The best, once upon a time. But you know how these things go. People grow apart," she said, shrugging.

Jory sighed, turning to leave, when she heard Nefeli whisper softly, almost as if she didn't want to be heard. "I think sometimes when you are hurting, it's the ones you know the best that you avoid. They can see you. Too clearly."

Jory looked at the blonde Greek beauty with her perfectly polished nails and lipstick and hair and saw for the first time the girl within. The phone in her hand was a distraction to keep anyone from truly seeing her. It suddenly became clear to Jory that Nefeli was hurting. She didn't know why, but she recalled the jealous way Nefeli had looked at her when Nico took her on the moped that first day, and the fight afterward that led to their passionate encounter.

And yet truly seeing Nefeli now, her cool exterior momentarily shattered, she saw a woman lonely, and hurting. A woman who hid behind her phone and her red lipstick to mask that pain. Why? Jory felt an innate desire to comfort Nefeli and reached out her hand.

But the guise was back, as Nefeli pulled herself together and glared at Jory. "See, it's good reading the horoscopes, gives one excellent insight," she said, rolling her eyes and pretending to read.

"Well, I hope we see you Saturday. I'm sure it would mean a lot to Cress. Have a nice day, Nefeli," Jory said, the door clicking behind her.

Thirteen

Nefeli watched Jory leave, the invitation tempting her. She picked it up, touching the sides, swallowing to try to keep the tears from coming. Finally, she took the envelope and locked the door to the shop, driving to the only place she wanted to be.

The famous Venetian Tower of Kokkos, built in the seventeenth century, had been Nefeli's favorite place as a girl. She loved the ruins, and fancied herself a princess in the tower, waiting to meet a prince. She had always felt a part of the place deep in her bones, in a way that was slightly different. Nefeli had always had those feelings, this knowledge of something bigger shifting, even if she didn't quite know what it was. She had started reading horoscopes at a young age not because she was trying to read the future, but because she was trying to figure out exactly how much what she felt made sense in the world. They helped guide her intuition.

She had also always loved the tower because of its local legend, as it was said to have played a part in the setting of a Romeo and Juliet–like love affair that involved members of the rival Kokkos and Barozzi families. Nefeli loved Shakespeare and drama and romance, but as she grew into a teenager, she dreamed less about a prince coming to rescue her and more about how she might rescue herself. The outside world was a big place and Nefeli wanted big things. She had the right foundation. She was beautiful for starters, the kind of beauty that had grown with her. She came from a wealthy family that had trained her properly for her place in society. She dreamed that one day she would leave the island and go to Hollywood to become famous, and once this was accomplished, she would come back to Naxos and restore the tower to become her own castle on the island. A true princess.

When Nefeli was eighteen years old, she awoke one morning with a pressing need to get to her place, the tower. She hopped on her bicycle without breakfast and pedaled as fast as she could, something pressing her to hurry, hurry. But when she arrived, nothing was out of the ordinary. Until she heard a voice behind her.

"Why do you come here every day?"

She turned, startled. The voice belonged to a boy so beautiful, her mouth went immediately dry. He was blond, like her. She thought she was the only person on Naxos with hair that shimmered gold in the sun, but he was like an Adonis, her perfect match, her male equal. As she looked at him, it was as if the sun itself was rising inside of her. She felt the rays drawing her to him.

"How do you know I come here every day?" she asked.

He pointed to a tiny shack at the end of the property. "That's where I live. My family and I help the owner of this place keep the grounds."

She scoffed, looking at the overgrown grass and ruins. "I'm sorry to say you are not doing a very good job."

But instead of being offended at her rudeness—a defense she was prone to use when she was feeling out of control and uncomfortable, as she was now—he laughed. "Apparently the rustic feel brings more tourists over the summer," he said, "so we try to keep it as overrun as possible without letting the elements truly ravage this place. But of course, that is just in our spare time. My father is a mechanic. I am a mechanic too."

Her heart sank. She was a Castellanos. Her family name meant something on the island—her father was running for mayor next year. A mechanic was not in the cards for a girl like her, and her parents would never allow it. Here she was, at her most magical spot in the world, having a magical moment with a boy about her own age, and he was completely off limits to her.

He seemed to read her thoughts and laughed at the crestfallen expression she wore. Who was he to laugh at her? She scowled at him and he laughed more.

"I know who you are. You are Nefeli Castellanos." He stepped forward, extending his hand. "I am Nico Remis."

She did not take his hand but allowed him a curt "Nice to meet you" before climbing back on her bike, suddenly feeling the need to leave.

"Shall I see you tomorrow, then?" he asked as she pedaled quickly away from him.

"No!" she called back behind her. And then softly, to herself, almost as if it were a promise, "I won't be coming back again."

It was a promise she broke nearly immediately and many times to follow. At first she told herself it was because she was not going to be kicked out of her favorite place in the world just because some boy was there. She would tell him to leave. And she did, every time she found him there waiting, which was every time that she went to the tower. She told him to leave, he didn't, and the next day she would arrive and it would be the same thing again. He never left and she always went back. She allowed this because she realized very quickly that whether he was a mechanic or not, he was wonderful. He called her his Juliet, as he knew her love of Shakespeare. He was funny and charming and he made her blood boil in every way, whether they were arguing about the history of the tower, or laughing at some bit of village gossip, or debating the best movies to watch.

"We could go to one, you know. A movie. Together," he said one day. "Nefeli, I lov—"

Nefeli felt her face grow hot. "Hush! Don't ever say *that*."

"But—"

"No," she said firmly. She felt shame but shame for what she was going to say. "You and I together will not be possible," she whispered.

"Why, because your parents won't think I'm good enough?" he asked, his voice rising slightly for the first time since she had known him.

"No," she lied, trying to control the longing inside her. *Say something cruel, Nefeli. Say something so that he will leave you alone and not tempt you. You deserve better, greater.* She took a breath. "Because I don't want you."

He strode toward her then, grabbing her shoulders. "I am the only thing you truly want," he whispered, kissing her then, fiercely, passionately. So great was their passion at that moment that they created little sparks, and no one in the village could understand why their fireplaces were lighting in the middle of a hot summer when they certainly hadn't tried to start one.

Their great hidden and secret passion smoldered all summer, the hottest Naxos had ever known. In fact, it smoldered so persistently that Nefeli was hardly surprised when in late August, it burst into flame and they were burned.

In early September, her period was late.

Everything happened very quickly after that. Nefeli's parents, after raging, crying and screaming that she was a good-for-nothing whore, put on an elaborate wedding with false smiles and toasts, complimenting the beautiful young match.

Her father won the position of mayor for the next four years, and her family set up the most popular mechanic shop on the island for Nico, renting bikes and motorcycles, all funded by her father.

Nobody on the island knew yet that Nefeli was pregnant when suddenly, she was not. The cramping started early in the day, with the bleeding following shortly thereafter. It was Nico who called in the doctor, who told them Nefeli had lost the child. Her parents did not visit.

There was but one person who held her head as Nefeli wept at the injustice of it all, losing her dream, her choice to marry and her unborn child all in one fell swoop. That person was her best friend, Cressida.

Nefeli sat at the Tower of Kokkos now, reading and re-reading the invitation in her hand to Cressida's opening of the *Taverna Mysticos Kypos*. She wondered how long it had taken Cressida to decide whether she was going to invite her. She had not lied to

Jory when she said that Cressida had been her best friend, but she did know why they had grown apart. After the miscarriage, Nefeli began the long, slow process of severing their friendship. And then when Leo died, Nefeli did not take the same loving approach Cressida had when she was so lost. She abandoned her friend because she could not bear to look at her, to hear her say over and over, "But I loved him."

Because that day Nico had tried to say "I love you" she stopped him. "Never say *that*," she'd said.

And he never had. She'd been lying when she said she didn't want to hear it. To him and to herself. All these years together now and she'd been waiting. After they made love the first time, after the forced wedding, after their miscarriage. Never once. Of course, she could never say it first. But the sad truth was, Nefeli loved Nico. She loved him with every ounce of her being. The loss of her baby, of her future, had left her cold and guarded, jealous and angry. She touched her flat belly and felt the longing there again. No matter their passion, they had never produced another child.

Nefeli could no longer wait and pretend that her husband loved her. She could not live like this, not anymore. And when she got the invitation from Cressida, she realized that if Cressida, after all her grief, could start anew, so too could she.

It was late when she arrived back home on foot. Nico was in the kitchen, eating what looked like a stew. His mother must have brought it by, knowing Nefeli rarely cooked for them anymore, though she was an exemplary cook. He looked up at her, the same look he always gave her these days. Wary and tired. She made him wary and tired. Unless she made him passionate, which these days was only when she was angry. For she too was wary and tired. Tired of feeling unloved. Tired of feeling alone.

"I'm going to bed," she said, sighing, walking past him, not seeing the disappointment in his eyes.

"You haven't eaten dinner," he said.

"I'm not hungry."

"You're never hungry."

She ignored him and closed her bedroom door, the one down the hall from the master suite. It had been three years since she'd slept there. She took a long bath, and when she began to cry so loud she was sobbing, she ducked her head under the water so Nico would never hear her heart breaking into a thousand pieces for not being next to him.

It was late in the night when Nico woke from his sleep, hearing Nefeli call for him. She never called for him anymore. She sounded distraught, like she was crying, so he went quickly to her room without bothering to put on a robe. But when he opened the door, she was sound asleep.

"Nefeli?" he whispered. But she was snoring lightly.

He turned to leave when he heard her call him again.

"Nico, don't leave me."

His breath caught with something he didn't want to think was hope as he returned to her, crawling into bed beside her. Still, she did not respond. She was asleep. Was he imagining things, hoping for the things he would never hear?

But at least while she was asleep, he could admire her beauty. She was so much prettier without makeup, he thought, looking down at her sleeping face. When she exhaled, her lip puffed out, like a fish. He used to call her his little piranha, as they fell into long, lazy naps when they were eighteen and used to make love.

"Piranha! But that is a terrible fish!"

"No, it is simply a very dangerous fish. Dangerous and beautiful. Like you for me. Because of how much I—"

"Shh," she said, putting her finger on his lips. "Don't say it. Don't ever say *that*."

And the saddest part about the story of Nico and Nefeli is that theirs was a love so great it made fires start and they had never once told one another the truth.

Nico placed his finger over her puffing mouth, touching her lip lightly, covering it, as she had then. "Nefeli," he whispered.

Nefeli woke then, her eyes wide. She took a deep breath and waited, but he could not say it, not now, not after all these years. Instead he pulled her in with a deep, longing kiss, taking off her nightgown and making love to his wife, his whole body saying the only thing he was never allowed to say out loud.

She was gone when he woke in her bed. The closet was empty of her clothes. The toiletries and lipsticks were gone from the bathroom. Her clothes had been packed, it looked like for weeks. There was no note. No scent of her still lingering. It was as if she had all been a dream he never truly had. And for the first time in his adult life, Nico sobbed, at the empty room without his golden match beside him.

~

"You look fantastic," Cressida said. "It was a great idea to wear the green dress I gave you. Shane will go mad." Jory flushed at the sound of his name which made Cressida smile. "I wonder how long you'll actually be *in* the dress."

"Cress!" Jory admonished, fanning herself. "Okay, I'm ready. I'm ready. I am leaving now. Like, right this second," she said, not moving from the mirror in her room.

Cressida handed her lipstick, which she put on with shaking hands. "You know what? I should cancel. I can meet Shane after the opening. We're too busy, Cress. I need to be here."

"Marjory St. James! As your friend I will lovingly say that I understand your fear. But Mago would tell you to quit being such a shitty chicken!" Cressida cried, pointing her finger threateningly.

Jory began to laugh. "Did you," she said, barely able to get out the words, "did you mean a 'chickenshit'?"

"Why would you be a chickenshit? Wouldn't shitty chicken make more sense?" Cressida asked in earnest. Jory had to sit, she was laughing so hard.

"You're completely right, it would make more sense that way. I actually have no idea where the word came from or what it means," Jory finished, wiping the tears from her eyes. "Oh gosh, that was good. I needed that," she sighed. "Are you truly sure you're okay without me?"

"Jory, we are ready, nearly ready at least, and the only thing left to do is cooking the food, which you are not allowed to be a part of anyway," Cressida reminded her. "The cutlery, glasses and plates are polished, the restaurant is set, the card machine ready. Jory, you are officially free to go. So please, get out."

Shane met her at the parking lot, looking as gorgeous as ever. He was pacing anxiously as Jory pulled up on her moped. She realized he was as nervous as she was, and suddenly she felt much better. He beamed when he saw her, and by the way his eyes raked over her body, she was feeling very happy she'd worn the dress.

"Hi," he said, coming over to her, his hands grasping her arms and rubbing them up and down as if to keep her warm. "Wow, you look beautiful."

"Thank you, so do you," she said, tilting her face up to his. "Where are we going?"

"Somewhere very special to me. Are you averse to boat travel at all?"

"I love being on the water."

"Of course, you're from Maryland. This is *Persephone II*," he said, pointing to a small boat on the dock.

Jory knew enough from living in Annapolis, one of the sailing capitals of the world, that this was a dinghy, or a small boat used to transport one to and from a larger yacht.

"If that is *Persephone II*, where is the *Persephone*?"

He shrugged, his hands in his pockets as if embarrassed. "That's what I'd like to show you, if you don't mind coming along."

Shane helped her onto the boat then secured her in the seat beside him.

"Warm enough? It's a short but chilly ride over this time of day."

Jory nodded. She felt warmed by him, and it took only ten minutes at full speed into the bay until they ended up docking beside a yacht. Shane turned off the engine and pulled the tender to the larger boat, tying it to the side. He climbed a small ladder before he turned back to Jory, his hand out.

"Come aboard, my lady."

Jory looked around in awe at the beautiful wooden yacht. It was dwarfed by the other large superyachts moored nearby, and yet none surpassed the simple elegance of the design.

"It's beautiful," Jory breathed.

Shane beamed. "It's a traditional wooden boat from Turkey, called a gulet. I was backpacking through Europe during college when I fell in love with these ships. Have you been to Turkey?"

"Only to Istanbul," she murmured, walking forward to look around further. Her throat was dry, a familiar uneasiness settling in. "That must have been some college fund."

He shrugged nonchalantly but averted his gaze, taking her hand. "I worked on this boat for a full summer actually, one of the most amazing summers of my life with Ilhan, our captain, and his wife and daughter and a few others. I was a solo backpacker and the youngest on the boat. Ilhan's wife, Kubre, was the cook, and an excellent one at that. They did a cooking show that year with Ilhan and Kubre on the *Persephone*, and their business flourished so much over the next six years that they decided to retire early." Shane grinned. "Imagine my surprise when six years after my young summer, Ilhan emailed me to offer to sell me his boat, as he promised he would if he ever sold it. I have such a sense of home here." He put his hands in his pockets again and bowed his head. "I could show you some of my sketches from that summer?"

The uneasiness lifted as Jory felt exactly what he must have felt then, and she nodded enthusiastically. She smiled and squeezed his hand. "Will you show me around first?"

The gulet was extraordinarily beautiful and yet simple. On the lower deck, white leather seats came together like a bed for sunbathing or reading. Behind that was a set of stairs which led to three bedrooms, all beautifully decorated, with a bathroom and one en suite room, which Shane said was his. At the helm of the ship was an impressive kitchen, a large table with bench seating, and a wine shelf filled with fine wines.

Someone had obviously been there to set up before they arrived. On the table was an ice bucket chilling a bottle of French champagne, and a platter of pita and mezze. Shane poured them each a glass of champagne and they sat at the back, staring at the sky, not speaking for a long while.

"Are you going to show me your sketches now?" Jory asked, breaking the silence, which was making her more and more nervous. And more and more excited at the same time. Her voice, she realized, came out in a squeak.

His face lit up and he went to go retrieve his sketchbook. Jory looked around, her heart racing. She'd never been on a yacht like this. She couldn't shake the feeling that she was betraying herself by being out here. She knew that her strong disdain for people with money and wealth came from her own uncomfortable relationship with her father and his family. Being around money made her anxious. It made her feel mistrust. It scared her, and she knew it could hurt her if she let it.

Jory poured herself a hefty glass of the French champagne and looked at the label. Laurent-Perrier Cuvée Rosé, one she knew was pricey. She downed one glass and poured herself another.

Shane returned to sit beside her and poured himself another champagne. "I'm really nervous, you know," he said. "I've never shown anyone my sketches before. You should have seen me in my hotel room in Athens after I sent you the first one. I couldn't sleep until I heard back from you."

Jory smiled, immediately relaxing into her seat, leaning back into Shane's arms as he opened the sketchbook.

As he went through each page, he told a story—of Ilhan fishing off the side of the boat for the night's dinner. One of Kubre, her short curling hair and her lopsided smile as she fried up the little fish from the Mediterranean in her fry pan. Jory laughed out loud at the one of their thirteen-year-old daughter, Mil, lying on her stomach, longingly looking at the boys on the other boats as they passed. There was the wallet man in Athens.

"Georgios!" Jory exclaimed excitedly as she turned the next page.

"You know him?" Shane asked. "He fascinated me!"

"Georgios is the oldest man in Potamia. And no matter the day or time, he always wears that suit and Panama hat and carries a cane. His grandson, Raki, just came back to the island, and he is being trained to be the new Georgios."

Shane laughed. "I had no idea you were in Potamia. I love that village, it's my favorite place in all of Naxos."

"Mine too!" she exclaimed. And just as she was about to talk more about Cressida and the village, she turned the page to see a beautiful sketch of *herself*. It was from the night at the restaurant Rigani, when they'd sat at separate tables outside. She let out a breath that was a little like a laugh.

"You weren't supposed to see that one!" Shane said. "I'm so embarrassed. But…don't you find it a good likeness? Is that why you're almost laughing but not really?"

She lifted her head to look at him. His expression was so concerned, she leaned over and kissed him gently. "No," she said. "I'm almost laughing because I *knew* you were staring at me that night but I never caught you!"

He laughed with relief. "How did you know I was looking at you?"

"Because," she whispered, "I could feel you. I can always feel you."

She barely finished the sentence before Shane's lips covered hers, his hand holding the back of her head and pulling her closer. Jory was so ravenous for him, she pressed her whole body against his as he lay back into the couch and their kiss deepened and took them toward the point of no return.

"Will you stay here with me tonight?" Shane asked, his voice husky, his beard rough against her throat.

As her heart began to race, she felt his match hers, pressed against her chest. "Yes," she whispered, and their mouths met once more, their touch so powerful that shooting stars seemed to appear overhead like fireworks over the yacht.

"This looks amazing, darling," Leo said, pulling Cressida toward him and kissing her forehead. "Everything we always dreamed it would be."

"Do you think?" she asked, wrapping her arms around his waist. "I keep feeling like I'm missing something, but I don't know what. I have the food, I have the wine, I have help… and yet it's not quite right. Why is that?"

"Because I am not here. I am dead. But you are not. Wake up, Cress. Wake up. Wake up."

"Cressida, wake up! Wake up!"

She jumped and looked at the clock. 5 a.m. Nefeli? What was her voice doing in the best dream?

"Open the door. Please!"

It was indeed Nefeli. Cressida wondered what she was doing at her home after all these years. When she finally opened the door, she saw that Nefeli's beautiful face was swollen from tears, she was still in her nightgown, and she looked desperate. Nefeli never, ever looked desperate.

"Nefeli, what are you doing here at this hour?"

"You are doing what you were always meant to do—opening this taverna. I know I failed you. I…I didn't know how…"

Cressida's heart lurched for this woman she knew so well, still, after all these years.

"Come in, Nefeli, come inside," she said, and Nefeli rolled her suitcase in behind her.

They sat at Cressida's kitchen table. It was still dark outside, but the smell of lemons let them know the sun was on its way up to chase the darkness of night away. Hope came with the sun. Hope was close.

They sat for long moments in silence before Nefeli spoke again.

"Please let me help you see your dream through. Please allow me back into your life, allow me to make up for the past years and be your friend again. I have missed you. More than you could ever know. I just didn't know how to ask to come back into your life until now." Nefeli held up the invitation Jory had given her. "I have read and re-read this invitation a hundred times and I knew that this was my last chance to find my way back to my best friend. The person who held my hand through grief, the person that may perhaps again. But I will not take your kindness this time without giving back. Let me help you."

Cressida was touched to her soul. She realized how much she missed Nefeli as well, but she did not know what she could offer outside of a room to stay.

"I am happy to have you stay in the guesthouse and shall make a room up for you now. But Nefeli, what of Nico? What of your husband?"

Nefeli stood for all of a few moments, before one tear spilled down her cheek. "I have left Nico. I have nowhere else to go."

⌒

"Wake up, beautiful."

Jory opened her eyes to a very naked Shane next to her. Before she could remind him that she had ordered no wake up call, his mouth was on hers, his perfect body covering hers yet again, warm from the morning sun beaming in through the cabin's windows.

When he rolled off her a good time later, they were both gasping for breath and laughing. Shane recovered his breath and pulled Jory toward him.

"What do you have going on today?"

Reality set in.

"What day is it?" she asked in a panic, her hair in a wild tumble of frizz.

"Thursday. Why? Is everything okay?"

That's what she had been afraid of. Suddenly it was Thursday and they only had two days to open. She had to get back. She had to get back *now*.

"Oh my god, I can't believe it's been two days. Shane, I have to go. I've promised to help Cressida and it's very important to her. I had no intention of being away two days. Not that it hasn't been the most amazing two days, of course."

Shane kissed her. "No explanations needed. If it's important to you, it's important to me."

In less than an hour, Jory was back on the dock. Shane pulled her in for a deep, aching kiss before he finally let her go. She hopped onto her moped and as she pulled out of the marina, she heard Shane call behind her.

"Jory!"

She turned.

"Those were the best nights of my life," he called.

"Really?" she yelled back, glowing.

"Really."

"Mine too."

~

When Jory hadn't returned the next day, Cressida figured a brunch would be in order when she finally did return. Jory had told her about the sunny late mornings in Los Angeles brunching with her best friends that almost always turned into hours of laughing and talking and rehashing their adventures from the evening before. Cressida pulled out an old waffle-maker she had in storage and was up early finding waffle recipes for her friend.

As she mixed the dry ingredients and whisked the egg whites separately from the yolks in order to make them more fluffy, Cressida realized that despite having an occasional woman friend—first her mother, then Nefeli, Mago and now Jory—she was only just beginning to understand the depth of those friendships, the true power among women. Once, long ago, the women of Potamia had come together and something magical had begun to happen. It was happening again now, Cressida believed.

She couldn't wait for Jory to come home so she could tell her everything.

When Jory arrived home that morning, a pot of coffee and homemade waffles with lemon curd, blueberries and cream were waiting. Her eyes lit up as she looked at the spread, breathing in the mouthwatering smell of freshly cooked waffles.

"It's official," said Jory. "I *have* died and gone to heaven. I'd been wondering the past couple of days," she added with a dreamy sigh.

"Good thing you were wearing such a great dress," Cressida teased.

Jory laughed and sat across from Cressida. "This is amazing, thank you."

"The occasion called for it," she replied, then leaned forward. "Tell me *everything*."

"Oh my god," Jory sighed, head in hands. "It was beyond wonderful."

Cressida's whole face lit up. "Look at you—you are glowing!"

Jory blushed. "I promise I'll tell you *most* of the details, but first I have to apologize. I'm so sorry I went missing for two days just before the opening. I feel like a terrible friend."

"Don't be silly," Cressida scoffed. "You are not a terrible friend but I must say, you did miss a dinner upon dinners."

In true Los Angeles brunch fashion, Cressida gave Jory a full account of the night before.

"So, Mago and Arie arrived shortly after you left," Cressida began, painting the night for Jory in detail.

Arie wore a dark blue shirt and light pants, a jacket over his shoulder. Mago was in a white dress with blue trim. Cressida had been honored to see them so dressed up for the occasion. The three of them would taste Arie's wines with some of her dishes to make final sommelier decisions for opening night.

She smiled widely as she invited them inside, taking Arie's jacket. As he took the wines into the kitchen to keep them chilled, Cressida lightly touched Mago's elbow, whispering in her ear, "I love how you and Arie match tonight. You look so lovely."

Mago seemed nervous, unsettled.

"It was not planned," Mago said, "but as soon as he arrived at my door, I knew tonight was the night." And without another word, she took herself out to the garden, murmuring.

"I knew something was going on," Cressida said to Jory, her tone rising with excitement. "But I had no idea what. Mago never stopped talking, and while she is always the life of the party, I am telling you, Jory, she was so nervous she kept forgetting to breathe. She even started fanning herself and still never stopped talking."

"What did Arie do?" Jory asked, the excitement catching.

"He just sat there, looking amused," Cressida said. "We finally finished our meals, so I went to clean up when Mago says to me, 'No, Cressida, I would like you to be here, please.'"

Mago stood and walked to Arie, taking his hand in hers.

"Arie, my Arie. I know what it is like to lose a spouse. When Kristopher died, I was devastated. I did not know what to make of my life. And then when I thought I was dying, I made a promise to myself that I would never marry again. I would choose to be alone. But I was wrong. I was frightened. I thought I was being brave by letting you go. But being brave isn't about not being frightened. Being brave means being terrified and jumping in anyway. I want to jump in with you. I want to belong to you, as you belong to me in my heart, and will for the rest of my days. I would be so honored, Arie, if you would be my husband."

Cressida's jaw dropped, her eyes widened, and she looked at Arie, expecting to see the same shock and surprise. But his face only creased with smiling joy and rightness, as if somehow he knew this would always be.

He stood to face Mago, and took her other hand, which was shaking, and simply said, "Yes."

"What?!" Jory exclaimed as Cressida finished the story. "But Mago said she'd never marry again. *She* asked *him*?"

"Well, it looks like she too has changed her mind about how to live her life," Cressida said. "But my friend, that is not the only big news. Nefeli is here," she said, nodding toward the room in the upstairs corner.

"Nefeli is here? Why?" Jory recalled what Nefeli had said about her and Cressida when she delivered her invitation. *But you know how these things go. People grow apart.*

"She's left Nico," Cressida explained. "She has nowhere else to go, and she wants to help open the taverna with us."

Jory sipped her coffee. "I think I need caffeine before I can process all of this."

Cressida nodded. "Yes, it was a big day yesterday for many. Mago and Arie, Nefeli and Nico, you, me. It seems the women of Potamia are resurrecting their powers."

"Am I a woman of Potamia?" Jory asked.

"My dear friend, I believe Potamia brought you here because you already were one of us, but we needed someone to reconnect us. So in that way, you will always be a woman of Potamia. And there is something very special happening right now, to us all."

"Magic?"

"Maybe a little bit like magic."

Fourteen

The last days before the opening were a blur. It looked as though they would have a full house as the RSVPs came in one by one in the letterbox or by hand, so they would be at the full capacity of thirty-six guests. Jory was busy running from one place to another, doing last-minute errands, constantly dropping off one thing they needed and returning only to go back for something else.

Finally, Nefeli approached her and thrust an old flip phone into her hand. "This is my old phone. Take it. It's ancient, but better than nothing. You need to be more efficient, and we need to be able to reach you."

Jory had been trying to get to the shop to buy a cheap phone, as she'd promised Shane she would. He'd given her his phone number as she'd left the boat and made her promise to text soon but she hadn't had the time, and she was finding it remarkably difficult to be away from him.

"Thank you!" she gushed to Nefeli.

"It's just a phone," she muttered, backing away as Jory reached out to hug her.

So, in between waiting for the stationery, and after going to Selene's brother for the large wooden boards he'd sanded down and cut to size, Jory managed to send a quick text to Shane.

Look at who has a phone to use! Can I just say I have not stopped thinking about you since I left the boat? Oh gosh, I feel silly. Okay I'm hitting send anyway.

Who is this?

Her heart plummeted before he sent a winking face and she laughed. He sent something else, but she couldn't open it on the old phone.

Um, it's an old flip phone. I can't open what you sent!

That's probably a good thing if you are in the presence of other people. You're all I can think about. I can't wait to have you in my arms again.

Jory's insides melted and she felt tingling everywhere.

In a few days I expect you to show me in person just how much. Xx Hurry!

Nefeli, as it turned out, was worth her weight in gold. She immediately took over the set up of the hostess station, adding links to make reservations on the taverna's Facebook page, and she knew everything about running the credit card machine without having to be taught.

She planned table maps and set up ordering systems on Cressida's iPad. She was shrewd enough to know every detail they were missing yet offered her insight with respect. Jory was surprised that after just the first day, she actually liked Nefeli. It was as if her harsh exterior was removed the second she took the bloodred paint off her lips and nails.

She'd also asked her nephew, Basil, a sixteen-year-old boy from Chora, to help Cressida prep and do the dishes during service.

"Jory, after we open, I want you to take these downtown," Nefeli said, handing her the brochures. "Drop them at the information center, hostels, to anyone who might be able to get the word out. Look at this place." She pointed around. "Rooms, empty rooms with no one in them. Cressida may as well get some summer staff in and have them work in exchange for accommodation."

Even Cressida had to admit it was a brilliant idea. "It would only be for a short season, though. I will have to figure out the situation with the guesthouse by the end of August," she had said quietly to Nefeli, assuming Jory could not hear her, but she could. Jory sighed.

Cressida began preparing the food. She went to the fish market and purchased *boquerones* and cod, fresh black mussels and prawns the size of her hand. On Friday she prepared the *boquerones*—little white anchovies that she cleaned and deboned, salted and then marinated in herbs and vinegar. With the cod, she made *bakaliaros*, where the fish was soaked in water and salted to be ready for the shallow-fry dish.

Every time Cressida finished one dish, she wrote it on her blackboard, with everything other than prices, which they would assess after opening night.

By Friday evening, everything was prepped, portioned, and ready for cooking on Saturday. The menu, Cressida thought, looking at the beautiful blackboard, was finished, and all that was left was to bake without incident and to get through her very first service.

~

"I have no idea why you asked me to help you. We know what happened last time I baked," Jory said at five o'clock in the morning, in her pajamas with Cressida in the kitchen.

"Because you calm me," she said softly, and Jory looked at her. "I need to be calm to make this bread. I need it to feel peaceful, and like coming home, for it is the first thing they will eat tonight. And I am afraid of what I might feel today if you are not here by my side."

"Well, I am here," Jory said, squeezing her hand. "And at the moment I'm far too tired to be able to bake any of my own stuff into this, so let's do it."

"What, no early morning dreams of your Shane?"

The sound of his name made her insides turn. "There is now!"

Cressida chuckled. "I think a little bit of hazy delight is not a bad thing for people to taste."

Jory scowled good-naturedly, and they baked together all morning. Jory finally went back to sleep for a few hours before they met again at noon, for the start of what was going to be the biggest day of Cressida's new life.

⌒

Taverna Mysticos Kypos

To share

Freshly baked sourdough w homemade olive oil

Cheese: Mizithra and Anthotyros

Dolmades

Marinated olives from the garden

Boquerones—Vinegar-marinated white anchovies

Warm mezze

Keftedes—Fried meatballs with mint and cinnamon
Piperies—Peppers stuffed with feta
Calamari w butter, garlic & lemon
Prawns w lemon & peri-peri

Fish

Bakaliaros Skordalia—Fried salt cod with potato mash

Meat

Whole leg of lamb w oregano and lemon

Wild greens

Artichoke and broad bean salad

Dessert

Loukoumi—Rose delight
Ice cream handmade with Georgios's poached quince

~

"Wow," Nefeli said, typing the names of the dishes onto the iPad. "That is impressive. I haven't found anyone else but Basil to help you in the kitchen yet, though I've had many emails from seasonal workers with good experience looking for jobs on the island for the summer. Should I call them?"

"No, tonight I can do this all on my own with the help of Basil and you two. Everything is to share, mezze style. On the blackboard it looks like a lot of food, but a serving board will be placed in the middle of the table, and then each person will have one to two servings of the dishes listed. Little nibbles, really. Nefeli, have you done the table plans?"

She nodded, pulling out place cards. Nefeli had taken on the job of putting tables together so that it was like a dinner party and she knew exactly who to pair with whom. "Easy. Here you are." She handed the table plan to Cressida, who nodded until her eyes fell on to one table in particular and one eyebrow raised.

"You actually want to put Phaedra on the same table as Matthaeus? After the last town meeting?"

"I wasn't there, I would have no idea," Nefeli said innocently.

"The same one since we were young," Cressida said with a smile. "His goats are *still* eating her olives."

Nefeli shrugged. "I just thought a moment together with your bread involved might finally make them stop hating and start...well, you know."

"Not tonight," Cressida said. "Tonight, I need everyone focused on the food and ambience."

Nefeli sighed and changed the place cards. "But next week, I am definitely making them rose-scented water to share," Cressida said. They both began to laugh.

"Do you remember the time they actually started throwing food at one another across the room?" Nefeli asked Cressida. Which began a whole round of "remember when" between the women, and suddenly it was as if not a day had passed since they were twelve and had planned to take over the world.

"I'm going to get ready for tonight," Jory said, but her words were lost in the laughter of the women. She felt the joy and lightness between them after so many years apart and she was happy that they had let old burdens go.

She ducked into her room for a shower and changed into the new dress she'd bought today from Madam Dionysia. It was still from her hidden bargain rack but Jory had spent a little more than usual. It had to be elegant yet easy to move in—the perfect dress for the hostess of an opening of a restaurant.

Her phone made a dinging sound and her heart skipped a beat as she glanced at the message from Shane.

I miss you beautiful.

I miss you too, she thought, starting to type her reply. There was a knock on her door.

"Jory, it's Cress."

Jory pulled the door open quickly, the back of her dress still unzipped. "Is everything okay?"

She was surprised to see Cressida dressed in an actual chef's uniform. Her pants were black and slim-fit, shaping her legs nicely, though they looked quite comfortable. Her black chef's jacket was both fitted and flattering, with three-quarter sleeves and her name stitched in white on the left breast.

Cressida caught Jory's surprised look. "Leo had this made for me just before he died. I've never worn it before. Do I look okay?" she asked.

"You look fantastic, like a true professional. How about me?"

Cressida chuckled. "Turn around, I shall zip you up."

Jory turned around and felt the blue fabric tighten around her waist.

"Now turn back and let's have a look," Cressida said. "Stunning!"

Jory beamed.

"Ah, my friend," Cressida began, taking her shoulders. "Before we open, I just want to say thank you for coming here, for your friendship and support, and all your work to make this happen for me. You are a conduit to make beautiful things happen because of your beautiful soul. This is not your home, and we are not your people, and I can see in your eyes that very soon it shall be time for you to move on, because you have done what you came here to do, even though you didn't know it was why you are here. But this is always your home now. You know how your mother says you're home wherever you go? I think your mother and you go from place to place creating homes. A whole big world of home, everywhere you go. That is who you are, and what you do. And that you found me, and I found you, has been one of the best things that ever happened in my life."

Jory's eyes filled with tears. She pulled Cressida in for a tight hug, and they both cried just a little.

"Come on, you," Jory said, dabbing under her eyes to try to keep the mascara she hardly ever wore from running. "It's time."

~

At 7:30 p.m. exactly, Jory and Nefeli were ready at the door. Jory nervously wiped her palms on her dress.

"You're getting sweaty prints on your dress," Nefeli pointed to Jory's damp hands. "You look nervous."

Jory *was* nervous. The importance of the night hit her and she wanted nothing more than to see it a success. She told Nefeli as much.

"It will be perfect," Nefeli said with certainty. "And I know this because I have known this night would come for a long time, and it is simply proving itself to be such."

Jory took solace in that. She'd learned not to doubt Nefeli's assuredness any more than she would doubt Mago's colors or Cressida's cooking. The women of Potamia were very special. Was she truly one of them now? She took a deep breath, looking around and seeing how right everything felt. Yes. She was. Perhaps she always had been. Perhaps everyone was, it was simply a matter of stories colliding in the right way to let what was meant to be, be.

"You look very pretty, by the way," she said to Nefeli. And she did. She was perfectly presented, hair and nails and makeup done, but softer somehow, in a pale pink dress Jory had never seen before. "Is your dress new?"

"Mago," she said.

"Ah. Will Nico be coming tonight?"

"He was not invited," she said, her voice tightening.

"Have you heard from him at all?" Jory asked softly.

Nefeli shook her head once, staring ahead. "Look, the first are arriving."

"I'll go get the wine," Jory said. Arie had been kind enough to donate enough bottles so that each of the guests would have a complimentary glass of wine waiting as they arrived.

As the guests trickled down the stairs to the garden, Jory and Nefeli greeted the guests warmly with a glass of Arie's rosé. Jory could hear them marveling at the decor as they arrived. It did look spectacular. They'd strung fairy lights through the garden for people to congregate under while they drank their wine outside, the evening balmy. The dining tables were covered with Mago's colorful tablecloths, creating a charm, a warmth, a welcoming atmosphere that made all the guests feel at home as they walked in. Guests trickled past the blackboard menu, murmuring their anticipation for the food to come.

"It had to be Mago that did the tablecloths," Jory heard a group of female voices whispering to one another. Jory smiled as she passed them, looking around the garden for Mago. She was standing with Arie and Mayor Andreas.

At the same moment, she noticed Basil waving to her from the kitchen that the first course was ready to send out.

"How's it going?" Cressida asked nervously when Jory came in.

"Brilliantly of course," Nefeli answered instead, following Jory into the kitchen. "Everyone is commenting on how beautiful the restaurant looks and on the menu on the blackboard."

"People have wine, it's a beautiful night, they are relaxed," Jory added.

"Okay, good, because I've changed my mind," Cressida said, pointing to the large wooden boards that had the cold mezze dishes in the middle ready to serve. "I think we'll keep it more casual and serve the mezze while our friends mingle and have wine, and seat only for the last courses and dessert."

"Excellent idea," Jory said, picking up the first very large tray and grabbing a handful of napkins. Nefeli did the same and they returned to the crowd.

Jory took her wooden serving tray to Mayor Andreas.

"Look at this, just look," his voice boomed. "Magnificent! It will be the best little taverna on the whole island and people will come for the food, and then they'll want to stay in the charming rooms. When is Cressida planning to open them?"

Mago motioned Jory over. "Jory, what do you have here?"

"Take the small plates and a napkin and fill your plate," Jory announced. "Dolmades, olives, cheese, bread and boquerones."

"Ah, Jory," Mayor Andreas exclaimed, taking a dolma and putting the whole thing in his mouth, closing his eyes and moaning. "Best little taverna on the island," he repeated.

"It certainly is, and with Arie's help, the tourists will learn soon enough," Jory agreed.

"People pass through our village. Sometimes they stop by the castle or the church, but they continue on," he said sadly. "Steady tourism could do wonders for our village. I still think we could advertise the sacred spring."

Mago gave Jory a pointed look. "Mayor Andreas brought some marketing people here once to show them the spring, but…"

"We could never find it," he said with frustration. "Every time I turned down what I knew was the right street, we ended up lost again. Very embarrassing."

Jory hid her smile. "I think maybe leave the spring out of this one, Mayor. It will be found when it wants to." She went back to the kitchen to pick up another platter.

"That one is the warm mezze, Jory," Cressida called from the kitchen.

She took the plate of warm mezze into the garden, where she recognized Georgios and Raki in their Panama hats. They were chatting with Phaedra and Matthaeus and a few others

Jory didn't recognize. Phaedra's voice was starting to rise as she pointed her finger at Matthaeus angrily.

"Can I entice any of you with keftedes and piperies?" Jory interrupted. "Or perhaps sauteed calamari or a peri-peri prawn skewer? There are small forks if you need."

Whatever argument they were having faded to nothing as they all bit into Cressida's dishes. In fact, Jory realized the whole garden was suddenly quiet but for the soft music they had on in the background and sounds from the kitchen. When she looked around, she found Cressida's friends savoring her food, their eyes closed before opening as if in surprise, smiling at each other then in shared delight. There were no words to describe the flavors that enticed their senses and then fulfilled them.

After a time, Nefeli went to each group and led them to their tables inside for the last three dishes as Jory topped up their wines, leaving the bottles in the middle of the table.

"Oh look," Jory heard one say. "Look at the label. What a beautiful photo."

"I wonder who the woman is," another commented.

"*Taverna Mysticos Kypos*, it says. Do you think this is the name Cressida chose?"

Jory smiled and went back to the kitchen. The two main courses were served; the salt cod with mashed potato followed by the lamb leg with greens and the fresh bean salad. There was very little talking in the restaurant during these courses, just the clinking sound of glasses and cutlery, the murmurs of appreciation, the sighs of pleasure.

When it was time to bring the rose delight and ice cream with quince, Jory, Nefeli and Basil all brought the plated dishes while Arie came and poured his Kitron, and finally, Cressida came out of the kitchen, facing her friends, her neighbors.

Jory nodded to her to speak.

"Thank you so much for coming tonight," Cressida said. "I could not have done this without your support. Welcome, to *Taverna Mysticos Kypos.*"

The room applauded and Cressida, blushing profusely, waved and walked back into the kitchen.

For everyone at the *Taverna Mysticos Kypos* that night, it was like coming home. Each guest relived their strongest memory of what home meant to them. For some it tasted like Christmas; for others, their mother or father baking, a holiday. For some it was the sound of their children. For some it was Sunday roast. The greatest memory that reminded them that they were home was in every bite, and it was indeed magical.

Cressida watched as the people she had known all her life savored her food. First in silence, later making speeches. She watched them drink wine and after dessert, she watched them begin to dance, led by Mago and Arie, as Basil played his guitar. She turned to Leo's ghost beside her and danced. His soul faded away from her and found its own home somewhere in the great beyond, while she found hers again here, joyously in this kitchen.

And when it was all over, they all went to their own homes, happy and sated, with hazy stories they would tell for years, for no one really remembered anything in particular. They only knew that the taverna was open, as if it has always been open, and that good food, good wine and good company were only a step away at the little Greek taverna.

Fifteen

Everything was changing, and while some of it was unexpected—like Mago asking Arie to marry her, Nefeli leaving Nico, the little taverna opening—these changes were still happening by choice. But there was one person who felt that her choice had been taken from her, and that person was Selene Leos.

Selene had made her choice the first time she laid eyes on Shane Deluca when he walked into her gallery. He was the man she wanted. Her heart was set on his looks, his money and his ability to get her off this island and into his bed. For as long as they both shall live.

Shane Deluca was one of the wealthiest men in America under the age of thirty-five, according to the *Forbes* article Selene had read nearly a thousand times.

If it was just about the money and looks, that would have been one thing. But as it was, Selene had also gained feelings for Shane. And emotion was something she had never entered into the equation. It made her attraction to him almost too irresistible.

At first, he flirted. There was a spark in his eye when she tilted her head and glanced at him sideways. There was a time when she was almost certain he was going to ask her out, that he felt what she did. And then it stopped. It simply stopped. It was sudden and jarring, but eventually she heard that he'd gone back to the mainland for a while. Selene responded by putting a tourniquet on her heart and telling Lucas to be on the lookout for when he finally returned to port, and to give her any information he found out.

She knew from the *Forbes* article that Shane owned a company called the Resurgence Hotel Group, though he did try to hide that fact when she first met him. He even lied to her and told her his name was Shane Matthews but Selene was clever and knew the right people to find out everything she could about him.

He was thirty-two years old, single, and was here on Naxos working with his lawyer, Michael, who apparently did all the legwork, to purchase the little property in Potamia that was Cressida's. She and Cressida weren't friends, but they had gone to school together and she used to dine at Rigani when Cressida was still a chef there. She thought that the Resurgence offering for Cressida's property was a perfect way out. Though no one talked about such things, most people knew that Cressida would have to do something soon. There was no way her husband's insurance money could last much longer.

She was surprised, then, when Jory came with an invitation to the opening of Cressida's taverna. She had said nothing then as it was not her concern, but she was curious. Had Cressida refused the offer? Was she going to try to open the business on her own now? What did that mean of Shane? Would he be leaving the island? This would have explained his sudden disappearance and she was worried he was not coming back, so her relief was palpable when she got the text from Lucas to say that he saw Shane and was checking in for gossip duty as promised.

The front door opened and Lucas came in.

"Well?" she asked coolly, though her heart raced in excitement.

"I saw him at the port a few days ago. Not sure what he was doing there but he bumped into his girlfriend. You know, that funny American girl you sent over that day?"

Selene felt a lump in her throat. Jory. Selene had known something was going on between them, and yet Jory denied it right to her face.

"Jory," she said, swallowing.

"Yeah, that one. Nice girl," Lucas said. "Pretty, actually."

She sniggered. "If you like that sort of thing."

"What's not to like? Blonde, long legs—"

"Got it, Lucas!" she snapped. "What exactly made you think she's his girlfriend?"

He shrugged. "Well, he came over as soon as he saw her, and they talked for a bit. Then they kissed. And it definitely didn't seem like the first time, if you know what I mean."

Despite her shaking hands, she shrugged Lucas away as if what he'd said didn't matter. She could fix this. Certainly, this… wisp of a girl with her frizzy hair could not undo everything Selene had set in motion by her desires long ago.

But then, a few mornings later, Selene was passing by the wharf early in the morning and saw Shane helping Jory off a dinghy, the kind they used as tender boats for the larger yachts. And he was kissing Jory the way Selene had dreamed of Shane kissing her as she lulled herself to sleep each night. A rogue tear had run down her cheek.

The soft open for Cressida's taverna had occurred the night after, but Selene did not attend. Instead she sat in her apartment, heartbroken and angry, hatching a scheme that would cause a blast of pain to Jory. If she'd had the gall to lie to Selene's face then she could be repaid in kind.

Jory arrived at the gallery all smiles, trilling, "Good morning, Selene!" and followed with, "We missed you at the opening last night. It was such a fantastic evening, everything went perfectly."

It was then that Selene snapped, perhaps without even thinking it fully through, "What is the point anyway? I thought she'd be selling to that hotel group that offered for it."

"What did you say?" Jory asked quietly.

"I heard the owner of the Resurgence Hotel Group is back and he is not leaving until he owns that property. No matter what it takes." The lie rolled smoothly off her tongue. "But surely Cressida has told you everything. You are so close to one another."

"I know a bit," Jory said slowly, swallowing. "But surely it's simply an offer. She can say yes or say no. But now that she's opened, I cannot imagine she would want to sell."

"What do I know? But I imagine a few weeks of a new taverna opening will not pay enough to win a bid against a millionaire company. And this man is determined. Never have I met a more determined man."

"You know who it is? The person wanting to buy the company?"

"Of course!" Selene said brightly. "Actually, come to think of it, so do you. He was in the gallery the first day I met you, you know, during your graceful moment with my display," she said, smiling sweetly. "That was him, Shane Deluca. American, like you."

What color there had been left in Jory's normally pink cheeks drained and her face went completely white. She licked her lips a few times as if they were suddenly dry, and blinked rapidly, as though holding back tears.

"Shane? Shane works for the group trying to buy Cressida's property?" Jory gasped.

"Works for it?" Selene gave a brittle laugh and got out her phone, opening the *Forbes* article about Shane. "Darling, he owns it."

If possible, Jory's face became even more pale as she glanced at the article and zoomed in on the photo. "But he said... I mean, the *Persephone,* yes. I did wonder. But he told me..."

"Ah, let me guess," Selene said, taking her phone back and shaking her head with false sympathy. "He told you he was someone else, right? You know, when I first met him he even lied about his name!" she laughed. "Shane Matthews, he said."

"That's his middle name," Jory said quietly, her breathing becoming more ragged.

"Look, you don't get to be one of the richest men in America by playing nice all the time. He knows what he wants, and he doesn't care how he gets it. That's probably why we hit it off so well," she mused. "Cressida probably hasn't even met him. I hear he has his friend Michael do a lot of his dirty work—sign his name on the paperwork, meet with clients, so Shane can find out what he needs to make his deal happen and nobody really knows who he is."

She was pushing it there, she knew, but instead of looking sad, Jory suddenly looked hard, cold. "And did he know when he met me that I was staying with Cressida?"

Selene hesitated for a moment, not meeting Jory's eyes, pretending to be busy. The ramifications of her lies would be sweet revenge against Jory, but the consequences would reach much further, she realized then. Still, she continued the lie. "Of course he did. I told him the very same day."

~

"Shane has known that I was working with you from the beginning and apparently he will stop at nothing to buy out your property."

It had taken Jory half an hour to get back to the taverna and sit Cressida and Nefeli down to convey everything she had learned about Shane from Selene. As she spoke, her voice was hoarse but her eyes were dry. She had cried enough on the way back, the feeling of hurt turning into betrayal, and betrayal bringing her right back to all those years ago, swearing to never trust anyone with money.

Jory was angry but she was also ashamed. She should have known, somehow, about Shane. And now she had to tell her friend that her own lover had lied to her about who he was, and for what? To buy Cressida's property? To get information? Just to get her into bed? Why?

Cressida reached out and took Jory's hands in her own and waited until Jory looked up at her. "Oh Jory, I am so sorry I did not tell you my financial situation. Leo's insurance money, along with some help from his family early on, has allowed me to stay on this past year and a half since he passed. But two months ago I realized I could no longer pay the mortgage. I did not know what to do, but when the offer came from Resurgence, I was truly thinking of selling. I even met with the lawyer, Michael, to find out more. But then you came."

She motioned around her.

"And you made me believe and we have done all this." Cressida paused. "I have ignored all their emails and calls. I should have picked up. I should have told them I was opening, that I was going to try to keep my home and dream." She shook her head. "Damnit."

Nefeli stood, pacing back and forth. "It doesn't matter," she said, shaking her head. "We will get the money, somehow. I can ask my parents—"

"You don't understand people with this kind of wealth. You don't know how ruthless they are, how determined." Despite Jory's passion, her voice came out in a hoarse whisper. "I know what this kind of money does to people, because it's the same for my father's family. I know not to trust it."

Abruptly, she sat again, exhausted and spent. "Shane never told me what he did. Or who he was. He told me he was a bartender! He lied to me. He lied, and I cannot accept that. I can't see any reason for his lying other than what Selene said— he is determined to get what he wants, and he wants this taverna, which has meant more to me than anything in the world." She started to break then. "I'm so, so sorry."

Cressida stood and took Jory into her arms. "This is not your fault! I will schedule a meeting with Shane."

"Invite him here," Jory said, her expression full of determination. "Invite Shane here tomorrow. I want to see the look on his face when he has to own up to what he has done."

Shane Deluca was good at one thing—he knew when to stay and fix something. It all started in Mexico nearly a decade before at a great little place in Tulum. He had gone over to visit a friend, Jonas, a chef he'd worked with in Pennsylvania. After one night dining in Jonas's place, he simply knew he needed to stay. He was hired as a bartender for the season, despite his parents opposing his decision. He was midway through college, but hospitality called his name, not banking. So he stayed. He became friends with all the locals, grew to love the terrain, the food, the people.

Jonas had set up a woodfire grill at one of the small hotels on the Avenida Boca Paila, and while the restaurant was succeeding, the hotel could not compete with the large resorts popping up all over the once small village, now becoming overrun with American tourists wanting an all-inclusive experience. The small guesthouse called Mi Casa, Su Casa could not keep up with the restaurant, and the bad reviews were starting to mount up. The owners were a charming couple, the man from the U.S. and his wife a local, and they had started when Tulum was still so small that a guesthouse like theirs flourished, which was why Jonas had gone there in the first place. But business was slowing, the rooms were dated, no air-conditioning, the internet was patchy, and while they had a prime location, they didn't have the staff to manicure their beach each morning of the seaweed.

When the season ended and the whole site was about to foreclose, Shane felt with every instinct within him that he could make this right. He did something he thought he'd never do—he flew home to Pennsylvania and scheduled a meeting with his father, an investment banker. Charles loved his wife and two children and while they were not wealthy, they were a proper white-collar family. When his son had found the world of restaurants and travel more to his liking than the high-end college education he was getting, Charles had been strict and set rules in place that Shane would adhere to, like staying in college. He had worked hard, after all, for his kids to have whatever they wanted. When Shane scheduled the appointment with him after that summer in Mexico, Charles thought he knew what to expect.

"You're leaving school." It was not a question.

"Well, that depends, actually. I have a business proposition for you." And that was when Shane outlined his idea for buying out Mi Casa, Su Casa. It did not displace the locals or compete with the resorts. It was a new and better way of attracting tourism in a growing economy. Shane had utilized all the business skills he'd learned at Penn State to create algorithms and spreadsheets that impressed even Charles, and most especially, his colleagues at the bank. They would need three million dollars to renovate, put the right staff in place, and open a niche for a more bohemian tourist who loved good food, a good bar and boutique-style accommodation.

The bank agreed. Shane did not drop out of school, but completed his degree, as that was part of the deal. He got his three million and got his friends from school together to do market research and design, and they reopened Mi Casa, Su Casa and Jonas's restaurant the following season and made back their money threefold. The Resurgence Hotel Group was born and Shane was a millionaire by the time he was twenty-five. He spent the next near decade finding places that needed a resurgence, and making them work both for the company and locally.

Shane loved his work and his lifestyle, but he was lonely. He had all the attributes that could allow him to live his life as a playboy—looks, wealth, lifestyle. But he had always wanted a long-term relationship, a partner to share in his life, not simply a fleeting affair in every port. He had met a few women over the years—lovely, smart women he'd imagined he could possibly build a life with. But the relationship always ended with an ultimatum—he had to stay. Not once had one of his few girlfriends held out their hand and said, "Take me with you." Which was all he'd ever wanted.

But the loneliness ended the day he met Marjory St. James, who was already traveling the world, already a person who didn't want to stagnate in one place. Suddenly there was no greater purpose, no greater goal, than to be with her. He knew it was crazy to be in love with a girl he'd only met a few times, but it felt that way every time he saw her—she made his skin feel like it was on fire. When they touched, when they came together, it was like they were meant for one another, and in those moments, she looked at him like he was the greatest man on earth. He wanted to be that man. More importantly, he believed he *could* be that man. So much so he'd completely fallen off course as to why he was even here in Naxos. He'd found a place that needed help and had put in a bid, leaving the details for Michael to sort out. He had a greater influence on the island than Shane would have on his own, as he was in some ways a local.

He'd always loved Greece and the islands, but the competition with large hotels and small guesthouses on islands like Santorini and Mykonos had put it out of his range. But here on Naxos, success was possible. Especially when he found the beautiful little guesthouse in Potamia, his every instinct kicked in that this place needed something and someone to let it become what it could be, to resurge, and he was the one that could do it. Close enough to be manageable, far enough from town to avoid any competition. And the fact that it was set up and ready to go, but with no guests and no staff and no part of it anything other than a woman's home, meant it should have been an easy buy. The poor woman's husband had passed away the year before and she'd been covering the mortgage with his insurance but was behind on her payments and the bank was about to foreclose. Michael had been calling and emailing to no avail after their first meeting, and Shane was just about to make contact himself when a very surprising email came through from the enigmatic Mrs. Thermopolis, inviting Shane for coffee and a conversation the following morning.

And so here he was, driving the nine kilometers to Potamia this Monday morning, a morning he did not know would continue the story of the most memorable summer in Potamia in a decade.

Shane was whistling as he drove along, so enthused was he to see the beautiful house again and to meet the very guarded Mrs. Thermopolis for the first time. He actually didn't even know her first name. He understood the impact it could have to come to her just as himself, not as a name or a company. Just a man who was honest about where he came from and how he came to be here and what he knew her property could become. He pulled up and parked across the street, admiring again the view of the beautiful house with the garden and taverna. It had felt like home to him the second he first saw it months ago. It felt like home now. Until he got out of the car.

Suddenly, a great gust of wind blew from the north. His papers flew from his hands and the wind was so strong that it actually forced Shane back against his bike as he kneeled to collect them. The wind made a hollow sound as it blew, almost as if it was pleading with him to leave. He ran around grabbing the drawings and photographs and shoving them back into his folder.

At that moment, the door of the guesthouse opened and a young Greek woman with long dark hair in a side braid emerged and met his eyes, her head tilting. In that exact instant, the wind died completely and he could hear his own breath again. He began to walk toward her but inexplicably stopped. It was as though he literally could not move forward.

"Mr. Deluca?" the woman asked.

"Yes. Are you Mrs. Thermopolis?"

She nodded briefly, and the air thinned and it was as if he was free from his bondage, allowing him to move forward. He started to follow her to the front door, but she turned, leading him to a white picket fence. She opened the gate and looked him directly in the eyes.

"My name is Cressida."

The air around him did not need to still this time to tell him that nothing would be the same now. This was Cressida, the magical baker he had heard about every day in the past few weeks he'd been with Jory. This was Jory's closest friend here. This was Jory's home in Potamia. And he'd had no idea.

Cressida nodded as she heard his gasp and indicated that he follow her down the stairs.

The garden flourished with the rich vegetation of olives, lemons, and herbs so tall they were like bushes, but it was also manicured, tidy, and there were tables set out. One, a charming white antique under a lemon tree, was occupied. Jory. She wore the same yellow dress she had worn the day he first took her to the ruins, but her face was now a stark contrast to that happy day. She sat on her hands, leaning forward, staring at him, her jaw set.

Shane felt suddenly very cold, her expression an impenetrable ice wall. Yes, he'd misled Jory into believing he was still a bartender. He'd withheld pertinent information about himself that could possibly look really bad to her and Cressida right now. Especially considering her early confession of her mistrust of people with money, like her father. But surely he could simply talk to her? This was Jory. She knew him. He'd had no idea that Cressida's property was the taverna Jory had been so passionately involved in.

"You've been busy," he finally said, motioning to the garden around him.

"As if you didn't know that," Jory replied, the muscle in her jaw tightening.

"I didn't know you had anything to do with this place," he said, meeting Jory's eyes. She looked at him directly, her gaze hostile and untrusting. He turned back to Cressida who was standing behind him. "I didn't know," he repeated, more clearly.

"I don't believe you," Jory said coldly.

"Jory," he turned to her, pleading, "you know me. You know I wouldn't lie to you."

A shocked laugh left Jory's mouth. "I most certainly know you now," she said, opening Cressida's phone to the *Forbes* page.

Shane flinched. He hated that article.

Jory continued, her voice bitter, brittle. "Let's see, Shane Deluca. Owner of the Resurgence Hotel Group, trying to buy my friend's property? No, I did not know that. Nor did I know that you happen to be one of the wealthiest men in America."

Shane tried to interrupt but she put her hand up and raised her voice.

"You wouldn't lie to me? But you have lied to me, every step of the way, Shane. A *bartender*? The last place you worked was

Mexico? I mean, the fact that that was a decade ago when you then became a millionaire probably wasn't an important piece of information to pass on."

"I didn't tell you because you told me pretty much the day I met you that you hated anyone with money and didn't trust them," he said quietly.

"And isn't it clear now," she said, walking toward him, "that the reason I don't trust people with money is because I'm from a family with money and they're exactly like you, putting on a face of the good Samaritan, Robin Hood, helping the poor, when the truth is all any of you ever do is step on every little person on the way to get what you want while refusing to own up to it!"

"Own up to what?" he asked, incredulous. "That I have money? Well, I have money, but I'm still me, not some evil villain in a movie."

Cressida finally spoke, her voice clear and calm. "We know, Mr. Deluca, that you knew about Jory and my relationship the day you met her in Selene's shop."

"That's not true!" he exclaimed. "Why would you think that?"

"Selene told me the truth. Did you not lie to her when you first met and told her your name was Shane Matthews so she wouldn't know who you were?"

Shane's face flushed. "Yes, I did, but only because—"

Cressida put her hand up. "I spoke to your lawyer at the beginning. You could have come here earlier and spoken with me, but you did not. Instead, you lied to my friend and therefore to me. You made her grow to care for you, with dishonor and deceit, and for what? Was it for this tiny, worthless property you do not even need?"

"I did not—"

"Please leave now, Mr. Deluca," Cressida said, crossing her arms over her chest.

Shane shook his head, the ground pulled from under him. "There is nothing I can say, is there? Jory..." he pleaded one last time, turning to her.

But she was immovable. "Leave, Shane. I don't want to see you again."

"Fine," he said coolly, turning to leave. At the base of the stairs he looked back at Jory, this time his eyes hard. "I guess neither of us knew each other then, Jory. Because right now, I'm looking at a stranger. The person I knew would never assume the worst of someone or dismiss them so completely. Especially someone you cared about."

He walked up the stairs.

"Goodbye, Jory."

Jory waited until Shane was completely out of sight before she put her face in her hands and let herself cry. They were big, hiccupping sobs of too much emotion in too little time—the betrayal, the incredible anger, the glimmer of hope at seeing Shane's face, the disappointment, the goodbye.

Cressida's arm came around her shoulders and Jory lifted her head out of her hands, her face wet with tears. "I'm sorry," Jory said. "I'm not a pretty crier."

Cressida smiled. "No, you are really not. I'm so glad you waited for him to leave."

This brought an almost genuine laugh to Jory, but then the tears began to stream more and she sat down, Cressida sitting beside her. "I thought I was falling in love with him," Jory choked.

"Are you sure you do not want to talk to him?"

"What on earth could he possibly say that would undo the fact that he lied about something so important? Which means there's nothing he can say now. Nothing at all," Jory finished, sniffling and wiping her nose on the back of her hand. "Ugh, I need a tissue."

Cressida stood. "I'll go grab some."

She was gone for only a moment before she returned and sat again beside Jory, handing her the box. Jory took one, then immediately another three after she blew her nose.

A long sigh came from Jory and she groaned and dropped her head back into her hands. "My heart hurts."

Cressida pulled her in for a hug. "I know, honey. I know."

Sixteen

The days were so busy at the taverna once they opened to the public that Jory was too busy to think about Shane most of the day. In the evenings, after the last of Arie's groups left and they cleaned up, she shared dinner with Cressida and Nefeli and often Mago, who talked of anything and everything except what happened with Shane, at Jory's request. But at night, she wept endlessly, questioned everything, went through emotions of anger and heartache so quickly it mentally exhausted her, but not enough to sleep. She tossed and turned and stared at the ceiling, going through every moment with him in her head, and having conversations and arguments as if he were there.

She was bone tired, pale with dark circles under her eyes, and strung tight with emotion, so when Jory saw Liz and Kate walk down the stairs of the taverna to surprise her, she nearly dropped her plates right then and there, running to them and crying and laughing at the same time.

After a warm welcome from Cressida, Kate and Liz were set up in their own rooms at the guesthouse. Though Cressida welcomed them as her guests, they both adamantly insisted on paying. The four of them were all in Jory's room, sitting around drinking Arie's wine.

"We want to be your first paying guests, so don't even think about arguing with me, Cress," Liz said sternly.

Jory winked at Cressida, who she could tell loved the way her friends adopted her new nickname on their own. "Listen to her, Cress, you do not argue with Elizabeth Mortimer. She always wins."

"I'm not surprised she wins against you. What terrible arguments you have for someone who was on the debate team in college," Cressida said, looking to Kate and Liz.

Kate rolled her eyes. "Tell me she hasn't done her adamant, 'Does that make sense?' routine on you?"

Cressida laughed. "She was getting better, but the first one did not make sense!"

Jory stood. "But I did win that argument, didn't I? I never should have gotten involved with Shane."

They all sobered.

"Admit it," Jory said. "Shane betrayed me, he hurt me, he is a lying, rich, holier-than-thou jerk." Her eyes welled up.

"Okay," Liz said. "You promised you'd tell us everything in detail as soon as we were upstairs with a wine, and here we are. So tell us what happened?"

Between Jory and Cressida—who had to fill in occasionally when Jory couldn't speak because she'd cry—they managed to get the story out of meeting Shane, of Jory's resistance, of her inevitable falling for him and giving into this amazing thing.

"And then he lied to me. Not simply omitted the fact that he was this wealthy millionaire, but actually lied about what he did. And why? Because of *money*. It always, always boils down to that with these people," Jory cried, falling back onto the bed. "I really thought…I don't know, that we could have something kind of awesome." She started to cry softly.

Kate came over and lay next to her, pulling Jory's head on her shoulder.

"I feel like this is my fault," Cressida said with frustration. "If I had not hidden the fact that someone was trying to buy my business and that I was very strongly thinking of doing so, this never would have happened. I never knew the man Shane was the owner, I only dealt with Michael, the lawyer from the Resurgence Hotel Group."

Liz jumped up excitedly. "Okay, let's get to work Googling the names we know." She grabbed her laptop out of her bag and brought it to the middle of the bed where they could all sit around it.

Jory stubbornly crossed her arms and stayed on her pillow. "I'm not interested."

Liz ignored her and typed in his name. "S-h-a-n-e D-e-l-u-c-a," she said out loud as she typed. "Of the R-e-s…"

"Why did you stop typing?" Kate asked.

"Because it's number one in the search engine already," Liz answered.

"Click the image first," Kate said, "I'm dying to see what he looks like."

It took only a second for the first photo to come up of Shane in his classic khaki shorts and white T-shirt, on a yacht called *Persephone*. It was a candid photo so he wasn't posed, and he looked young and happy.

"Holy fuck, he's hot." Liz whistled.

"Liz!" Jory protested from the pillow, still refusing to join them. "Not helping!"

"He's pretty spectacular-looking," Cressida admitted, "even for a wing bing."

The two girls turned to Cressida, confused. Jory spoke up. "*Bigwig*, Cress."

"Don't worry, Cress," Liz said. "Jory makes up words too."

"What?" Jory sat up, confused and offended. "Like what?"

"Like when you say 'miss you like a rogue limb,'" Liz clarified. "We all know what you mean by it, like a phantom limb. But it's not a real phrase. Your mom said you made it up when you were younger and we all just say it now."

"I love when Jory says that," Cressida admitted.

Jory simply looked dumbfounded at the fact as Kate patted her shoulder.

They all turned back to the screen. The photo, when Liz clicked on it, was from the now infamous *Forbes* article from a few months prior.

"Funny," said Liz after reading a while, "he's the only one who did not pose for the photo shoot, nor did he offer an interview. They had to put one together themselves. Let's see. From Pennsylvania, went to Penn State. Jory, you said that's what he told you, right?"

She nodded, finally giving in and scootching up to sit with her friends and look at the article. But seeing his photo made her insides hurt so much, she shook slightly when she exhaled.

"At least he hasn't lied about everything then," Liz said. "Let's see, opened his first place in Mexico when he was still in college—"

"Uh!" Jory interrupted, sounding furious. "'My last bartending job was in Mexico,' Shane told me. Probably first and last bartending job, which he refused to follow up with, 'oh yeah, after that I bought the business and became a rich asshole overnight and never had to bartend again'!"

"Oh Jory, honey, I'm sorry," Liz said. "We can stop if you want."

She took a deep breath. "No, go ahead. I've read it a million times anyway."

"Okay," Liz continued, "… 'first place in Mexico, Mi Casa, Su Casa.' Oh wow, I stayed at that place a couple of years ago!" Liz exclaimed. "It was amazing. Awesome restaurant, still really boutique and small, family-run, but boho chic. Loved it."

"He is single now, Liz, if you're interested," Jory said sourly.

"Oh, shut it. This is important! Let's look at the other properties the group owns," she said. They scrolled through photos of little hotels in Argentina, Bali, Thailand, Turkey and two others in Mexico, all similar, family-run places that had kept their original charm. But every time they scrolled through another photo of a shining, smiling Shane at one of these places, shaking hands with the staff and laughing with them, it made Jory simultaneously sad and angry. It didn't matter the smile, the charm—he was a rich man buying these people out of their livelihoods.

Jory reached over and closed the screen. "You guys can Google him as much as you want, but I'm done now."

"Of course, honey," Kate said, "we just wanted to try to find out if perhaps there'd been a mistake. That maybe he wasn't so bad."

"I can't imagine anything other than what it is, so I'd rather put it behind me. You girls are *here* and we can all have a fantastic holiday together for the first time ever! So, let's go get Mago. Cress, shall we meet at the taverna in an hour?"

"Yes, and I'll make dinner. We are so glad to have you girls here," Cressida said, smiling at Liz and Kate before she left.

Liz grabbed her laptop and kissed the top of Jory's head. "Sorry, honey. I thought it would help. You know we love you more than life."

Jory smiled. "Yeah, I know. Go on, go back to your rooms and Google away without me." She laughed. "I'm going to Arie's to buy an extra case of wine for the week so we don't accidentally drink the taverna out of all of its stock. I'll see you back soon. Oh and I am so, so glad you're here."

~

Cressida's guesthouse was full. Or nearly so. It took only a week after the taverna had opened before the lunch sitting filled up each day. The guesthouse now had Jory and Nefeli in two rooms, two new staff members that were working in exchange for accommodation in another, and now Liz and Kate in two more rooms—her first paying customers—leaving only one room left. Everything felt like it was heading in the right direction, except suddenly, since Selene's news of who Shane really was, something felt wrong somehow.

So Cressida did the only thing she knew how to do and pulled out her Callas book of recipes, flipping to the page of the Vasilopita her mother used to make. It was a bread usually served during the holidays, and often a coin was baked in to bring good luck.

"Make it right," she breathed in and breathed out, over and over, as she was guided to what was needed until the recipe was perfect, and when she knew it was right, she put it in the oven. A Callas didn't need a coin or a trinket. They *were* the luck within.

It had been nearly a week since Shane had broken Jory's heart. The moment she saw Kate and Liz, she had exploded with joy at seeing them there. She had been so happy, had had the most amazing month with Cressida in Potamia, but when Shane walked away and she hadn't heard from him, she didn't realize how huge a part of her heart he had become in such a short time. Now, surrounded by her friends—all of her friends—laughing and drinking wine as they nibbled on olives, she felt a bandage on her heart she didn't realize she'd needed so badly.

"Mago," Nefeli asked, "how are the wedding plans going?"

"You're getting married?" Kate trilled. They had both fallen completely in love with Mago from the moment they met her.

"Yes, to my Arie." She filled Kate and Liz in on the details of their love affair as Cressida served them bowls of huge black mussels steamed in wine with peppers and feta. "We've decided we have waited long enough. We are going to get married at the end of the month on the vineyard. Just a quiet wedding. My two boys are coming from the mainland. Cressida will cater, of course, and you girls will be more than welcome if you are still here then."

"We're staying for the rest of July, so absolutely. I love that you actually asked a man to marry you. Were you nervous?" Liz asked.

"Haven't been so nervous since my first wedding night, and much like with the proposal, I shouldn't have been. What a romp that was," Mago said, and they all laughed.

"Oh my god, this is amazing," Kate said to Cressida, who'd been quiet much of the time. "Jory was not kidding when she said you were the most extraordinary cook." Cressida beamed and began telling her about the small farm where the feta was produced.

"Do you like to cook?" Cressida asked Kate.

"I love cooking. I'm obsessed with cooking shows. Sometimes on the weekends, I get up in the morning and put on one of my favorites and then spend all day working on the recipes. Everything from scratch."

"Do you still do that, Kate, even living with Mark?" Jory asked, leaning forward. "We all lived together for years," she explained to the others.

"More than ever."

"She's not kidding, Cressida," Liz said, smiling. "Do you remember the Thanksgiving dinner Kate cooked, Jory?"

She chuckled. "You mean the one where you and I came out with our weapons in the middle of the night to catch the intruder who was breaking into our apartment?"

"Who turned out to be Kate, who was following Martha Stewart who insisted that getting the turkey in by 4 a.m. was the only way it would be cooked in time." They were practically in tears laughing at the memory, even the Greek women who weren't there at the time.

"What weapons did you actually bring out? Is it true all Americans have guns?" Nefeli asked.

"No," Kate said, "that's a bit of an exaggeration. But Jory brought out a blow dryer."

"It was the first thing I could find," Jory protested.

"The point is," Kate said, raising her voice, "I was not an intruder, I was cooking, and my Thanksgiving was absolutely perfect. Unlike the time Jory tried to do Thanksgiving. What was the thing she tried to make, the chocolate gravy?"

Jory blushed as Cressida gave her a look. "It was in that movie, *Chocolat*. It looked so good—this like, chocolate gravy on turkey or something."

"Did you use a recipe?" Cressida asked.

"Well, no, I just watched the movie lots and figured if I melted chocolate, it would be great."

"It was not great," Kate said adamantly, shaking her head.

"Definitely not great," Liz agreed. Jory scowled good-naturedly at them.

"Come, Kate," Cressida said, "you can help me finish the pork."

Kate followed Cressida into the kitchen where she pulled a leg of pork out of the oven. It had been cooked with fennel, dill and wine for an hour. "It's nearly ready to go, but for the final step. It's quite a rich dish, this pork, as we add an egg into the sauce to finish cooking. It's a very important process and you must be fully paying attention to be sure you don't scramble it."

"A bit like carbonara?" Kate asked.

"I suppose so." Cressida broke the eggs into the bowl for Kate to whisk. But she hadn't just brought Kate back there to be her sous chef. "What more have you found out about him? Of this Shane Deluca?"

"From our research, he seems like a perfectly good guy. He started in hospitality. He actually did work as a bartender in that place in Mexico that Liz has been to. When it fell into trouble, he went back home to get a bank loan for the money it needed to survive and grow, all while keeping the locals on board. It seems his ethos is to keep the local community involved in order to stop big hotel groups from snagging them at their weakest. Jory doesn't want to hear anything about it, of course, so we've not tried to talk about it with her again. But here, this is what we found." She handed Cressida her phone to read through articles she'd saved. Kate then added the meat juices to the eggs in the bowl, whisking continuously as Cressida had said so that the heat wouldn't scramble the eggs. "I think I've got it."

Cressida came over and took the pan off the heat, adding a splash of lemon preserve, her secret ingredient. "This is actually very good, Kate. You should think about cooking for a living."

They poured the mixture into the pan with the pork and Cressida put it on the lowest heat possible, stirring continuously as Kate watched the egg sauce thicken. "It looks amazing."

"I never would have been able to do any of this without her," Cressida said softly. "Look around you … at this taverna, at this food, at me. This is because of Jory."

"Yes, Jory has a great gift, I knew that from the moment I met her. I think we all have great gifts within us, and it just takes the right person or the right moment to allow us to become the best version of who we truly are. Jory's great gift is helping people find their own. But I think—and don't get me wrong, she is one of my best friends in the world—she uses that as an excuse not to find her own way sometimes."

"And you think Shane is her way?"

Kate looked thoughtful. "It's possible. Perhaps if he could explain …"

Cressida nodded. "If only anyone would let him."

~

Just a few blocks away on the other side of the village, another man had been waiting for his chance. Nico Remis woke with a start in the middle of the night, his head on the kitchen table, the two plates in front of him uneaten, the romantic candles he had lit nearly burned down. Every night since the day Nefeli had left, he came home from work, he made dinner for them both, which he'd never done before, and he set two plates, and he waited.

He had wanted to go to her immediately, but everyone kept telling him, just wait, she will come home. She will come home to you, and when she does, you must be ready. His mother told him that when she would bring pots of food over for him to heat, on the days he did not know what to make. Nefeli's parents told him that too. *Just wait*, they said. *She will come home to you.*

But she did not come home. He waited every night until midnight, and every night when he saw the lights of the taverna go out, he would clean up the kitchen and go to bed in the room where Nefeli had slept, wishing her home.

But this night had been different. He had closed the shop early, found one of Nefeli's recipes she used to make on special occasions, and followed it to the letter. By seven o'clock, the Kotopoulo Kritharaki was ready. He'd had the butcher cut the whole chicken for him, but he added the garlic and onions himself, the cinnamon stick and allspice, covering it with orzo and tomatoes and putting it in the oven for nearly an hour. While it was cooking he had a long shower and pulled out his recently dry-cleaned tuxedo, the one he had worn to their wedding, and lit the candelabra they'd gotten as a gift and had never used. He even lit all seven candles, and then he waited.

For surely, this was the night that Nefeli would come home. It was, after all, their anniversary. She had always been the dramatic sort, and this was exactly the kind of thing that would make her love him again. He was certain. But the hours passed, one by one, and even at midnight, he did not give up but sat, waiting, until eventually he fell asleep on his arm at the table, trying not to cry.

At three o'clock in the morning, when Nico woke, he was refreshed. Not tired at all, not tired like Nefeli said she had been of him, of them. He was not tired of his golden match, and she was not tired of him. He knew that, with every fiber of his being. But he was tired of waiting.

At that same moment, Mago slept soundly next door, her breathing even and calm, the anxiety of her up and coming wedding eased. Kate and Liz slept deeply and dreamlessly in a coma of travel and food. Even Jory and Cressida fell into a peaceful sleep. But one room was filled with quiet restlessness.

Nefeli had immersed herself in the taverna and its opening, and the success had managed to dull the pain of the fact that she had left the man she loved so greatly. Her friendship with Cressida was a calming, healing presence again in her life, which she was eternally grateful for, and Jory and her friends were like a night-light in a dark place.

But when she was alone, in the dark of night, she missed Nico. And on this night, the night of her anniversary, she only wanted to go home. But she could not. She could not simply walk back into the marriage that was loveless, no matter how long she'd waited. Nefeli sighed, giving up on sleep, and went to put on her dressing gown.

"Juliet! My Juliet! Nefeli!"

Nico? She quickly rose and pulled her dressing gown around her, coming out onto the balcony that faced the street, wondering if she was dreaming.

But she was not dreaming. There he was, Nico, her husband, her beautiful golden match, who had not sought her out since she'd left, nor had ever tried to say that he loved her at all. Now he was here, in the wee hours of the morning, dressed in a tuxedo, the one he wore at their wedding, with wilted flowers in his hand.

"What do you want, you silly fool?" she whispered loudly.

He raised his arms, showing her the flowers. "Alas, my Juliet, she comes."

"Stop calling me that," she hissed, "and stop yelling. Do you want to wake the whole town?"

"Yes, actually, I do. *Juliet*!" he called loudly.

Lights came on then, starting with the rooms of the taverna, then Mago's, before they began to trickle on and on through the town.

"It is the west, and Juliet is the sun!" Nico yelled.

"Ah hm…" Mago coughed, beckoning Nico to her. "It's actually the east. Where Juliet is the sun."

"Oh. Do you think anyone will have noticed?"

"Just in case, now that the town is awake, perhaps start again," she advised.

"*Juliet*! Nefeli!"

"Nico, I am actually standing right here. My balcony is less than two meters from you," Nefeli cried desperately.

People began to walk outside now in their nightgowns. "Nico? Nico, is that you? What in the good lord's name are you doing out here yelling in the middle of the night?"

"I am here to see my Nefeli, who is the…"

"Sun," Mago whispered.

"Sun…and Juliet is the east!"

"That didn't really work either," Mago said. "Perhaps, Nico, forget Shakespeare. Just speak from your heart."

He nodded and turned to Nefeli. "I don't know Shakespeare. I never did, not when you told me about it at the old castle when we first met as teenagers. I was a poor mechanic and you were the great Nefeli Castellanos. I didn't know anything except that I loved you."

Nefeli pulled her robe closer to her.

"I loved you then, the moment I first saw you. I loved you the day I first kissed you. I loved you the day I married you, the luckiest man on earth. I have loved you for more than ten long years and I will love you for the rest of all my days. You said never to say it. I didn't. I was an idiot! I love you, Nefeli! I love you and I will love you till the day I die."

Oddly, no one stayed outside to see how it ended. For the townsfolk were reminded that they should always say the thing they sometimes forget to say, and that they should say it right now.

And so by the time Nefeli came downstairs, with the help of Jory, Cressida, Liz and Kate, she walked to the middle of the empty street where her husband waited. She said nothing until she reached his open arms, then simply said, "I love you too, you silly man."

And then she kept on kissing him until morning.

Seventeen

The weeks that followed were filled with new stories, moving onto the next chapter.

Nefeli moved back in with Nico, though she continued to work at the taverna every day. She was not so much needed for marketing because word passed around, for one reason or another. Sometimes a couple would be driving and they would suddenly find themselves winding up the road just nine kilometers away and happening upon a secret garden and a little taverna that felt like just the right place to go.

Nefeli and Cressida's friendship was back to how it had been, as if nothing had ever happened in between, when everything had.

The three American girls stayed at the guesthouse through the month of July and helped in the restaurant and supported

Cressida, though Cressida forced them to go travel together, something they had never done before. They explored the island, Liz trading in her rental car for a two-seater scooter for her and Kate, that they rode all over the island, Jory on her moped as their tour guide.

They took day trips and a few overnight trips to islands nearby using the ferry. They went to Pano Koufonissi's pristine beaches, to Paros and Mykonos. On one Sunday when the taverna was closed, Cressida even came with them. They took the early morning ferry to Delos, where they could explore and have lunch and come back in the late afternoon.

"I haven't been off the island for four years," Cressida said as they left the port. She leaned over the rail, the wind picking up her hair, and she felt like it blew through her and made her feel young again. "Which one is his, Jory?"

The girls all looked out to the yachts sitting in the bay.

"That one," Jory pointed as they passed the *Persephone.* Shane had not tried to contact her, as she'd asked, but she knew he was still on the island every time she saw the red motorbike parked and the *Persephone* in the water.

"It's pretty," Kate said, "compared to the other ones, I mean. Jory, it looks just like the one in that picture you showed us when you told us you were coming here."

"Actually," Liz said, "it is." She pulled out the travel brochure. "Look. The *Persephone.*"

Jory glanced at the picture in surprise, and back to the *Persephone*. She almost allowed herself a small smile to think of what Shane would say if he knew about that moment which seemed so long ago now. Fate, he would call it, grinning at her with that smile that always melted her. And she would have wanted to deny it, just as she'd denied it that day when Liz and Kate had toasted to her fate and she said she didn't believe in it.

But that was before. That was before Potamia and Cressida and the magic they shared, and that was before Shane. She looked around almost in awe of her, Liz and Kate on a ferry in Greece, gazing out at the yacht that had inspired Jory to come, that turned out to belong to the love of her life.

The thought made her gasp inwardly and she turned away from the deck. Did she love Shane? She knew she did. But the love of her life? Destined to be together? That was a crazy notion.

Wasn't it?

She didn't want to tell her friends, but she'd been wondering the past few weeks if she'd been wrong. She'd stare longingly at her phone, waiting for a text from Shane that never came. She was hurt and betrayed, but at some point in the past days, she realized she'd never actually let Shane tell his side. Yes, he said he was a bartender and omitted the important details about his wealth, who he was. But did he have good reason? She had been so adamant about her mistrust of anyone with money because of her father's family that it was no wonder he hadn't told her. Would she have continued to see him? Probably not, she answered herself honestly.

First rule of debate, you listen to each other's sides. She'd never even heard his. What if she'd made a *bad* argument?

It's not considered an argument if the other person never has a say answered that part of her that missed and longed for Shane.

No, she thought, looking back out to the *Persephone*. He knew about her helping Cressida and he'd never said a word that he was trying to buy it.

"Probably making her do all the hard work and then snatching it from under her," she muttered.

"What was that, Jory?" Kate asked.

She hadn't realized she'd spoken out loud. "Oh, just thinking of where to go next," she lied. "Surely someone out there is just waiting to be found and I can help!"

They smiled a smile that did not go to their eyes. For they all knew, all of them but Jory, that the only person in this story left to be found was her.

~

"So?" Cressida asked Nefeli a few days before the wedding and the departure of her friends. "How are we doing?"

Nefeli sat at the large desk in the office, printing out the profit and loss report Cressida would not have known how to do without her.

"Very good. The sales reports are much higher than I would have expected. I think we will be able to cover the costs of the taverna this month, and if business continues, it will balance nicely."

"For the taverna," Cressida stated. It was not a question. "But not for the whole property."

"I think the profits look promising enough to start paying back your late payments," Nefeli said carefully. "If that is what you want to do."

Sudden insight flooded her and she knew the Vasilopita bread had worked. She knew the truth, she knew only what was right. Cressida now knew what she needed to do about her taverna.

⌒

The following morning, Jory, Liz and Kate were heading out for the day on their last trip together before the holiday ended. And much like before, Cressida put on a fine summer dress, white with a tan and yellow design, that had been a favorite of Leo's.

As she left her home, Mago threw a long white silk jacket over the balcony, scoffing, "I don't know why you need to wear this, but you do. But not to my wedding. Only the bride can wear white!"

"Are you wearing white?" Cressida asked, picking the jacket up from the dewy grass and shrugging it on.

"Of course not, what do I look like, the Virgin Mary? I'm wearing red."

"Then why can't I wear white?"

"It's still the rules," Mago said. She sounded nervous.

Covered by the white silk, Cressida got into her truck and drove down to Chora, to a small office where Michael greeted her at his desk. He still had the same kind smile and small glasses, and something just a little funny was happening in her stomach at seeing him.

"Mrs. Thermopolis."

"Michael."

He smiled and nodded. "Cressida, then. Thank you for calling. I understand you've had quite the busy time since we last met."

Everything felt so easy then, as she sat across from Michael at the desk and told him all they'd been up to at the taverna. She had the sales reports in an envelope in her bag but felt no need to open them yet. They talked for nearly a half hour, mostly about business, but about other things as well. She couldn't believe she was opening up to a man, one whose company was trying to buy her business, but she liked this Michael. He was a lawyer, but a good one, he claimed, and his interests were always in favor of the underdog. He based himself in Naxos part of the year, where he met Shane and discovered his interest in the taverna.

"It's always been a favorite spot of mine, that guesthouse. When Mr. Deluca found it so as well, I knew it would find its way to where it needed to be. Which it looks like it has." He nodded his head at her. "I've heard the best things about your food and look forward to the day I can come as a guest."

She blushed, but he just smiled. "Will he see me?"

Michael stood then. "Yes, if you're willing to come out to the yacht? He's waiting for you."

Michael took her on the dinghy out to the beautiful yacht where Shane helped her onto the boat. He really was a beautiful man, brown curling hair and tanned skin, and as Jory always described him—in khaki shorts and a white T-shirt. He smiled at her as if she'd never said the horrible things she did, though he had the same drawn look that Jory did, with circles under his eyes and a smile that never quite met his eyes fully.

"Mrs. Thermopolis," he said as she balanced herself onto the boat. "Welcome to *Persephone*."

She walked around the sundeck. "It is a beautiful ship."

"Thank you. Has Jory told you much about it?" he asked, sounding hopeful.

Cressida spoke carefully, finding she did not want to hurt the man who was obviously as heartbroken as Jory. "No, she has not. But her friends have come to the island and they were wise enough to Google you." She smiled when he laughed, a sound that seemed to surprise himself. "It is a Turkish sailboat, is it not?"

Much of his hesitation passed as Shane took her around the yacht and explained his history working on it, his enthusiasm seeping through, his love for what he did. "I know it's only a boat, but I feel such a sense of home here. I had hoped…"

Cressida felt as though she were talking to Jory, the way he spoke, the way he loved his boat, the way he worked to help and not to hurt. Would he be so open to her? Had his intent always been to help and not to hurt? She got up her courage and pulled out the reports and her photos.

"Mr. Deluca, I have a proposition for you."

She and Shane and Michael sat on the boat for hours, looking over prospects. She brought every report, every sale, every loss, the mortgage, every photo Jory had ever taken, as she outlined her ideas. Shane looked through and pulled out his own ideas, placing them side by side. They all compared notes and ideas as lunch came out, and they found they were not arguing at all but enjoying each other's company. Together, they might just be able to create something even more magical.

It was late afternoon when they shook hands. "You've done a really extraordinary thing with the restaurant, Cressida," Shane said. "You should be proud."

"I am. But I did not do it on my own. Without Jory, I would not be here. She has a knack for helping people find their way."

His eyes both tightened and softened at the same time. "I got that from her too."

"Shane," she said, using his name for the first time. "I know that it was never your intention to hurt Marjory. I can't explain how I know this but I do."

"Perhaps you baked another truth serum into your bread and accidentally ate it," he teased with a grin.

Cressida laughed. "I did not actually bake that into your bread that day, just to let you know. That was just you and Jory, two people who wanted to know one another. You must come and see her. Explain things."

He shrugged. "I'm not sure anything I'd say would make a difference. She'll always have a shadow of a doubt because she doesn't trust me. Even if she did trust me, she still wouldn't take my hand and get on this boat and sail away into the sunset. This life I have is not for her. But it is for me. So...where do we go from here?"

"Home," Cressida said, and smiled.

Eighteen

Mago and Arie's wedding was on July 28 in the afternoon. It was running forty-nine minutes late, as weddings tend to do. Mago's sons, Jase and Zach, came over from the mainland. They and the girls from the taverna were the only people invited, which of course meant the entire three hundred inhabitants of Potamia showed up at the Vineyard Diamantés.

It was a simple affair. Mago wore a bright red suit dress and hat and Arie wore a black tuxedo with a matching red tie that Mago had given him months before without knowing why she was giving it to him. Arie had always hoped it would be for the day he would finally dance with his lady.

The ceremony was perfect and by 4:38 p.m., they were married, and it was time to celebrate. Cressida and Kate pulled out large pans the size of tables to finish the traditional Gamopilafo, wedding rice made with lamb, like a Spanish Paella.

Later the classic music began, and then the Sirtaki, the famous Greek wedding dance. All three hundred uninvited guests joined in, their arms around each other as they danced in celebration.

There were two people who did not join in the dancing. Jory slipped past the group of revelers toward Cressida, who was tapping her foot and smiling at the group.

"What a pair we are," Jory said, inching in beside her.

"Lives of the party, really," Cressida laughed. "I'm not quite ready to dance yet. Soon though. Soon, I shall dance again." She turned to Jory. "And so will you."

Jory looked out to the dancing and felt a longing for Shane, to be dancing with him. But that was over, and she had to move on. She sighed, taking Cressida's elbow and turning away from the party. "Shall we get these dishes cleaned up while we can?"

Cressida shook her head but followed Jory into the kitchen.

They carried the large bowls into the kitchen of Vineyard Diamantés and began to do the dishes. Jory poured them both glasses of the white wine to sip while they cleaned up, comfortably silent. The kitchen was just behind the cellar door tasting room so both were surprised when they heard the bell at the door, a sign someone had arrived.

"The party is outside!" Cressida called. "Just follow the music and dancing."

"Actually, I've come to see you," a female voice called.

Cressida and Jory both turned to see Selene in the doorway. Selene, usually so put together, was dressed in simple pants and a loose top.

"Selene, we did not see you at the wedding," Cressida said.

"I…" She fidgeted with her hands. "I did not feel comfortable coming. But I have to speak with you, Jory."

Jory turned to Selene. "Yes?"

"I lied to you," she blurted, her relief at exposing the truth nearly pushing her forward. "Jory, Cressida, I lied. About Shane. I knew he was in town trying to buy Cressida's business but I didn't know about your involvement with Cressida until you came with the invitation for the opening. So I… I never told him that you two knew one another. I never knew there was even a connection. Nor do I think did he. Not that I would know. I had not seen him since that first day you met in my shop."

Jory swallowed a lump in her throat. "He still lied about who he was," she said, but without conviction.

"Wouldn't you, if you were constantly meeting women like me who saw an opportunity in a man with that kind of money?"

Jory stopped doing the dishes. "But why did *you* lie?"

Selene looked away, taking a breath. "Because…"

"Because you're in love with him," Jory finished, taking her own breath and sitting down.

Selene met Jory's eyes briefly, her shoulders back, head high.

"I am sorry I lied to you," Selene said. "I never meant for all of this to happen. He was always very secretive about his money. That is why he lied about his name when he first met me. But I was too clever."

Selene forced a brittle laugh, trying to keep her eyes from tearing, but it did not work.

"I had hoped to be free from this island by marrying a wealthy man. Shane was as good-looking as he was rich. I did not expect to have more feelings for him than that. But he was charming and kind and when he looked at me and spoke to me, it was like I was a person of value. I have not felt that before. Nor did I expect to have feelings like this guilt for hurting the both of you."

Selene paused, her eyes glistening. "This guilt is unbearable."

Cressida met Jory's eyes, and they could not help but allow a smile. "You may as well embrace it and get out there to that wedding and dance," Cressida said, turning the tap back on and returning to the dishes. "Seems like you are a part of it all now too."

"A part of what?"

"This summer of new beginnings."

"This is our last morning together," Jory said to Cressida as they made coffee the following morning.

Cressida looked at her friend. "You are not usually up this early."

"I couldn't sleep," Jory admitted.

"Arie's Kitron will do that to you. Too much sugar." Cressida paused. "Though I'm guessing it was more along the lines of thinking about a certain American man who might just be the one you love?"

"You can't fall in love after a couple of dates," Jory said.

"Who made this so?" Cressida asked. "Me? I was in love with Leo after a week. Arie has been in love with Mago since they were ten. Nefeli fell in love with Nico the second she met him. Sometimes love hits hard."

Cressida paused again to take a sip of her coffee. "You know, I like your Shane."

"You don't even know him," Jory scoffed. "And he's not my Shane."

"He's always been your Shane to me. And he could be—you are the one who can make that so. What have you decided?"

Jory sighed. "You mean after staying up all night? I've decided to get on the plane back to the mainland with Liz and Kate and see where the road leads."

Cressida pursed her lips at this.

"Can I tell you, Jory, you follow your instincts and your gifts around the world, you are the most brazen adventurous spirit I know, you are willing to do anything, to try anything, to help anyone. But you won't go on the one adventure of your own."

"Oh, good! Coffee!" Liz exclaimed, coming down the stairs right at that moment.

Relieved for the timely interruption, Jory stood. "I'll get you a cup. And Liz, you forgot your glasses."

"Oh, I thought that's what morning without coffee always looked like. I should start putting them on earlier." She sat beside them and gratefully accepted the steaming mug Jory held out to her. "What's for breakfast?"

"Wedding rice," Kate's voice called from the kitchen seconds before she appeared with small bowls. "Sans the lamb. I think you have enough left for a week, Cress."

Liz looked disappointed. "I wanted some of Cressida's famous bread or cake."

"Jory forbade it," Mago said, coming down the stairs into the garden.

"Mago!" the girls all called at once.

"How was your wedding night?" Jory asked, grinning.

"Ongoing, so I need sustenance," Mago said, to which Liz and Kate laughed uproariously.

"Wait," Liz said. "Why did Jory forbid your bread?"

"Because she's too afraid Cressida will encourage her to throw all caution to the wind and find Shane," Kate said.

"Which she should," Liz added.

"Girls, it is never in good form to judge your friends' decisions. They will do that to themselves when they are old and look back with regret," Mago said serenely.

"Mago!" Jory cried. "You are not helping my case!"

"I'm just teasing you, my dear." Mago laughed, hugging Jory, and then pulling them all in for a hug. "You go left, then the world gives you all that left has to offer. You go right, you get all the choices going right has to offer. There is no right or wrong. If you follow your heart, no matter what it says, or how many other things stand in the way, you will find your way home."

Cressida looked up at Jory then and their eyes met, and they smiled. And they said their goodbye for now without ever saying a word.

~

"Last call for boarding! Chora Naxos to Athens departing at eleven-thirty!" the voice called over the port's loudspeaker.

A tug sounded. Liz, impatient, grabbed their suitcases and started loading them onto the boat. Cressida, Mago and Nefeli had all come to the dock to see them off and have a tearful goodbye.

Kate hugged each of them at length, crying freely, far from the briskness that Liz displayed, coming in for a quick hug, then grabbing the bags as she went.

"Don't be too eager to get back to normal," Cressida said to Liz with the seconds she was given to embrace her. "This adventure you girls had together should happen more often. Promise you'll try?"

"I promise," she said, holding Cressida for another moment.

"Being in your kitchen is such an inspiration," Kate said to Cressida. "I don't want it to end when I leave Greece, so I've signed up for a course at the Culinary Arts Institute in Los Angeles. Will you stay in touch and give me tips as I become a chef?"

"How exciting, Kate! And of course I will," Cressida said, hugging her one last time.

When Liz and Kate were finally on board, Mago and Nefeli started walking for the car. There was only Cressida and Jory left in the final moments before the boat left.

"I will have you to blame for the rest of my life," Cressida said, taking Jory's hands.

She grinned. "Likewise, friend. I promise to visit soon. In the meantime...I'll miss you, Cress."

"I'll miss you like the limby rogue," Cressida said, pulling Jory in and hugging her tight, trying to keep the tears from falling.

"The what?"

"Like you and your friends say to each other. The phrase you made up."

"Oh, like a rogue limb?"

Cressida nodded.

"You know…that expression…even if I did make it up, when I say it, it's supposed to mean that there will be a part of me that's always missing without you there," Jory said.

Cressida pulled away abruptly, wiping her eyes. "Another missing part is here," she said softly.

She nodded over Jory's shoulder and when she turned, there he was.

"Shane," she gasped, out of breath from surprise. "What are you doing here?"

"A little birdie told me I might find you here," he said, keeping his distance.

"Who?" Jory asked.

"Me." Cressida smiled warmly at Shane, who smiled back at her.

Jory looked back and forth between the two of them.

"I don't understand," she said.

"Jory, allow me to introduce you to Shane Deluca of the Resurgence Hotel Group. My new business partner," Cressida explained.

Again, Jory looked between them both. "Your *what*?"

"I have decided to sell the property to the Resurgence Hotel Group that Shane owns. We will be business partners. This will be an excellent way to bolster our town. I am very pleased with the development."

"But … you … your taverna," Jory stuttered.

Cressida gave Jory's hand a squeeze. "Jory. You know this is right. Can't you feel it?"

"Is *that* what you baked in that bread?"

Cressida simply laughed and put her hand on Jory's shoulder. "Remember Marjory—'the life you have led doesn't have to be the only one you lead.'"

And then she turned and walked away, leaving Jory alone on the dock with Shane. He looked at her expectantly.

"I'm sorry I planned to leave without saying a proper goodbye," Jory began.

"Yes, that really put a wrinkle in my plan to explain myself," Shane said. "Do you even know anything about what I do?"

Jory stepped back from him. "I do know, no thanks to you. You never told me anything. You skirted away from the truth, left yourself shrouded in mystery. How could I have known?"

"You could have Googled me," Shane suggested. "It worked for Liz and Kate."

Despite herself, Jory laughed and Shane smiled to hear it.

"But you're absolutely right," he said. "I know that it was wrong to have lied to you about what I did for a living. I only wanted to keep getting to know this amazing woman whose presence made me excited, inspired and just all-round happy. I didn't think that you'd give me a chance, and Jory, I wanted that chance more than anything. I *still want* that chance."

Seeing her resolve waver, Shane stepped forward and embraced her, holding her tight, the warmth seeping through her. It felt so good, she wanted to cry. "And while we're on it," he said into her hair, "you weren't so forthright with me either. I had no idea about everything *you* were doing. You made magic happen here."

Her eyes began to fill, feeling overwhelmed. "From what my detectives were able to uncover, you are no slouch at turning places around as well. I'm sure you'll do a beautiful job with the guesthouse. You won't try to make it too fancy, will you? It should be simple. And you must have Cress keep cooking. And—"

He put his hand on her lips. "I will do everything with the greatest of care and respect for what you and Cressida have built, I promise." He rubbed his thumb over her lips, his hand behind her neck, and finally pulled her in for the softest, sweetest kiss. "As I will with you, and what we have built between us, if you'll let me."

The horn for the ferry blew loudly, giving its last call.

"I want to see you again, I do," Jory said desperately. "We can stay in touch. Maybe when you get back to the States, or if we end up in the same city, we can see one another. Go on a date."

"I don't want to text you, or call you, or bump into you here and there. I want you. I want to dive in, all in, with you."

"Shane, you are asking me to change the course of my life to stay here with you. That's a scary thing for me," she said quietly. "Does that make sense?"

Out of nowhere, there was a loud collective, "NO!" shouted from the boat. Liz and Kate and a group of onlookers stood watching.

Shane was laughing. "Thank you," he said, waving to their audience. Jory's lip quirked and she shook her head at Liz and Kate, who grinned down at her.

"You are losing that instinct of yours, Marjory St. James," Shane said, bringing her attention back to him. "Stay?" He pulled her close and kissed her again. "No one said anything about staying. This is still a morning to leave, Jory, only you leave with me this time. Every time. Every morning we are in a port and the air stirs, and we know it's time to leave, we sail away. And every time we land in a port and know it's time to stay, we dock. Home is wherever we are, on the *Persephone*. Home with me, Jory."

As Jory processed what Shane was telling her, she realized his words were everything she wanted to hear. Had always longed to hear. Home. Wherever they made it.

Jory stood on her toes to press her forehead to his, and they smiled, their eyes crinkling, their lips nearly touching.

"How could I possibly refuse that offer," she said, "when it's—"

"Fate?" Shane supplied hopefully.

"I was thinking a little more like magic," said Jory.

And then they were kissing as the port cheered, as the ferry sailed off from the dock, and it was every bit like the real-life end of a silly Hollywood movie.

Standing at the boat's bow, smiling happily at the couple, Kate turned to Liz. "So we sail off into the sunset and they live happily ever after?" Kate asked.

"It appears so, although that's the most cliché ending I've ever seen in my whole life," Liz said.

"Maybe," Kate replied, wrapping her arm around Liz and lowering her head to her shoulder. "But it's still a pretty good ending."

On a planet with 195 countries and a human population of eight billion people, there are a lot of places to see and stories to tell. Sometimes those places and their stories collide, like a beautiful accident nobody ever saw coming. This collision may not cure cancer or alter the paths of most of the eight billion people. But occasionally it will alter the paths of the people it was intended to change. And this makes for a very good ending indeed.

And so ends the story of the Little Greek Taverna.

YOUR
BOOK
CLUB
RESOURCE

Visit **GCPClubCar.com** to sign up for the GCP Club Car newsletter, featuring exclusive promotions, info on other Club Car titles, and more.

 @GrandCentralPub

Reading Group Guide

Discussion Questions

1. The novel opens with Jory, Kate and Liz planning Jory's summer trip to Greece. What do you make of their friendship dynamic and what role do Kate and Liz play in Jory's trip?

2. Readers get to see a vivid glimpse of Cressida's passion for cooking at the beginning of Chapter 2 when she finds an urge to bake a honey cake. What do you make of Cressida's instant need to bake? Do you think there is a specific reason behind her baking?

3. In Chapter 3 at the gallery and Chapter 4 at Madam Dionysia's, do Jory's interactions with the employees remind you of any moments from your own life?

4. Mago explains her sad family upbringing, including losing her mother and grandmother. How does Mago's personality

change throughout the book? Is her personality assisted through her own independent choices or does she need to rely on other characters, like Cressida and Jory, for her happiness?

5. The end of Chapter 5 sees the first intimate interaction between Cressida and Jory in the form of a hug. To what extent does this gesture set up the long-lasting relationship between the two throughout the book?

6. Cressida teaches Jory how to make olive bread and Jory, though she struggles, has an enjoyable time with her. How does Cressida's cooking affect their relationship? Do you see Cressida as more of a mentor or friend to Jory, or both? Explain.

7. How does the public perception of Shane change throughout the novel? Given his wealth, do you believe that Shane was treated fairly? Why or why not?

8. Throughout the book, different characters talk about their family backgrounds. How does learning about their histories change your perspectives of each character?

9. Toward the end of the book, it is revealed that Shane is wealthy and he wanted to get involved in the taverna with the intention of reviving it. However, Jory and Cressida interpreted his actions as dishonest. Do you think Jory and Cressida misjudged Shane's intentions or were they justified in their reactions? Explain.

10. At the end of Chapter 17, Cressida answers Shane's question, "Where do we go from here?" with the word, "Home." What do you think "Home" is to her? What does home look like for Jory? For Shane? For Mago?

Author Q&A

Q: What was the inspiration behind this book? Was it based on an experience that you had abroad or did you hear about a similar experience from a colleague or friend?

A: I started writing this book just after we went into lockdown on April 1, 2020. Originally, I was working on a travel memoir—piecing together all the blogs, emails and journals I'd written over my many years of traveling. But I just couldn't feel the excitement to work on a nonfiction book about a world that suddenly didn't exist anymore. I wanted to write something charming and delightful, a book I would want to escape into, so I decided to write a fictional book instead, but with a character who was an avid traveler and loved to experience the world! So first I had to pick a favorite location of mine...

Q: Why did you choose Greece as the location for this book? What about Greece was alluring to you?

A: On my first trip I began in Europe and I traveled in the Greek Islands. Naxos was one of my favorite places ever! I took a moped and explored and ate beautiful food. Naxos is a unique island in the Cyclades because it is so large and they grow so much of their own food and produce, unlike some of the smaller islands, so it feels more authentic and real. Fun fact: I actually did get locked in the bathroom of my guesthouse in Naxos, so I think that story might have inspired the story and location in the beginning!

Q: Was there any specific or special research that you needed to do while writing *The Secrets of the Little Greek Taverna*?

A: When I first visited Naxos in the early 2000s people didn't have smartphones and on that first trip I didn't even take a guidebook! I really did wing it like Jory did. Because I couldn't hop on a plane and return to Naxos during the pandemic, the internet and my old journals became my best friends for researching this book when it came to descriptions of the island and locations. The research necessary for the food and restaurant aspect of the book was, thankfully, located within my own house.

Q: Did any of your loved ones inspire the personalities of the characters in your book or did you come up with all of the characters from your own imagination?

A: Most of the characters in the book are from my imagination. But Cindy, Liz and Kate were partially inspired by real people. The brunch scene in Chapter 1 was based on two of my closest girlfriends, Jaime and Blakeley, and our time together in L.A. In the end, the characters of Liz and Kate, and later Cressida, are the embodiment of the amazing women friends I have in my life.

Cindy St. James is in one way inspired by my own amazing mother—she actually can take any space and make it feel like home within minutes! I loved the idea of turning this gift into something just a little bit magical.

Q: Throughout the novel, Cressida cooks up several dishes unique to Greek culture. How did food inspire you while writing?

A: Food and wine have been two of my great passions since I started in hospitality when I was eighteen years old and now my partner, Dan, (who's a chef) and I own and operate three restaurants in Nelson, New Zealand. But how it inspired the book was out of writer's block! I was lost as to where to go in the story and wandering around my house when I stopped in front of my boyfriend's 300+ cookbooks. I sat down to write a Greek recipe and suddenly Cressida, a minor character at that stage, became a magical baker! *The Secrets of the Little Greek Taverna* suddenly had a title, a plot, a dream and a vision.

Q: Your novel is unique in that it is not only a story about friendships and betrayal but also the impact of magic on one's relationships. Why did you decide to incorporate elements of magic into your book?

A: Some of my favorite stories have aspects of magical realism—*Chocolat*, *Practical Magic*, *Like Water for Chocolate*, *Garden Spells*. I love that the story takes place in the real world and so the magical aspect feels believable and real. These books are ones I can stay up all night reading, feeling charmed, delighted, transported, and when you close that book with a smile you just feel happy and think, "I just loved this book." I've always wanted to write a story that made others feel that way too.

Q: Did you always want to be a novelist or was creative writing an interest that you developed later in life?

A: I have wanted to write for as long as I have been reading. Books were some of my best friends as a child. I lost myself in the worlds of the characters in books and I wanted to become a storyteller, too—to be a part of the world of people who could create magic with words. I wanted to be able to give others what books gave me. I can feel that happening sometimes—moments when characters and the scenes seem to write themselves—that is when the true magic happens for the reader—and for me!

Q: How do you think this book will change the way readers view both food and their family dynamics? What is the most important lesson that readers should take away after reading your book?

A: Food is one of the most important parts of our culture—bringing families, friends and communities together. Food connects us, it inspires us, it satiates us, makes us hum and desire. Cultures are bound together by flavors, foraging, sharing recipes, passing down from one generation to the next. Food is life, and as Cressida says to Jory on page 144:

"The magic does not come from within, it comes from the whole story put together on a plate with appreciation and love of all the stories that came together to make it so. We, as cooks, are the storytellers. We weave and mend the flavors together into a novel. It isn't a skill that is learned. It is a gift of allowing the flavors to come through you, not from you."

I love that there are aspects of this novel that people may take with them—the food or family dynamics, the power of female friendship, the magic that can happen in everyday life, grief and healing, falling in love. But there is really only one thing I want my readers to take away: I want them to close the book with the same smile I have when I read a book that delights me, and say, "I loved that book."

Q: What was the easiest part and most challenging part of writing this book?

A: The hardest part of writing this book was the second draft. About a third of the way through the first draft the book changed from being a contemporary romance to being a magical realism story about friendship, love, food and travel. I kept writing as if the book was always that way. But the second draft, when I had to look at a novel concocted of different stories and styles and merge them into one, was challenging. The easiest part of writing this book was sitting down every day and writing. The moment I got home, opened my computer and started writing, I was in my happy place.

Q: What's one thing that you want readers to know about you?

A: I want my readers to feel connected. If you read a character of mine and you relate to them, then we are connecting. Or a sentence that describes how you feel, or a recipe that makes you feel at home. That is the magic of books. We are sharing parts of our souls and I believe that is why we love books, why books are our friends, how they help us through toughest times. It is us connecting with each other, knowing we are understood and not alone in the world. If you connect with my words, you are connecting with me, and that means I, too, am connecting with you, and that is why I write—and read.

Traveling Like Jory St. James (and Me, Erin Palmisano)

Spoiler alert! While the character of Jory St. James is not in any way autobiographical, travel tales she has had that are mentioned throughout the book are all true from my own travels (including the fact that I was, in fact, attacked and robbed by a baboon in Victoria Falls!).

In some ways this book was a love letter to the twenty years of experiences I had traveling the world. So for any of you who were inspired by the location, or by Jory, to get out there and book a destination, I have made a little guide of travel tips to help make the most out of your next trip.

Tip 1: Get a little bit lost.

"I thought I'd meander and get a little bit lost ... it's my favorite thing to do in a new place."

—*Jory, page 23*

Don't worry, it's nearly impossible to *really* get lost in this day and age with smartphones. For the experience of getting lost but knowing you can always find your way back, download the map of the town, city or country where you are traveling either on Google Maps or Maps.me. Once downloaded, you can use these maps offline at any time or place.

Then, step out your front door and wander! In a small town like Potamia or even Chora Naxos, this is easier than in a large city, but in a large city just ask your hotel or hostel to show you some highlights and meander in that direction, once the safety of areas has been confirmed. But the point is, don't just Uber to whatever destination you want to see. Walk! Peek into shops that look interesting, try a vendor, check out a cafe that looks cool. See the streets, the architecture, the people. Let yourself be surprised.

Some favorite places to meander and get a little lost:

1. The labyrinthine walkways of Venice, Italy, that always end up at the canals.

2. Meandering the souqs in the ancient Islamic Cairo, Egypt.
3. The alleyways large enough only for people and motorbikes in Varansi, India, that lead to the ghats on the River Ganges.
4. Put on a pair of walking shoes in Manhattan and just walk! If you go too far you can always get back by the subway or a taxi.

Tip 2: Stay a little longer.

"You are staying a week?... That is a long time for a girl like yourself... Most people come through."
—Mago, page 32

The days of thirty countries in thirty days are well over. If you've got a week, choose a city and its surrounding sites. Three weeks? One small country or part of a big one. Three months? A small region. Longer? Endless possibilities.

In a week in one place, you find yourself feeling like a local rather quickly. You learn your neighborhood. You give other tourists directions and tips. You learn the best places to eat. You always discover new places. The bartender remembers your name. You can't do this in a day, so take time and let yourself fall in love with one place instead of many.

Best places to stay a little longer:

- Nelson, New Zealand
- Jerusalem, Israel
- The Lakes District, Argentina
- Rome, Italy
- Naxos, Greece
- Cape Town, South Africa

Tip 3: Go on an adventure.

"I remember the first moment I glimpsed the Treasury in Petra, I felt like all my childhood dreams had just somehow come true."

—Jory, page 153

Everyone has something on their travel bucket list, whether they ever get to it or not. A piece of history—Petra, Jordan, the Pyramids of Egypt, Angkor Wat. Or art—seeing the Mona Lisa, the Vatican Museum, an Opera at La Scala in Milan. Or perhaps it is for the great outdoors—seeing Everest, hiking to Machu Picchu, surfing in Costa Rica. Whatever it is, let yourself dream big and go on an adventure.

Here are a few highly recommended adventures I have personally loved:

- Riding on a felucca down the Nile in Egypt for four days.
- Sleeping outside in the dunes of the desert of Wadi Rum, Jordan.
- Hiking the four days to Machu Picchu.
- An overland or glamping safari in Africa (I did both).

Tip 4: Take the local transport.

"I love that story. Is it the one where you hopped on the local train in Egypt...?"

—Kate, page 8

Taking the local transportation is the epitome of experiencing a country at its most authentic. Travel by train, by bus, by share rides and collectivos. Talk to the person sitting next to you. Buy food out of the window on the stops. Take your headphones off. Relax into someone else's daily life. You will never experience local culture more authentically than this.

Some iconic local transport ideas:

- The subway in New York City
- Long-distance sleeper trains around India
- The chicken buses in Central America
- The ferries around the Greek Islands

- Tuk tuks around Bangkok (and motorcycle taxis on the Thai islands!)

Tip 5: Get off the beaten track.

"I happened to be talking about the train trip in England when I hopped on and stayed until the tracks ended and found myself in one of my favorite places in the world."

—Jory, page 10

We often have a good idea of the things we want to see and experience when we get to a country, but some of the best experiences you will ever have will be to get off the beaten track and go somewhere many travelers don't find themselves.

Here are some of my favorite off the beaten track places and how I ended up there:

- Riding the train from London all day until it ended in Pembroke, Wales.
- Taking a postcard to the tourist information desk and buying a ticket to Val d'Aran, Pyrenees, Spain.
- Wandering to the wrong tea plantation in Darjeeling, India, and ending up in a small village celebration with the local shaman blessing me.

- Helping a local carry his groceries onto a ferry to Elephantine Island off Aswan, Egypt, who became my local friend and tour guide.

Tip 6: Eat and experience the food of the culture.

"To truly be a cook is to appreciate that food is, from its beginning to its execution, a story within a story within a story. It is the story of the growers, the farmers, the fishermen. It is the story of the people as much as the product. The magic does not come from within, it comes from the whole story put together on a plate with appreciation and love of all the stories that came together to make it so. We, as cooks, are the storytellers. We weave and mend the flavors together into a novel. It isn't a skill that is learned. It is a gift of allowing the flavors to come through you, not from you."

—Cressida, page 144

Food is who we are, culturally as a species. Cressida and Jory's love of food is not unique. When traveling to a new country, food is at the heart of who we are. So eat at a local spot, taste the street food, dine alone, go to a high-end restaurant, try something different or a local specialty, take a cooking class.

Some do not miss foodie experiences (and if you don't think you're a foodie, you will be after these):

- Afternoon gelato in Italy
- Tapas in Andalusia, Spain
- Eating noodles out of a plastic bag—Thailand's famous street food
- A huge prime steak and a glass of Malbec in Buenos Aires, Argentina
- Taking a cooking class in Hoi An, Vietnam
- Eating roti and curry from a fire in the earth in the desert in Rajasthan, India
- A chocolate-making class in Cuzco, Peru
- A street food tour of Mexico City

Some extra travel tips:

- Always try to speak at least a couple words in the language of the country you are in.
- Practical tip: Get a guide, join a guided tour or purchase the audio tour if you are especially interested in learning more about a place or the artwork. You will never find out that information by looking around alone.
- If you have a long layover, look for an airport lounge! Most international airports have lounges you can pay for either

an hourly or daily rate, where you can use showers, watch television, get free Wi-Fi and eat food and drink (even alcohol) for free the whole time.

- Finally: Immerse yourself in your surroundings, in the culture, food, people, language, way of life, without judgment, comparison or opinion. Most of the world lives life much differently than we do in the western world. To explore it, to be a part of it, is not to compare it. It is not to judge it. It is simply to see it and be grateful to be invited into a moment of another person's life or story, their world. Let yourself be part of a story.

"Sometimes stories collide, like a beautiful accident nobody saw coming."

—*Prologue,* The Secrets of the Little Greek Taverna

Dan and Erin's Rolled Eggplant Bolognese (Serves 2)

This recipe is more like an Italian involtini with eggplant and meat sauce instead of ricotta, but the ingredients and preparation are very similar to the moussaka Cressida makes at Mago's request for her and Jory. This is a dish of ours that is about utilizing our favorite leftovers in a new and tasty way.

Ingredients:

4 medium-sized eggplants, cut lengthwise into ¼ inch slices
2 7-ounce balls fresh mozzarella, sliced
2 ½ cups of your favorite leftover Bolognese meat sauce

You can use any favorite meat sauce recipe for this dish—but our preference is a slow cooked classical Bologna recipe, made with a combination of pork and beef mince, white wine, milk, tomatoes and beef stock. The end result should be a rich, well flavored mixture— and the quality of this mix makes all the difference in the final dish!

For the tomato sauce:

Olive oil

Salt

2-3 cloves garlic

14 ounces canned whole San Marzano tomatoes (the quality of the tomato is very important—if you cannot find San Marzano's, a high quality canned or passata di pomodoro will do instead)

For the white sauce:

1/8 cup white flour

1/8 cup butter

2 cups whole milk

1-2 fresh bay leaves

¼ white onion

To garnish:

Fresh basil

Grated Parmesan

Preheat your oven to Bake at 450° F

While your oven is heating, slice the eggplants. On 2-3 large baking trays, rub garlic on the base, adding salt, and a very small amount of olive oil.

Line the eggplant on the trays and bake for 15-25 minutes on one side only. You want the eggplant to brown on one side, but not burn. Depending on the size of your oven and how many baking trays you have, you may need to do this in batches. This is fine—the eggplants should be cooled to room temperature once you are ready to roll them.

At this stage you will want to bring your leftover Bolognese out of the refrigerator to soften on the counter while you are cooking.

Making the tomato sauce:

While your eggplant is cooking, make the tomato sauce. Because of the quality of the San Marzano tomatoes or high quality passata, this is a fast, fresh sauce to make that you can make in bulk and freeze, as it can be used as a pasta sauce on its own, pizza sauce, or base for other dishes.

In a medium saucepan, add 2-3 tablespoons of olive oil, a dash of sea salt, and grate 2 large cloves of garlic into this before you heat the pan (*cooking hack—add a splash of water to help cook the garlic more quickly without browning it).

Cook on medium to high heat until garlic sizzles, then raise heat until the water has burned off.

If your tomatoes are whole, blitz them first to get a chunky puree (in a blender for about ten seconds). Not necessary if you are using a passata. Add the 14 ounces of tomatoes and cook on medium heat for about ten minutes, adding salt to flavor if needed.

Making the white sauce

In a small stainless-steel saucepan, add the flour and butter on low heat, stirring constantly until the mixture takes on a sandy look and texture. Set aside to cool.

In a separate medium-sized saucepan, add the whole milk with 1-2 fresh bay leaves and ¼ white onion, infusing the flavors into the milk. The milk should be heated gently, until just about hot enough that you can't put your finger in it.

Then sieve mix removing the bay leaf and onion from the milk and bring gently up to a boil as you whisk in the now room temperature roux. It is important that you continually whisk and do not let any of the roux stick to the bottom of the pan and burn, or you will have to start again! Once it starts to bubble, it is ready to go—with no further cooking needed!

Prepping your leftover Bolognese:

Once softened, check the seasoning, adding salt and pepper—we also add a little ground cumin, but season to your taste!

Rolling the eggplant:

Lower temperature on the oven to 350° F.

Create a thin base layer in a 12-inch oval ceramic baking dish of your tomato sauce, grating a small layer of Parmesan over top.

Layer two slices of the cooked eggplant (the eggplant should be cool, soft enough to fold—but not so soft it will fall to pieces). Scoop a large spoonful of meat sauce in the middle. Roll the eggplant around the meat sauce and fold underneath. Then place them in the ceramic dish, and line them up like enchiladas.

Once the dish is full, top with the white sauce, then another layer of your tomato sauce, and finally the slices of fresh mozzarella on top.

Bake at 350° F for 30 minutes.

Let rest for 5 minutes until it has cooled slightly, and the cheese is no longer bubbling. Serve immediately or refrigerate as is and reheat the next day.

Garnish with fresh basil and Parmesan.

And now, eat and enjoy!!!!

Important note: Where possible, we use stainless steel or heavy "Le Creuset" type cookware—don't use aluminum for this recipe!

—*Erin & Dan*

Acknowledgments

Thank you to everyone at Moa Press and Hachette New Zealand and Australia for making this dream a reality. Dianne Blacklock, for the wonderfully thorough and insightful copyedit; Dom Visini, thank you for your work getting this through the production process into publication! Also thank you to Libby Turner for her proofread.

Most notably, to Kate Stephenson, who gave this novel a chance. Never could I have anticipated a better editor, publisher, agent and all-round champion to this book. Kate, I thank you eternally.

To the team at Grand Central Publishing in the U.S., led by the dynamic Kirsiah Depp: thank you, Ivy Cheng, Leena Oropez, Shreya Gupta and Stacey Reid. And to the team at

Headline UK—your commitment to this book and its potential is staggering. I can't wait to meet you all in person!

To Andrea Phillips, my wind and wings since we were twelve years old. Ange, this book would not have gotten this far without your dedication to editing it into the best possible version to submit. I cherish every moment we worked on this together.

Another sincere thank-you to Blakeley Vaughn, who also took the time and energy to read and give brilliantly detailed editorial notes.

To my photographer Victoria Vincent at A Beautiful Photo —thank you for such an amazing shoot and my portrait in this book. You have a gift for helping women embrace their confidence and beauty that is so inspiring—and fun!

Tremendous love to my family—all of you—for giving me the best support system in the world and always believing in me. And Dad, even though you aren't here for this, I think of you every time something exciting happens and know you would be so proud. I miss you every day.

And to all the amazing women in my life. I am lucky to have so many of you (you know who you are) who have affected my life so much that I inadvertently became a writer of women's friendship!

To my partner in life, Daniel. Thank you for encouraging me to treat writing like a job, for helping me write recipes and find the correct terminology with cooking and for your love and support for the past fourteen years together. I feel so lucky to spend every day with my favorite person.

One final shout-out to the Mighty Moas! This journey has been at times electrifying, other times terrifying, overwhelming, joyful. Being able to share our mutual stories has been an honor and a gift.

And most especially thank you to all of my readers. I can only hope that this book brings you some of the joy that reading books has brought to me. Thank you for your support.

About the Author

Erin Palmisano is a dual New Zealand and U.S. citizen. As an avid reader, she always wanted to write stories where her passions of food, wine and travel come together with a hint of magic. Erin and her chef partner live with their two cats in Nelson, New Zealand, where they own and operate three restaurants. *The Secrets of the Little Greek Taverna* is her debut novel.

**GRAND
CENTRAL**

Your next great read is only a click away.

 GrandCentralPublishing.com

 Read-Forever.com

 TwelveBooks.com

 LegacyLitBooks.com

 GCP-Balance.com

A BOOK FOR EVERY READER.